AT LAST

BARBARA BRETTON

BERKLEY BOOKS, NEW YORK

AT LAST

A Berkley Book / published by arrangement with
the author

PRINTING HISTORY
Berkley edition / November 2000

All rights reserved.
Copyright © 2000 by Barbara Bretton
Cover illustration by Arthur Gager

This book, or parts thereof, may not be reproduced
in any manner without permission.
For information address: The Berkley Publishing Group,
a division of Penguin Putnam Inc.,
375 Hudson Street, New York, New York 10014.

The Penguin Putnam Inc. World Wide Web site address is
http://www.penguinputnam.com

ISBN: 0-425-17737-8

BERKLEY®
Berkley Books are published by The Berkley Publishing Group,
a division of Penguin Putnam Inc.,
375 Hudson Street, New York, New York 10014.
BERKLEY and the "B" design
are trademarks belonging to Penguin Putnam Inc.

PRINTED IN THE UNITED STATES OF AMERICA

10 9 8 7 6 5 4 3 2 1

This one's for you, Daddy, with much love.

ACKNOWLEDGMENTS

The list remains long; the gratitude endures. With thanks, as always, to:

Steve Axelrod, Judith Palais, and Leslie Gelbman, for support and encouragement and guidance.

My husband, simply for being.

My father, Mel Fuller, and my mother, Vi; Tim Bowden and his virtual and non-virtual family; Jim Selkirk and his son David; Joyce Bradsher, actress/artist/auctioneer; Kay Butler and her son Wendell—all of whom display enormous grace under almost unbearable pressure.

Gene Haldeman, for his friendship.

Cathy Thacker, for making me laugh.

Bertrice Small, for so much.

Tom E. Huff, who always believed.

Robin Kaigh, for knowing even before I do.

Tracey Robinson, because sometimes the second time is the charm.

Debra Matteucci, for fifteen terrific years.

Willa Cline, Web Goddess (and Pye).

The wonderful members of MERWA who shared with me their love of Maine.

Rita Bowden, who showed me this year what love and courage are all about, and Don Hilton Bowden (1946–1999), whose stories and wit and brilliance continue to warm my life. I miss you, old friend.

PROLOGUE

The last person to actually see Graciela Taylor on the day she left Idle Point, Maine, forever was old Eb at the Stop and Pump. Maybe if she'd planned her getaway a little better—or had any idea at all that she was going to leave her fiancé standing at the altar—she would have seen to it that her gas tank was full. As it happened, the needle on her fuel gauge hovered over the E, and she was forced to make a right into Stop and Pump and pray old Eb wasn't in a talkative mood. She might have taken her chances that she'd make it to Portland before the engine sputtered then shut down, but that was too risky. The last thing she wanted was to run out of gas on Main Street and bump into Noah on his way home from the wedding that wasn't.

Old Eb peered out from his office, then did a double take, which didn't bode well for her speedy getaway. He'd been around since long before Gracie was born, and he'd seen everything there was worth seeing around Idle Point and a few things he'd rather forget. He was the one who'd found Gracie's mother dead at the bottom of the ravine, trapped in that old Chevy with the horn blaring. He was the one who'd found Gracie, thrown clear from the wreck and crying to beat the band. He was the one who wrapped her in blankets and held her close while they waited for her father to identify his wife's body. She and Eb had a history. If he had any idea what she was up to, it would be all over.

"You forgetting where you're supposed to be?" he asked as he ambled over to where she stood next to the old Mustang she'd bought four years ago with the money she'd saved working in the kennels for Dr. Jim. "They're down at the cove waitin' for you, Gracie. I'd be there myself if I didn't have to earn a living."

She smiled, wishing she'd taken time to exchange her short lacy white dress for a pair of jeans and a sweater. She looked like exactly what she was: a runaway bride. "I'm on my way," she said, carefully not specifying her destination. She was too fond of Eb to lie to him.

Eb checked his pocket watch. "Thought the clambake began at two o'clock," he said. There was a sharp note of curiosity in his voice as his faded blue eyes took in her outfit. "It's near to half past. You can't be late for your own good-bye party." Eb knew that she was due to leave for Philadelphia the next morning to begin her first year of veterinary school at the University of Pennsylvania, the goal she'd been striving for since she was barely old enough to walk.

"I know," she said, "but I'm running on fumes and . . ." She shrugged. "You know how it is. There was so much to do." He was a native New Englander, same as she. Didn't he know New Englanders were famous for minding their own business?

Eb checked her oil and cleaned her windshield while the tank guzzled down the gallons. If he wondered why Sam the Cat was grooming herself on the passenger's seat, he never said. Gracie peered nervously over her shoulder every time she heard a car approach. A clean getaway, that was all she wanted. When the dust cleared and the hurt feelings mended, maybe then they could talk. She'd left a note for Noah on the kitchen table. She told him that she was sorry, that she hadn't planned on any of this, but wasn't it better to put an end to it now before it was too late?

Besides, how did you explain to the boy you'd loved since kindergarten that leaving him was the best thing you could ever do for him?

Eb screwed the gas cap back on good and tight.

"What do I owe you?" she asked as she reached for her purse through the open car window.

Eb plunged his gnarled hands deep into the pockets of his overalls. "Just get yourself a good education, girlie, then come back home to us where you belong. I've waited a long time to dance at your wedding. I want to see you all set up with a job and a husband and a few babies."

He didn't have any idea what he was saying.

You don't understand, Eb. There was supposed to be a wedding today, but I backed out. We were going to throw aside all of our plans and run away to Paris together. Can you imagine, Eb? I love him, and he loves me, but we don't have a chance in the world of being happy together. His father has seen to that. That's why I'm going to get behind the wheel of my car and get away from here before I start believing in fairy tales.

Noah had been part of her life for as long as she could remember, and he had owned her heart almost as long. Even during those years when he was away at boarding school, he was never far from her mind. Not that he'd known she existed until he came back to Idle Point after his father's heart attack and everything fell into place. Loving him seemed as right and natural as breathing; marrying him was simply the next step.

Noah and Gracie had been together since senior year

of high school, and they had stayed together despite the best efforts of their families to break them up. You wouldn't think their fathers' paths would have crossed very often, not even in a small town like Idle Point, but the hatred between the two men was legendary, and the poison spilled over onto their children. They had learned through experience to keep their love hidden away from their families. When they went off to college—Noah to B. U., Gracie to the University of Pennsylvania—everyone was sure distance would put an end to their teenage love affair. Nobody but Noah and Gracie knew of the weekends spent sharing pretzels on the steps of the museum in Philadelphia or strolling near Independence Hall, talking about the home they would build together, the family they would raise. Gracie would join Dr. Jim's veterinary practice while Noah wrote the Great American Novel.

She'd heard the whispers from some of her so-called friends, the ones who wondered how a plain girl like Gracie who lived over by the docks managed to land someone like Noah. Gracie was serious and ambitious and poor. Noah was a rich man's son who thought life was his for the taking. He'd flunked out of B. U., and if he had some game plan for his life, he wasn't sharing it. He wasn't serious about anything. Didn't Gracie know that? One day he'd call her up and say, "You know there'll never be anyone else like you, Gracie, but I've met someone else and . . ."

Everyone but Gracie knew that was going to happen one day. Why couldn't she get it through her head that she was fooling herself? Their poison-tipped words hurt, but a long time ago Gramma Del had taught her how to deflect the sting and hold her head high. They never knew how good their aim was. Noah loved her for who she was inside, not for how she looked, not for what she owned.

He didn't care that she was tall and skinny and blessed with brains, not beauty; with a heart, but not a bank account. They loved each other, and up until last night, she had believed that was all they needed.

Whoever thought it would be Gracie who broke Noah's heart?

She had Simon Chase to thank for ruining their lives. He'd shown up at her father's house an hour ago. Sixty minutes was all it took to shatter her dreams. Her future father-in-law was an imposing man, tall and white-haired and blessed with the natural arrogance of the born Yankee aristocrat. His bad heart had slowed him down, but the fierceness of his gaze when he looked at Gracie hadn't softened a bit. She had always suspected that Simon didn't like her, but she'd never imagined the depth of it until that afternoon.

Simon had connections up and down the coast of Maine and right across into lake country. Noah and Gracie had slipped down to Portland last week to apply for their wedding license, figuring nobody in the city office would pay any attention to them. They were wrong. A clerk recognized the Chase name and mentioned it to his superior, who happened to mention it over lunch to a friend, and an hour later Simon's office phone was ringing with the news.

"You'll do the right thing," Simon had said as he rose to leave. "If you love my son the way you say you do, I know you'll do what's best for him. There's really no other way, is there, Graciela?"

It wasn't until Simon and his late-model Lincoln disappeared down the road that she found the envelope propped up on the kitchen table between the sugar bowl and the salt and pepper shakers. Ten thousand dollars to leave his son alone. Ten thousand dollars to keep her from ruining Noah's life. Apparently that was the going rate for betrayal in Idle Point.

"I mean it, girlie," Eb was saying. "Save your gas money for when you're filling your tank in New Jersey. Nobody gives anything away in New Jersey."

"I can't let you do that," she said. "You already gave me that beautiful silver mirror that belonged to Sarah when I started college."

His eyes glistened with tears. "Sarah loved you like one of her own grandbabies. You know she always prayed you and Noah would end up together one day."

Oh God. Can this get any worse? Let me get out of here before what's left of my heart breaks in two.

She knew when she'd been bested, and kissed Eb on a weathered cheek. "Thank you," she said. "You're very dear to me."

Eb turned red beneath his gray whiskers. "You make us proud, Gracie. Understand?"

"I'm doing the right thing," she said as she climbed behind the wheel. "This is the best thing for both of us." Simon Chase had proved that beyond a doubt less than an hour ago.

"What did you say?" Eb asked, but she only smiled at him. She'd said too much as it was.

She gunned the engine and reached into the glove box and withdrew an envelope thick with bills. "Here," she said, handing it to Eb through the open window. "Now you can take yourself on that vacation you and Sarah always talked about."

Her wheels spun on the gravel as she roared out of the gas station.

"Hold your horses!" Eb's voice floated after her. "There's money in this envelope! What do you—"

The last thing Gracie saw in her rearview mirror was

old Eb standing in the middle of the road with Simon Chase's blood money dangling from his fingers like a flag of surrender.

She didn't slow down again until she reached Boston.

ONE

Gracie Taylor fell in love with Noah Chase on the first day of kindergarten. She was five and a half years old and so homesick she thought her heart would stop beating when Gramma told her that she had to stay there in that cold and scary schoolroom and that she wouldn't come back for Gracie until two o'clock. She was standing near the coatroom and trying very hard not to cry when he appeared at her side. "You'd better hang up your sweater before the bell rings," he said, "or else Mrs. Cavanaugh'll give you a black star." He had bright blue eyes and thick dark lashes, and when he smiled at her, she thought her heart would float up to the ceiling like a birthday balloon. She'd never seen anyone like him before in her entire life, except in storybooks where beautiful children lived in beautiful houses with parents who loved them forever and ever.

He tugged at her sleeve, and his smile grew even brighter. "Better do it," he said. "I'll save you a seat."

Gracie, who never said a word unless she had to, looked deep into those twinkling blue eyes and said, "How do you know about the black stars?"

"Everybody knows," said her new friend. "Gold stars

when you're good. Black stars when you're bad."

Gracie didn't care a bit about black stars, but if he thought they were a bad thing, so did she. She hung up her favorite red sweater on the last empty hook in the coatroom. Gramma Del had given her that sweater for her last birthday, and she loved it. It had always seemed special, but now it only looked shabby and not special at all, hanging there with the other kids' sweaters. Theirs were hand knit of the softest wool, with tiny ducks and bunnies embroidered along the edges. You couldn't buy sweaters like that at the discount store where Gramma Del bought Gracie's. Gracie was sure that each one of those special sweaters had been made by a mommy.

The classroom was filled with noisy, laughing children, all pushing and shoving each other like puppies in a basket. She lived out by the docks, an only child in a world of adults. Her best friends were her books (especially the ones about animals), her goldfish, and her beloved hamster named Wilbur. She felt like herself around animals, not shy and quiet the way she did around people.

Gracie jammed her hands into the pockets of her corduroy jumper. Her feet felt big and heavy, too heavy to move her into the room. Why did she have to go to kindergarten anyway? She already knew how to read, and she could print out her name and her address and her telephone number with her favorite Crayola. Who wanted to sit around with a bunch of dumb kids, playing with blocks and finger paints when you could be reading about Lassie or the cat in the hat?

The boy with the bright blue eyes twisted around in his seat, then pointed at the desk next to him. He smiled at her like it was Christmas morning and having her sit next to him was the best present under the tree. Suddenly she was moving forward, her eyes locked with his, moving right past the other kids just like she was one of them.

She slid into the cold wooden seat and folded her hands on top of the desk.

"What's your name?" he asked, leaning across the aisle.

"G-Gracie," she said, wishing she had a pretty name like Tiffany or Marisa. "What's yours?"

"Noah," he said, screwing up his face like a dried-up lemon.

She giggled. Two of the other little kids turned around and saw what Noah was doing, and they giggled too, and before she knew it, she was right there in the center of a group of laughing children, almost like she belonged there.

It was the best day of Gracie's life. When Mrs. Cavanaugh said "Class dismissed!", Gracie wished she could blink her eyes and start the day all over again. She followed the other kids into the coatroom to claim her sweater, and the buzz of talk and laughter all around her felt like a big hug. They all liked Noah, and since Noah liked Gracie, they opened their circle wide enough to let Gracie in, too. It was like being welcomed into a magic circle where only good things happened, and she hated to see it end.

Gramma Del was waiting for her by the gate. She had Mondays off from her job as cook for the richest family in Idle Point. "You look real happy this afternoon, missy," she said, tugging on Gracie's stick-straight ponytail. "Did you have a good first day of school?"

"I taught them double dutch," she said, bouncing in place with excitement. "We have a class parakeet and two gerbils. I had milk and cookies. We took a nap on squishy pillows, and I even had my own blanket." She hadn't closed her eyes once, not even for a second. She didn't want to miss a thing.

"Your own blanket!" Gramma Del nodded. "Now that's

something." She took Gracie's hand, and they started walking.

Gramma Del was old, and she didn't walk real fast, which was fine with Gracie. She wanted the day to last forever. "Did you make any friends?"

"Terri and Laquita and Mary Ellen and Joey and Tim and Don and Noah." She almost wasn't going to tell Gramma Del about Noah. In a way she wanted him to be her very own special secret friend, but she couldn't keep anything from her grandma.

Gramma Del stopped walking. "Noah?"

"Yes," said Gracie. "He held a seat for me."

Gramma Del's lips all but disappeared. "Did you know I cook for Noah's daddy?"

"No," said Gracie. "He has blue eyes, Gramma."

"Well, those blue eyes won't be around too long, missy. His daddy has big plans for that little boy."

Boarding school.

Prep school.

Ivy League.

Gramma Del's words swirled over Gracie's head, but she wasn't paying much attention. She was thinking about Noah and the class parakeet and the gerbils and taking in all the sights as the other kids met up with their mommies or big brothers and sisters. Laquita was standing at the corner all by herself, looking like she didn't mind being alone one bit. She was a very quiet little girl with a round face and long black hair that spilled down her back. Mary Ellen and Joey, redheaded twins, waved at Gracie from the backseat of a big green station wagon. Tim and Don's big brother was yelling at them to get in the car right this minute, but they were talking to Terri near the school bus. Most of the kids lived in town and had been playing together since they were little babies.

Across the street, Noah walked quietly next to a well-dressed woman. The woman looked straight ahead as they walked. Noah looked down at the ground. For some reason Gracie's heart hurt as she watched them. That couldn't be his mommy. A mommy would hold your hand and ask you about your day and look happy to see you again, like Gramma Del did but better.

Gramma Del was daddy's mother. Gracie knew she did the best she could, because that's what Gramma Del was always telling her. "You should have better than an old woman taking care of you," she liked to say when she was giving Gracie her bath. "Things aren't meant to be this way." She lived out back in the small cottage behind the house and mostly minded her own business when it came to her son's comings and goings. She looked the other way when her son rolled home smelling all dusty like beer at all hours of the day or night and only spoke up when he didn't come home at all.

"This child deserves better," Gracie had heard her grandma say more than once. "She deserves a real family." Sometimes Gramma Del came into the house very late and carried a sleepy Gracie out to the cottage to spend the night. "I had a bad dream," she liked to say as she made room for Gracie in her narrow feather bed. "Glad you could visit." Gracie always laughed, even though she knew that wasn't the reason at all.

Maybe that was why Daddy had brought home that skinny red-haired woman at Christmastime and said, "Graciela, meet Vicky. She's your new mother." Gracie had burst into tears, then run from the room as fast as her new sneakers would carry her. Daddy had yelled at her to come back and apologize—"right this second, young lady!"—but Gracie didn't care. She threw herself on her bed and sobbed until her eyes hurt so bad she couldn't see. She didn't want some stranger coming in and pretending to be her mother. She wanted her real mother, the brown-haired woman with the gentle smile who looked down at her from the photograph on her nightstand.

Gracie wasn't sure how she knew this, but somehow she understood that she wasn't supposed to talk about the nights when her daddy fell asleep on the floor with an empty bottle beside him or how the redheaded woman walked out one day at the beginning of the summer and took everything that wasn't nailed down along with her. Gracie had been in her room, pretending to be sound asleep, but she'd really been watching through a crack in the door while the woman and her squeaky-voiced sister took money from Daddy's pockets and the bottles off the shelves.

No, she'd never talk about any of that. Not with anyone. People whispered enough about the Taylors anyway, about how her daddy couldn't seem to hold down a job and how he should be ashamed to have his mother working as a cook to keep a roof over his lazy, no-good head. She hoped Noah wouldn't stop liking her once he found out about her family, because if he did, she would never go back to school again, and nobody, not even Gramma Del, could make her.

But then, maybe Noah already knew. If Gramma Del worked for Noah's daddy, maybe Noah knew all about her family and liked her anyway.

She hugged that thought close all the way home.

"Change your clothes before you have your snack, Noah." Mary Weston took off her hat and placed it neatly in the center of the hall table with the red feather pointing toward the door.

"Yes, ma'am."

"Your parents will be home from their trip sometime this afternoon. We don't want them finding you looking like a hooligan, do we?"

"No, ma'am." He didn't have any idea what a hooligan looked like or why they wouldn't want him to look like one. *Hooligan.* The sound of it inside his head made him smile. *Hoooo-li-gin.* Somehow he'd bet hooligans had more fun than he did.

"Is something funny?"

"No, ma'am."

Mary's sour face puckered even more. "Then why aren't you upstairs changing clothes?"

Noah didn't have to be told again. He turned and raced up the steps two at a time, putting as much distance between himself and the housekeeper as he possibly could. He wished school could last twice as long. It was a lot more fun playing with the other kids than being alone in this scary old house. He ran down the second-floor hallway, making sure he didn't catch sight of the pictures on the wall. His mother said those were his relatives, the people his father came from, and that he should be proud, but Noah was mostly scared. They were all old and angry-looking, and sometimes he thought they'd reach right out of their picture frames and spank him just because they could. He'd never told that to anyone before. He knew what they'd say. "You're letting your imagination run away with you, young man. Paintings can't hurt you. Now stop being silly and practice your piano."

He didn't want to practice his piano. He wanted to tell stories about monsters who ate stupid grown-ups and wizards who rose up from the rocks out beyond the Point and turned lonely little boys into knights in shining armor. He had already decided that that was what he would do when he grew up. He wanted to live in a crowded house with lots of brothers and sisters and noise and music and laughter and dogs. Maybe a dog in every room and parents who let you play in the mud without yelling at you.

Noah's parents loved him. They told him so all the

time, like when they were heading out the door for a night in Boston or a weekend on the boat. Sometimes days would go by when he didn't even see his father, and that made the rare nights when they all ate dinner together special. He watched his father very carefully and tried to imitate the way he held his knife and fork, the tilt of his head when he spoke. His father was the smartest man in the entire world and, with one exception, Noah wanted to be just like him when he grew up. Noah would make sure he had plenty of time for his kids.

"What is the problem with you, child?" Gramma Del planted her hands on her hips. "There's nothing wrong with that blue jumper."

"It's not pretty enough," Gracie said, scowling at her reflection in the small white-framed mirror nailed to the wall over her dresser. "I want to be pretty."

Gramma Del sighed, and Gracie pretended she hadn't heard the sound. She knew just what it meant. She wasn't pretty like Laquita or Mary Ann—the face in the mirror told her that—and most likely she never would be. Her face was small and narrow. Her eyes were plain ordinary brown and big like cartoon eyes. Her clothes always looked like they'd belonged to somebody else, even when they still had Dotty's Discount Dress Store tags on them. Even Laquita, who had all those brothers and sisters, had nicer dresses.

More than anything, Gracie wanted to fit in. She'd been in kindergarten for three weeks now, and she had learned a lot. As much as they liked her, she was still an outsider who couldn't quite figure out why. It was more than the lookalike dresses from the big store down in Portland and the *Partridge Family* lunch boxes. Maybe it was that they all had mothers who took them to school in the morning and waited outside for them in the afternoon. Even Noah's mother showed up more often than not, all dressed in her fancy clothes that made Gramma Del roll her eyes when she thought Mrs. Chase wasn't looking. "Doesn't have the sense the good Lord gave her," Gramma Del said, tugging at the hem of her gray sweater.

Gramma Del walked Gracie to and from school most days, but every now and then her father took over the job. Gracie hated it when her father waited for her at the corner in his dented pickup truck with the sign Taylor Construction written on the driver's door. Her father didn't like to talk much in the mornings, and he didn't understand anything about matching your tights to your jumper or why peanut butter and jelly sandwiches should be on fluffy white bread, not rye with the little seeds that got between your teeth.

But oh how she loved school. For a few hours every day it didn't matter that she wasn't like the rest of them. In that little classroom, she was one of the gang. She could read what was on the blackboard before Mrs. Cavanaugh explained it. At first Laquita and Noah thought it was some kind of magic trick. Then, when they realized she could read *and* write, the looks on their faces made her laugh. She knew the mama gerbil was going to have babies before Mrs. Cavanaugh did. Mary Ann saved a place next to her at nap time, and even though she'd much rather nap on Noah's side of the room, she didn't want to hurt Mary Ann's feelings, so she stayed where she was. Besides, she could watch Noah from over there and not be afraid he was going to catch her doing it. She loved the way his thick dark lashes rested against his cheeks, the way he smiled a little in his sleep. Sometimes he seemed ashamed to be her friend, but that was okay, too, because she knew that when Don and Tim and the others ran off, she'd still be there waiting for him.

• • •

Noah's parents didn't argue very often. The sound of their cultured Yankee voices, raised loud enough to be heard from the hallway, scared him. He pressed himself against the wall near the kitchen and tried hard not to listen, but their words found him just the same.

"Del brought her here when she was a baby," his mother said. "I don't see the difference, Simon. She was no trouble then, and she'll be no trouble now."

"I have nothing against the child," his father said, "but I don't want to open the door to her father."

"She's a little girl. Do you want her safety on your conscience?"

"I'll agree," his father said, "but only as an interim measure. Del has two weeks to make other arrangements."

The silence was long and dark, and Noah wondered what it was about Gracie's father that made his own father sound so serious. Noah had seen Gracie's father three times in front of school, hunched behind the wheel of a truck with swirly letters painted on the side. He didn't walk Gracie to the steps like her Grandma Del did. He didn't meet her at the corner like Noah's mother. Instead, Gracie's father stayed in the truck and drummed his fingers on the steering wheel, and when Gracie waved goodbye, he just gunned the engine and drove off without waving good-bye right back.

Noah knew that there were rich people and poor people in the world. His parents had explained it to him when he'd asked why their maid cleaned their house and her own, while his mother went to lunch and didn't clean anything at all. What he didn't know was why Gracie didn't have a mother or why his father didn't like her.

His parents' voices grew softer again, and the shaky feeling inside his stomach went away. His mother appeared in the doorway. She smiled at him, but he saw that her eyes looked sad. "There you are," she said, holding out her hand. "Breakfast is ready, then it's off to school with you."

"Are you and Father mad?" he asked as he slid his hand into hers.

The smile faded. "Why would you ask that?"

"I heard you talking," he said as they walked down the hallway to the breakfast room.

"Grown-ups sometimes sound very serious, honey, and it can sound like we're angry. It's just our way."

"Is Gracie in trouble?"

She stopped and crouched down next to him, taking his face between her hands. "Nobody's in trouble," she said, and he noticed the shimmer of tears in her big blue eyes. "It's just that Gracie needs a place to play after school, and Del thought it might be nice if the two of you played together."

"Here?" In his whole life he'd never had a friend come over to play, and the idea made him want to turn somersaults up and down the hallway. Even his birthday parties were held at a fancy restaurant in Boothbay Harbor on the water.

His mother nodded. "Not as a permanent thing," she said. "Just until Del can make other arrangements."

"Can Laquita and Don and Tim come home with me, too?"

"Maybe someday," his mother said, the corners of her mouth angling down toward her chin. "Right now, Gracie is as much as your father can handle."

Sometimes Daddy slept in his Laz-y Boy with his feet pointed right at the TV screen and a shiny mountain of beer cans on the floor near the lamp with the shredded shade. Grandma Del said he worked too hard and that the sandman's job was over before Daddy could even make it to his bedroom. He sprawled across the chair with his arms flung out over the sides and his feet hanging off that funny little leg rest that hung off the end of the chair and snored like a summer thunderstorm. She didn't mind the fact that he fell asleep in his chair. Other daddies on TV did that, too, so she knew it was okay. That was how Gracie knew the way things were supposed to be.

Gracie hated the way the beer smell clung to his skin. It made him smell like a stranger, like somebody she didn't want to know. She'd asked Gramma Del if maybe they could hide his six-packs, but Gramma Del just shook her head and said the world wasn't big enough to hide temptation from a man bound and determined to fall.

Five times in the last two weeks he'd forgotten to pick up Gracie from school, and Mrs. Cavanaugh had to call Gramma Del at work. Gracie had sat quietly on the front step while Mrs. Cavanaugh paced the sidewalk, glancing at her watch as she peered up and down the street. The worst part of all was the way the other parents looked at Gracie. Their eyes would get all big and sad-looking, and they'd quickly turn their heads away and walk a little faster.

"We're going to make a few changes around here," Gramma Del said as she walked Gracie to school the morning after Daddy drove his truck onto the McMahon family's lawn and hit a sugar maple. Gramma said that Daddy wouldn't be picking her up after school anymore. From now on, Gracie would be walking home with Noah and Mrs. Chase.

Gracie stared up at her grandmother. "I'll go home with Noah?"

"Yes," Gramma said. Her mouth was so tight the word barely squeezed itself out. "Mr. Chase said you can sit quietly in the kitchen with me while I fix their supper."

"I can't play with Noah? He has electric trains."

Gramma's grip on her hand tightened.

"Ouch!"

Gramma's fingers loosened a teeny bit. "You are to stay in the kitchen with me, missy, and that's an order. Mr. Chase doesn't much like strangers in his house." She laughed one of those grown-up laughs that Gracie didn't understand. "Except the ones on his payroll."

It was said about Simon Harriman Chase that what he didn't own wasn't worth owning. His family had founded Idle Point before the Revolutionary War, and it was his family who had kept it going through good times and bad. They had started out as shipbuilders and were modestly successful until Josiah Chase discovered a vein of tourmaline on his property and the family fortune was made. The Chase influence was still felt in shipbuilding, in tourmaline mining, and in real estate, but for the last sixty years, the Chase family had been synonymous with journalism. The *Idle Point Gazette* had achieved a national reputation for fair, incisive reporting and had the awards to prove it. Simon's father handed over the reins of leadership to his eldest son eight years ago, and so far Simon had managed to maintain the same standards of critical excellence his readers had come to expect from the *Gazette*.

He ran the paper, chaired the local Chamber of Commerce, volunteered his time and money to the school board, hospital, and church. He was a model citizen, an accomplished man who hated a child with an intensity that sometimes scared him.

The sight of poor plain little Graciela Taylor with her brown hair and brown eyes and skinny little body filled him with helpless rage. He didn't wish her dead. He simply wished she had never been born.

TWO

~~~⟨e⟩~~~

She was such a little thing, Ruth Marlow Chase thought
as she took Gracie's hand in hers. The child's hand was
tiny, much smaller than Noah's, and he was only six
months older. The bones felt so fragile to Ruth that for a
moment she longed to gather the girl close to her and tell
her everything would be all right. God knew, she hadn't
wanted to feel anything for Mona Taylor's only child, but
Ruth was a kind woman, and it was impossible for her to
steel her mother's heart against a child, especially one as
small and easily forgettable as Gracie.

Gracie had brown eyes, brown hair, and skin as pale as
milk. Tiny face no bigger than a minute with features so
regular they barely registered on you. Her clothes looked
to be plucked from the box in the rear of the church
marked For the Poor. The child was plainer than plain,
not at all like her mother, and that struck Ruth as terribly
unfair. Mona had been blessed with the heart-shaped face
of an angel. Wide brow, delicate chin, full lips, and huge
brown eyes that drew you into their depths against your
will. Sweet-faced and sensual and—

Ruth stopped herself. She had been trained never to
speak ill of the dead, and Mona had been gone five years

this past May. So much had happened in those five years: Noah was in their life, and she had discovered a happiness neither she nor her husband had believed attainable. All of those years spent searching for the answer, and it had been right there, hiding behind a wall of disappointment so high she thought they would never get past it.

It all changed the day Mona Taylor died.

Ruth's face burned with embarrassment. How could she think such a thing with Mona's little girl walking next to her, as quiet and drab as one of those little field mice Ruth saw scampering across the lawn in the morning? She had wished many times that Mona and Ben Taylor would pack their bags and leave Idle Point forever, but she'd never once wished the woman dead, not even in her darkest moments. You couldn't build a good life on a foundation of hatred. You couldn't raise a healthy, happy child in an atmosphere of anger. There was so much sorrow and hatred in the world. Was it so wrong of her to want to keep it as far away from her family as she possibly could?

Maybe Simon was right, and she shouldn't have said yes to Del's request. Certainly the good Sisters of the Blessed Virgin would have opened their doors to Gracie for a few hours each afternoon. She knew Del was a Catholic, one who probably gave away much too much of her salary to the church. The old woman kept a blue rosary in the right-hand pocket of her apron and fingered it nervously like one of those Greek fishermen with the worry beads Ruth had seen on their vacation last year. Certainly if Del had approached the nuns, they would have found it in their hearts to help out.

"Family first" was Simon's motto. Nothing came before the sanctity of the family. He hadn't always understood that, but since Noah's arrival, he was a different man. Ruth knew she would be a fool to rock the boat, but she was very fond of Del, and there were times when she felt she owed the Taylors something. She wasn't exactly sure what or why, but a nagging sense of guilt was always there when she thought of what had become of Ben and his family. Somewhere along the way there must have been something she could have done to change things. Maybe if she'd stood up for herself with Simon or challenged Mona or been a better wife, a better woman, there might have been enough happy endings to go around.

But she hadn't. Ben was a drunk who lived off the money his elderly mother made cooking for the Chases. His wife was dead and buried while his sad-eyed little girl clung to the hand of a stranger with the kind of trust that the world would knock out of her before too long. And then there was Ruth, queen of the house on the hill, blessed with a husband who was the most powerful man in town and a beautiful little boy with the face of an angel—and all because she'd opted for silence, for the status quo. In the end there had been just one happy ending to go around, and it belonged to her.

Del was waiting for them on the front steps. Her hands were buried deep in the pockets of her apron, and she didn't smile until Mrs. Chase let go of Gracie's hand.

"In the house, child," she said to Gracie with a nod of her head toward Mrs. Chase and Noah. "We've been enough of a nuisance for one day."

"Not at all," said Ruth Chase, her pale blue eyes widening with surprise. "Gracie was great company, wasn't she, Noah?"

Noah was six years old and had other things on his mind.

"Cookies and milk on the table, same as always," Del said as the little boy ran toward the kitchen door. "Wash your hands first."

"You take such good care of him," Ruth said. She still had the same nervous smile she'd had as a girl. Del remembered that smile from the days when Gracie's father was captain of the high school football team and all the girls in town vied for his attention

"It's my job," Del said, her fingers tightening around her rosary beads.

"You treat Noah like one of your own."

"He's a good boy."

Ruth glowed with pleasure. She adored that child, which was a point in her favor as far as Del was concerned. Maybe if people paid more attention to their own, the world would be better off.

"Gramma Del." Gracie tugged at the sleeve of her gray sweater.

"Go inside," she said, patting the child's soft brown hair. "I'll be right there."

"Gramma Del!" More urgent this time.

Ruth smiled knowingly. "There's a bathroom right next to the kitchen," she said. "I'll show you."

Del stepped between the woman and child. "I'll show her, thank you kindly."

"You're busy," Ruth said, the nervous smile flickering. "Besides, I love having a little girl around."

"If you don't mind me saying so, missus, Mr. Chase doesn't feel the same way."

Ruth waved her hand in the air. "He's all bluster, Del. Surely you know that. He's just one for schedules and appointments. I wouldn't worry about him."

"I wouldn't either if he was my husband," Del said, although that wasn't entirely true. He was the kind of man who demanded obedience from everyone. "I need this job, Mrs. Chase. I can't afford to make him angry."

She didn't wait for an answer. She turned instead and shooed Gracie into the house.

• • •

By the time Gracie settled in at the kitchen table, Noah had finished his milk and cookies and gone upstairs to play. Gracie painstakingly colored some pictures in the Barbie coloring book Gramma Del had given her for her last birthday, but secretly she was listening for Noah. The house was as big as the school where she went to kindergarten, almost as big as the food store on Main Street. You could fit her room at home into the bathroom and still have space enough for the kitchen and hallway, too.

She'd never thought about what it meant to be rich. Gramma Del and Daddy said the Chases were rich and that they were poor, and when she asked why, her daddy had just said, "Because that's the way it's always been," and opened another bottle. It was very quiet in the Chase house. The only sound was Gramma Del singing to herself as she washed lettuce at the sink and sliced red, juicy tomatoes.

"Can I play with Noah?" she asked, pushing away the coloring book.

"You stay right here and keep me company," Gramma said.

"I want to watch cartoons."

"You'll watch cartoons when we go home."

"The cartoons'll be over when we get home."

"Then read one of your storybooks, Graciela. I'll be finished here in two shakes of a lamb's tail."

She didn't want to read a storybook. She wanted to find Noah and watch cartoons and turn somersaults down the long hallway.

"Does Noah have a puppy?" she asked, swinging her legs back and forth.

"No puppies," said Gramma.

"Bet he has kittens," she said. "Lots and lots of kittens."

She would fill up the big house with puppies and kittens and parakeets.

"No puppies, no kittens." Gramma wiped her hands on the dishrag tucked into the waistband of her apron and turned toward Gracie. "Mr. Chase doesn't like disruption."

"What does that mean?"

"It means he doesn't like dogs or cats or nosy little girls who should mind their own business."

"Is he a bad man?"

"He's a man," Gramma said with a sour look on her face. "That's all you need to know."

Most days, Mrs. Chase was there waiting at the bottom of the school steps for Gracie and Noah. She had asked Gracie to call her Aunt Ruth, but Gramma Del had said, "Not while I'm breathing," and that was that. Gracie had been afraid that Mrs. Chase would be angry, but Noah's mommy never seemed to be anything but sweet and pleasant, just like all the mommies on TV. Nobody ever yelled in Noah's house. They all whispered. The air never smelled of cigarettes and beer. It seemed to Gracie that all the flowers in Idle Point found their way to Mrs. Chase and made the house smell like springtime. Gracie asked Gramma Del if they could have flowers, too, but Gramma made one of her faces and said she didn't have time for such nonsense. Then she bent down right in front of Gracie's nose and said, "Don't you go getting too big for your britches, missy," which puzzled Gracie for days.

She hated it when Mrs. Chase was busy and she sent that prune-faced housekeeper instead. The housekeeper didn't even hold their hands when they crossed the big street between the school and the post office. The only good part about housekeeper days was the way Noah always reached for Gracie's hand as they stepped off the curb and held it tightly until they made it safely to the other side. Other than that, he didn't pay much attention to her in school or at home. She told herself she didn't care, but that was only because she would die if he knew how much she wanted to be his friend. Everybody liked Noah. They all wanted to be his best friend and sit with him at lunch and nap next to his blanket in the afternoon. Gracie wanted that, too, but she didn't think it was ever going to happen.

Halloween came and went. Thanksgiving, too. One snowy afternoon in early December, Noah and Gracie were walking home with Mrs. Chase when they saw Laquita standing at the corner near the hardware store. Her bare hands were clenched into fists, and she looked like she'd been crying.

"Isn't that the Adams girl?" Mrs. Chase said. Her voice sounded like a hug to Gracie, and instantly she felt jealous. Nobody had ever sounded that way about her.

She met Noah's eyes behind his mother's back and made a silly face. He laughed, and Mrs. Chase gave him a sharp look. "Stay here, children. I'll see what's wrong."

The wind off the water was high. It smelled to Gracie like salt and snow. Next to hot chocolate and puppy breath, that was her favorite smell in the whole world. She loved the way Idle Point smelled, all salty and sharp. She couldn't imagine living anywhere else in the whole world. Sometimes she heard Gramma Del and Daddy talking about how all the youngsters were up and leaving Idle Point for the cities where all you could smell were cars and people, and she wanted to say, "I won't be like that. I'll never leave here." She loved the sound the wind made on winter nights when she burrowed deeper under her blankets, the way the sea spray kissed her cheeks and nose as she walked to school, the way the waves exploded against the jagged rocks that outlined the shore. Idle Point wasn't soft and pretty like the storybook towns in picture books. To Gracie it was better: It was perfect.

She and Noah stood close together as they watched Mrs. Chase speak with the dark-haired little girl who kept brushing at her eyes with the back of her sleeve. They both knew that Laquita never cried, not even the time Buddy Powell pushed her off the swing and she cut her knee open. Laquita was only six years old, just like Noah, but she already had four brothers and sisters trailing behind her like the tail on a kite.

Mrs. Chase walked back toward them, holding the girl by the hand. "We're going to walk Laquita home," she said in her sweet voice. "Gracie, you take Laquita's hand. Noah, you come around this side and take my hand."

Big ugly spears of jealousy stabbed Gracie in the chest. She was supposed to be holding Mrs. Chase's hand, not Laquita's. She didn't care if the little girl looked sad enough to cry. It just wasn't fair. Wasn't it enough that Laquita got to play Mary in the school Christmas play next week, while Gracie was just a stupid shepherd? She didn't have the right to just show up there on the corner and push Gracie aside that way. And why did Mrs. Chase have to use her mommy voice anyway when everybody knew Laquita had a mommy of her own? It just wasn't fair.

It was the worst day of Laquita Adams's life, worse even than when she'd wet herself when her cousin Ellie tickled her and wouldn't stop no matter how loud Laquita yelled. She didn't want Mrs. Chase to walk her home. She didn't care that it was freezing cold outside or that her hands had turned into twin Popsicles. Sooner or later Daddy or Mommy would remember to come and get her. She didn't need for Noah and Gracie to see that all the stories about her family were right, that her parents didn't know how to take care of children, that they couldn't be trusted. Her parents loved her, even if they did sometimes seem to lose her in the crowd of kids. She just wished nobody else had to know about it.

Laquita knew the way these things worked. As soon as Noah and Gracie saw the love beads and smelled the incense and met her parents with their long, long hair and soft voices and strange ways, they'd go running right back to school with stories about the hippies over by the river and how they had too many babies and too little money, and maybe somebody should do something about it, help them out maybe, remind them that the world already had too many children.

Laquita didn't know much about the world, but she was sure her parents had too many children. There were babies everywhere you looked and smelly diapers and blankets and banana squished into the rugs. And with each new baby it seemed she got more forgotten. Why couldn't they be happy with just one or two babies like everybody else? Why did they think they needed so many? She couldn't imagine Noah's mommy with a houseful of babies all crying at once. She couldn't imagine Noah's mommy even visiting a house filled with babies, but that was just what was about to happen.

"You children stay here," Mrs. Chase said when they approached the rickety front porch, and suddenly Laquita saw her house the way it must look to her. The missing step. The collapsed pumpkins left over from Halloween oozing seeds and smelling like barf. The baby shoe on its side near the door. Worst of all was the noise! Crying babies and the television and Daddy's voice sounding louder than she'd ever heard it.

Laquita stood near the top step and rested her hand on the splintered wood. Noah and Gracie stood close together a few feet away. They all turned slightly when they heard

Mrs. Chase's voice, then Daddy's. Gracie's and Noah's
eyes grew wide. Laquita felt the knot of fear in her tummy
begin to untie just a little bit when her Daddy pushed open
the front door and stepped outside. He scooped her up in
his arms and said, "We're sorry, Quita, but your mom
went into labor around lunchtime, and we've been pretty
busy. We knew our grown-up little girl would find her
way home somehow."

He told Gracie and Noah that Laquita had a new baby
sister and invited them all inside to meet Cheyenne Marie.
Mrs. Chase said she needed a cigarette and would wait
for Noah and Gracie on the porch. Laquita noticed that
Mrs. Chase's hands were shaking, and her mouth was set
in an angry line.

Gracie's and Noah's eyes met, and Laquita almost burst
into tears. Cheyenne! Why did her parents like such stupid
names? Why couldn't she be Annie or Mary or Sue like
the other girls in class? Why couldn't she have brothers
named Jack and Bob instead of Sage and Morocco?

Her parents never did anything normal, or so it seemed
to Laquita. She loved them, but they always made her feel
like she wanted to hide in the back of the station wagon
and pretend she wasn't with them. Nobody else's parents
painted hearts and flowers on their car. She hated the long
black ponytail that swung between her father's shoulder
blades and the way her mother would feed one of the
babies any time she felt like it, sometimes right in the
middle of the candy aisle at the food store. Noah's
mommy would never do something like that, and she had
seen the way Gracie's Gramma Del looked at her parents
like they were the bad guys on a TV show. Why couldn't
they just be like everybody else?

When she grew up, she would have her own house and
she would live in it all by herself. Her house would have
white walls and white carpets and a white cat with blue

eyes, and it would smell like the beach roses that grew by the fence. Her parents and her brothers and sisters could come for visits, but they would have to sleep at the motel over near Eb's Stop and Pump because there would be only one bedroom in her house, and that bedroom would belong to her.

Gracie wanted to hate everything about Laquita's family, but she couldn't. She loved the noise and the baby smells and the way everyone seemed to really love each other. Laquita's mommy had let Gracie snuggle right in the bed with her, then placed the brand-new baby girl in her arms. Gracie had thought her heart would burst with excitement. The baby was so tiny, so perfect, and when she reached up and wrapped her tiny fist around Gracie's finger, she felt like she did on Christmas morning, only better. Imagine living like this all the time!

She looked at Laquita and wished they could change places. Laquita got to hold the babies and feed them and play with them every single day of the week. There was always somebody to hug or to talk with and a mommy and daddy who really seemed to like each other and their growing family. Laquita's mommy was full and soft like a pillow, and her daddy liked to make everyone laugh. The house was small, almost as small as Gramma Del's cottage, too small for the shadows and secrets that filled the house where Gracie lived. It seemed to Gracie that there was just room enough in Laquita's house for love.

"Quita," said the father after awhile, "why don't you take Graciela and Noah out back and show them Moses and the kittens."

Laquita didn't say anything. She just made a face and motioned for Gracie and Noah to follow her. Gracie didn't want to leave Mrs. Adams and the new baby, but the thought of kittens was more than she could resist. The only thing better than kittens was a basket of puppies.

She climbed off the bed and hurried to catch up with Laquita and Noah. They walked through a hallway plastered with drawings Laquita had done in kindergarten, stepped over two sleeping toddlers, and stopped to pat a big dog with red and white and black fur who was sprawled across the entrance to the kitchen. One day Gracie would have a dog just like that one, maybe even three of them! She'd have cats and kittens and a parrot named Walter and maybe one named Groucho, too. She would keep hamsters and gerbils, and there would be a tank of goldfish in every room.

Gramma Del wouldn't let her have a dog or a cat until she was old enough to take care of them. Gracie thought she was old enough now, but Gramma wouldn't budge. "I have enough work, thank you very much," Gramma said the last time Gracie asked, "and I don't need any more." Noah didn't have pets either, not even one measly goldfish in a round bowl from Kmart. They said his father was allergic, but Gracie didn't believe it. Mr. Chase probably just didn't want to be bothered.

She was surprised to find Noah's mommy sitting at the kitchen table with two other women. They were all smoking cigarettes, and a cup of coffee sat on the table in front of each of them. The two women looked a lot like Laquita's mommy with the same wide green eyes and curly hair. They even dressed like her in hand-me-downs that made Gracie think of old movies from back in the sixties. Mrs. Chase's fancy dark blue coat had slipped off the back of her chair and fallen to the floor where one of Laquita's baby brothers had claimed it for a blanket. Gracie would have figured Mrs. Chase would hate all that baby slobber on her coat, but she didn't seem to mind one bit. She even reached down to make sure the baby was covered with one of the sleeves. Gramma Del would have done something just like that.

"We'll be leaving in five minutes," Mrs. Chase called to them as they trooped out the back door after Laquita. Then she said something low that made the other two women laugh. Noah looked startled by the sound, as if he had never heard his mother laugh before.

They followed Laquita out to the shed where a mama cat named Moses greeted them with a loud meow while her five kittens answered back from their cozy straw-lined bed in the corner. "Moses was supposed to be a boy," Laquita said, cuddling the large gray cat, "but she fooled us when she had babies."

Noah and Gracie looked at each other, then laughed when they realized Laquita thought it was funny, too.

"You're lucky," Gracie said. "Now you get to have kittens."

"Uh-uh." Laquita shook her head. "Mommy says we have to find someone to adopt them."

"I know what that is," Gracie said. "You go to the place where they keep the lost pets and you take one home with you and take care of it forever."

"You could have a kitten if you want," Laquita said.

Gracie's heart beat so fast that it hurt. "Really?"

"Sure. You can pick whichever you want."

Gracie knew right away which kitten was the right one: the little white and gray one sitting alone in the corner of the box, looking like Gracie felt sometimes.

"He's so tiny!" She cradled the kitten against her chest. "His eyes are all wet. Does he have a cold?"

Laquita didn't know, and neither did Noah.

But that was okay. Gracie would keep the kitten cozy and dry. She would feed him warm milk from a teaspoon and sneak him scraps from her dinner the way the children in her storybooks cared for stray cats. She would make him all better and love him and take care of him just like her mother would have cared for her if God hadn't called her back to heaven.

THREE

Gracie wasn't the prettiest little girl on stage or the most talented. Ben Taylor didn't want to notice that, but he couldn't help it. She had never captured all of his heart, not since those heady first weeks after her birth when he'd still believed in miracles. He sat in the third row of the Idle Point Elementary School auditorium on the Friday before Christmas and watched as Gracie, dressed in shepherd's robes and carrying a staff, looked up toward the sky. "Behold!" she said in a clear, sweet voice. "A star rises in the east!"

It seemed to Ben that she'd been a baby the last time he'd looked at her. He turned away for just a moment, and the baby was gone, replaced by the child who stood before him. He'd spent most of her life swimming through a sea of booze, doing everything he could to blunt the sharp bite of pain that followed him through his days. She was so quiet around the house that he sometimes forgot she was there, a little mouse who spent her time with her nose in a book. He'd thought she was looking at the pictures, but Del said she'd been reading for almost a year.

He wasn't one for books. He'd rather work with his hands. Back in the early years of his marriage to Mona, he'd always had five or six projects in the works at any one time. Cupboards for her collections, toy boxes for the family they were trying to start. As the years went on and the children didn't arrive, he spent more time on cabinetry, more time away from the house and the pain that seemed to be everywhere.

Then one day in the twentieth year of their marriage, Mona told him she was pregnant. From the ashes of their dreams, they had their miracle. Six months later, Graciela Marie Taylor was pushed kicking and screaming from the world of angels and into his heart. "She has your eyes," Mona said, and oh how he'd wanted to believe that. Everyone in town wondered about the truth. He saw it on their faces when he shot the breeze with the folks down at the coffee shop next door to the *Gazette*. He saw it every time Simon Chase walked by.

He'd been working on a cradle for baby Gracie the day the accident happened. He and Mona had been talking about what kind of stain he should use on the wood just before she kissed him good-bye. If he closed his eyes he could see her as she'd been, lush and womanly with that sweet face and those big dark eyes that turned men into fools. He was no exception. He'd loved her enough to forgive her. He'd loved her enough to stop asking questions. The one thing he hadn't been able to do was love her enough to let her go.

She was taking the baby to the pediatrician for a booster shot of some kind. "Don't forget to buy milk," he had said to her as she went out the door. His last words to her: *Don't forget to buy milk.*

The chief of police, Joe Winthrop, had broken the news to him. Ben had been cleaning some paintbrushes in a mayonnaise jar filled with turpentine when he heard Joe's squad car crunching across the gravel driveway. He'd laid the brushes down on top of some newspaper, wiped his hands on the sides of his pants, then stepped out of the garage to see what Joe wanted. It was unusually hot that day in Idle Point. He'd never seen a May as hot as this one. They all said it was going to be a wicked summer. The sun was high in the sky, and he shielded his eyes with the back of his hand. His skin smelled like turpentine. He still remembered that fact. Even when he couldn't remember his own name, he remembered the dizzying smell of turpentine.

"What brings you out this way, Joe?" he asked, moving toward him. "Is it lunchtime already?" Mona had said she and the baby would be home by noon. He glanced up. The sun was directly overhead but leaning westward. "You're mighty quiet today."

Joe's face seemed to fall in on itself. "Jesus," Joe said, and his voice cracked on the word, tore itself right in two. "Jesus, Ben, I—"

Mona's purse, the straw one with the leather cords. Joe was holding Mona's purse in his hand.

"I'm sorry," Joe said. Those were the last words Ben remembered for a very long time.

He viewed the rest of it as if it had happened to someone else. The crushing pain of those first few days came close to killing him. A part of him wished it had. He wouldn't talk about a funeral, wouldn't let them start digging a grave at the old cemetery behind the church, wouldn't even care for his own daughter. The talk swirled all around him, white-hot and ugly. Mona was leaving him . . . somebody saw her at the outskirts of town . . . she had a suitcase all packed and in the trunk . . . poor Ben . . . poor, poor little Gracie . . .

He curled himself around a bottle of Scotch they kept in the cupboard above the refrigerator, and he tried to drink himself into oblivion.

He'd been working on that steadily ever since.

"Don't look now," said his mother Del when the show ended and they were waiting for Gracie, "but here comes trouble."

He turned his head in the direction Del indicated and saw Nora Fahey gliding toward them. Nora was a good-looking woman if you liked them racehorse lean and edgy. She had long, dark blond hair parted in the middle, tucked behind ears that sported long, dangly silver earrings. She wore a fisherman's sweater, a long gauzy skirt, and a denim jacket that looked like it had belonged to somebody else. He and Nora had been sleeping together since the night back in October when they hooked up at Rusty's over a game of eight ball. She taught art at the high school, owned six cats, and was looking to get married. He'd made two mistakes since Mona's death and he wasn't looking to make a third, but sometimes not even booze could ease the ache inside his heart. He'd been sober since Thanksgiving and was trying hard to make it to the New Year. He didn't want to rush into anything, not this time. He was getting close to fifty, and the mistakes were too hard to undo. The thing about being sober was that it made you see things you didn't want to see. Booze was a cloud of forgiveness between you and everything ugly. Booze was better than the confessional. It absolved your sins before you even had the chance to commit them.

Sober, he had to face up to the fact that he was flushing his life down the toilet. Taylor Construction was a joke. A name on the door of a truck. If he fielded six calls a year, that was cause for celebration. Add to that the fact that the kid needed a mother and Del needed to quit working for those bastards on the hill, and you had a life pretty well fucked up beyond repair.

Nora kissed him lightly then said hello to Del. His mother, never one for small talk, turned away.

"Gracie was wonderful," Nora said, linking her arm through his.

He nodded. "Came as a surprise to me." So did the fact that she was growing up.

"Why don't the three of you come back to my place for hot chocolate?" Nora suggested. He knew what this meant, bringing his mother and Gracie to Nora's place.

Nora was thirty-eight years old, divorced, and lonely. She was also soft and kind and womanly, and he ached for all of that and more.

He was forty-seven, widowed, and going down for the count. He did the only thing he knew how to do. He said yes.

Mrs. Cavanaugh made sure all the costumes had been collected before she gave out the Christmas cards and candy. Gracie and Noah waited their turns with Laquita and Mary Ellen. Don and Tim were always first on line, and they tried to grab two bags each when Mrs. Cavanaugh wasn't looking, but she put a stop to it. Gracie didn't mind so much, because she knew that the two brothers didn't always get as much to eat as the rest of them did. Besides, the longer it took to reach the front of the line, the longer the night would last.

She loved the way the auditorium looked with the bright red and green Christmas decorations and the big tree in the corner of their classroom. She loved dressing up in her shepherd's costume and stepping right up to the front of the stage when it was her turn to say her lines. For a moment she was so scared she didn't think she'd be able to push out the words, but then, like magic, something happened, and she wasn't Gracie Taylor any more but a real-life shepherd in Bethlehem, heralding the magical star in the first Christmas sky. At first she didn't see Daddy and Gramma Del in the audience, but then all of

a sudden her eyes landed right on them, and she was so
happy she thought her heart would burst. Gramma Del
blotted at her eyes with a handkerchief, and Daddy smiled
at her in a way he hadn't smiled in a long, long time. She
saw Nora Fahey sitting alone near the back, and she wondered if Miss Fahey wasn't speaking to Daddy anymore.
That happened a lot.

If only he could marry someone like Noah's mommy.
The thought made her feel all dreamy and sad at the same
time. Why couldn't Daddy find a wife who actually liked
little girls?

"Merry Christmas, Graciela." Mrs. Cavanaugh handed
her a small bag of hard candies and a Christmas card.
Gracie ducked her head and mumbled thank you, then ran
over to where the rest of the kids were trading for their
favorite flavors. She knew she couldn't stay much longer.
Gramma Del and Daddy were waiting for her outside, and
Daddy always got mad when Gracie dawdled. She had to
admit it had been better lately. He didn't smell like beer
anymore and he was always awake when she and Gramma
Del came home at night. Once he'd even started the meat
loaf heating up in the oven and set the table. Gramma Del
said he wasn't to go patting himself on the back for doing
what needed to be done, but Gracie could see it made her
very happy.

The last few weeks had been the very best in Gracie's
short life. She still loved school, and it showed. When
Mrs. Cavanaugh opened the Christmas mailbox yesterday
afternoon, Gracie had more cards than anybody but Noah.
Every time Mrs. Cavanaugh called her name, she felt her
heart swell with happiness. Noah turned bright red when
he opened the card Gracie had made for him. Gramma
Del had helped her cut green construction paper in the
shape of a Christmas tree and she'd decorated it with gold
and red and silver stars from the five-and-ten, then written

"Merry Xmas Noah Love Gracie" along the bottom. He'd bought her a real Hallmark card from the drugstore near the *Gazette* and signed it "With Love Noah." He'd made a mistake on the word "Noah" and had to cross it out and write it again. She promised she would keep the card forever and ever.

Laquita's mommy showed up in the doorway with the new baby in her arms and said it was time for them to go. Don and Tim had already left. So had most of the other kids. Finally Mrs. Cavanaugh said it was time for her to close up and that they shouldn't keep their parents waiting any longer, so Noah and Gracie put on their coats and mittens and started for the front door. They were halfway there when Mrs. Chase appeared, looking just like an angel from a Christmas card. Her blond hair looked like a halo, and she wore a white wool coat and a soft white scarf around her neck. The scarf twinkled with little gold stars that matched the sparkly gold star pinned to her collar. When she bent down to say hello to Gracie, Gracie reached up and touched her cheek with a mittened hand. Mrs. Chase laughed softly, then gathered Gracie close to her in a hug that smelled like cinnamon and chocolate—a mommy smell that made Gracie bury her head deep into the soft folds of her coat and wish she could stay there forever.

"I'm so glad I found you, Gracie," she said while Noah looked on. "We have a gift for you." She reached into the leather bag slung over her arm and pulled out a package wrapped in shiny red paper and tied with a big green and gold bow.

Gracie immediately tried to pull off the ribbons, but Mrs. Chase stopped her.

"No, no," she said. "I want you to wait until Christmas morning."

Gracie promised, but in her heart she knew that the

second she was in the backseat of Daddy's truck she
wouldn't be able to resist. Mrs. Chase turned to talk to
Mrs. Cavanaugh, who had joined them while Gracie and
Noah made faces at the teacher's back. The best thing
about Noah was the way he could be just as silly as the
rest of them. They were just about to take off their boots
and play skating rink in the hallway when Gramma Del's
voice sounded.

"Graci-*el*-a! You come out here this instant."

Gracie's heart sank. Gramma Del sounded like she was
in one of her moods, which meant that she'd had a fight
with Daddy or knew that Gracie was in here with Noah
and his mommy.

"Uh-oh," she said to Noah, then grabbed her Christmas
presents and card and ran toward the door.

"Hurry up with you," Gramma said, taking her hand.
"We're going to Nora Fahey's for hot chocolate, whether
we like it or not."

Gracie didn't much like Nora Fahey, but Nora had a
lot of cats, and that almost made up for the fact that she
would probably end up marrying Gracie's daddy. Ever
since Sam the kitten had come to live with her, Gracie
had been a lot less lonely. Sam shared everything with
her. He sat on her lap when she watched cartoons and
slept with his tiny head on her pillow at night. She told
Sam all of her secrets and most of her dreams. Gramma
Del hadn't been very happy when she saw Sam peeking
out of Gracie's coat pocket the day Laquita's sister Cheyenne was born, but after Mrs. Chase put in a word,
Gramma came around. She told Gracie she could keep
Sam as long as the kitten stayed in her room and didn't
get underfoot. "That's a lot of responsibility for a little
girl," Noah's mommy had said to her. "Are you sure you
can take good care of your kitty?"

Gracie swore to her on a stack of Bibles that she would.

Every day after school, Noah's mommy asked her about Sam the Cat. "Gracie, I was reading about cats last night in the newspaper. Did you know that chocolate is very bad for them? Cats love fresh drinking water. Did you know that, Gracie? You must keep the litter box clean, or Sam will look for someplace else . . ." Gracie tried to remember all of the things Mrs. Chase told her by writing down some of the words in the notebook she carried to school every day, but she didn't know how to spell all of them.

Mrs. Chase was Noah's mommy, but she seemed to love Gracie, too—at least a little. Mrs. Chase had a special smile for Gracie that made her feel wanted, and now this present proved it! Gracie settled into the backseat of the truck and started to slide the ribbons off the package as soon as Daddy started to drive away.

"What are you doing?" Daddy asked as the sound of ripping paper filled the truck.

"Nothing," Gracie said.

"She's opening a present," Gramma Del said. "That Mrs. Cavanaugh was mighty generous. Candy and a gift."

"Ooooh!" Gracie's heart almost burst through her chest. "Gramma, look!" She pulled the sweater out of the box and rubbed it gently against her cheek. The wool was cool and soft and smelled like cinnamon and chocolate, just like Noah's mommy. "A mommy sweater," she whispered. Her very own mommy sweater, just like all the other kids in school had, one of the special kind that hung proudly in the coatroom.

Gramma Del leaned over and inspected the sweater. Her fingers poked at the fine stitches and tugged at one of the pearly white buttons. "Your teacher made you this sweater?" She looked like she didn't believe such a thing was possible.

Gracie knew Gramma Del wasn't going to like the answer, but she'd been taught to tell the truth.

"It isn't from Mrs. Cavanaugh," Gracie said proudly. "It's from Noah's mommy."

"What did you say, Graciela?" That was Daddy from the front seat, and he didn't sound happy.

Gracie hung onto the sweater, and she didn't say a word.

"I asked you a question, Graciela."

Gramma Del poked her, but Gracie wasn't talking.

"Mrs. Chase gave your daughter a sweater," Gramma Del said in a voice Gracie had never heard before. It sounded like glass breaking.

"Son of a bitch!" Daddy screeched the truck to a stop, and Gracie closed her eyes as it fishtailed wildly across the icy road. Daddy hadn't been like this in a long time, and it scared her. He turned around in his seat and looked at Gracie. "Let me see that sweater."

She clung to it more tightly. "It's mine."

Gramma Del poked her again. "Let your daddy see it."

"No," Gracie said. "Noah's mommy gave it to me. It's mine."

"The hell it is." Ben leaned over the back of his seat and snatched the sweater from Gracie, who let out a high keening wail. He gunned the engine and started back in the opposite direction.

"Where are we going?" Gramma Del asked. She sounded as scared as Gracie felt.

"Where the hell do you think we're going?" he shot back. "We're going to return that goddamn sweater."

Ruth was just about to serve the cake and cookies when the doorbell rang. She put down the tray, carefully wiped her hands on a linen dish towel, then moved swiftly through the long hallway toward the front door. She heard Simon entertaining their guests in the front room with stories about Noah's tour de force appearance as Joseph in tonight's Christmas pageant at the school. She smiled at the note of justifiable pride in his voice. Noah was the light of his father's life, the reason he got up in the morning, the reason for the long hours spent at the *Gazette*, building a future for the boy who would carry on his name.

She wouldn't dwell on the dark years before Noah. What was done, was done. They were a family now, and nothing would ever change that. Out of terrible pain had come their greatest pleasure, and Ruth believed it had been worth every year of struggle.

He was such a popular little boy. It made her heart sing to watch the way the other children seemed to flock to him. He was a natural leader. Anyone could see that. She probably shouldn't have singled out Gracie Taylor the way she had, but she told herself nobody had seen her hand the gaily wrapped package to the little girl. There was something so touching about Gracie. She clung to Ruth's hand each afternoon as if she never wanted to let go. The poor thing was starved for a mother's love, and Ruth felt guilty for every day of happiness she had been afforded. Her own life had been restored to her the day Mona Taylor died, but at such a terrible cost to the child.

The doorbell rang again, and she bit back the slightest prickle of annoyance. Some people had no patience, but not Ruth. She knew how to wait. She had been practicing for most of her life. She ran a quick hand through her hair, blessing Alma at the Idle Point Beauty Salon, then swung open the door.

Ben Taylor stood there on the top step with the snow swirling around him. He looked almost violent, and she took a step back. "Ben," she said in her most polite and controlled voice. She prayed Simon hadn't heard the doorbell ring. "Can I help you?"

He tossed the sweater she'd picked out for Gracie at her feet.

"Graciela isn't a charity case," he all but spat in her face. "You can shove your presents up your—"

"Is there a problem?" Simon appeared at her side, and Ruth's knees almost gave way.

"Stay away from Graciela," Ben said, leveling a dangerous look at Simon.

Simon's expression gave away nothing. He took in the man on the doorstep, the ruined sweater lying in the snow, and the ashen look on Ruth's face in an instant.

"You have thirty seconds to leave," Simon said in a pleasant tone of voice. "If not, I'll call the police."

"There's been a misunderstanding," Ruth said as she picked up the sweater and brushed off the snow with trembling fingers. "This was just a little token of friendship from Noah. Nothing more."

"Stay away from Graciela," Ben repeated, "or I swear to God, I'll—" He stopped cold, and Ruth murmured a silent prayer of thanks. She knew her husband. One more word, and he would have had Ben Taylor behind bars before the next snowflake fell.

"Fifteen seconds," Simon said, still sounding pleasant and in control.

"She's mine," Ben said. "Remember that. Mine and Mona's."

His words found their mark. Simon's mask slipped just long enough for his wife to see his pain. Not even death could break the hold Mona Taylor had on these two men.

Ruth went back inside the house. She knew it would be a long time before either man realized she was gone.

FOUR

Noah had been away with his family all summer, and Gracie counted the days until school started and he came home again.

"But where is he?" she asked Gramma Del when she heard he wouldn't be coming back to Idle Point. "Why isn't he coming home when school starts?"

Gramma answered the way she always answered. "Because he's going to boarding school in New Hampshire, missy."

The answer made no sense to Gracie. Why would your parents want you to live far away at a sleepover school when you already had a gigantic room of your own and every toy in the Sears catalog? For a few weeks, Gracie badgered Gramma Del with the same questions about why Noah had to go away until Gramma Del finally said, "Because he's rich," then turned back to the dish-filled kitchen sink.

She never forgot Noah. The years passed, but the memory of those afternoons spent with the blue-eyed golden boy who lived in the big house on the hill never dimmed. Sometimes she would drive past the house on her way to Idle Point High, and she could almost see herself and

Noah running up the driveway with Mrs. Chase laughing behind them and Gramma Del waiting at the back door.

She loved school and threw herself into her studies wholeheartedly, the same way she did everything. She was rewarded with straight A's. She spent hours studying at the makeshift desk in her room with Sam the Cat draped across her shoulders. Sam was her best teacher. Gracie had filled notebook after notebook with her observations of Sam's behaviors, and those notebooks were the first small step on the road to achieving her dreams.

Gracie had a lot of friends at school, but it was understood that she couldn't invite any of them home with her. The bad thing about living in a town as small as Idle Point was that everyone knew everyone else's business. The good thing was you never had to explain. Mainers never asked questions, mostly because they already had all the answers right at the tips of their fingers. Everyone knew that the only thing Ben Taylor liked better than liquor was marrying the wrong woman. Gracie didn't have to say a word. Her friends invited her to parties and clambakes, and she went to as many as she could, but her free time was limited.

When she wasn't studying, she was working with Dr. Jim, who owned the animal hospital. Gracie had started cleaning cages for him when she was ten years old. She'd always been more comfortable around animals than people. With the exception of Gramma Del, animals were more dependable. They didn't drink or yell or forget to pay the bills. They didn't run hot and cold with their emotions. If they loved you, they loved you all the time, not just when it suited them.

Gracie was gentle with the animals and serious about her responsibilities, and it didn't take long for Dr. Jim to see that she had a gift for dealing with both the pets and their owners. He teased her about her ever-present notebook, but he always gave her a half-dozen new ones for Christmas every year. He said he'd never met a girl so young and so focused, and it was true. Gramma Del never had to tell her to pick up her room or hang up her clothes or do her homework. It made her feel good to know that in the middle of chaos, she could create a small oasis of order and dependability for herself.

Nobody was surprised when she announced that she wanted to be a veterinarian. Medical school cost money, and Gracie had always known that the only way she'd be able to attend college was if she paid for it herself or won a scholarship. When the other kids were off swimming away their summers on Hidden Island across the harbor, she was at work.

"You're early," Dr. Jim said on Monday morning. "I barely had a chance to start the coffee."

"You're not supposed to start the coffee," Gracie said, slipping into the pale blue smock that served as her uniform. "That's what you pay me for."

"I wish I could pay you to take some time off, Gracie. You're only young once. You should be out there on the beach with your friends, not cooped up in here with an old coot like me and some badly spoiled house pets."

"I like badly spoiled house pets," she said.

"You like anything with fin, fur, or feathers," Dr. Jim said, shaking his head. "I don't know how I got so lucky."

Gracie went about her business, opening blinds, checking for messages, making sure to feed the goldfish in the waiting room. She and Doc had been down this road many times before. She needed both the money and the experience working at the animal hospital afforded her more than she needed beach parties and proms. This was her ticket to the future. "A woman needs her own," Gramma Del had been telling her since Gracie was a little girl. Her own home. Her own money. Her own future right there in Idle Point, working side by side with Dr. Jim one day as his equal.

Dr. Jim didn't know it, but sometimes she managed to sneak away at lunchtime to her secret spot, a crescent of beach tucked away beyond the lighthouse where nobody but Gracie ever went. Her friends all rowed across the inlet to Hidden Island or drove up the coast to one of the fancy resort towns that dominated the economic land-scape. The adults spread their blankets on the smooth sands of the town beach. Nobody bothered with the for-bidding curve of coastline she'd claimed for her own. The current was strong there, and the rocks were so slippery and forbidding that Gracie always had the place to herself. She'd perch on an outcropping of rock, wrap her arms around her knees, and look out toward the horizon. Some-times she brought a book with her or a sandwich. Most times she brought nothing but a deep sense of belonging.

Idle Point was home.

The last time Noah Chase spent a summer trapped in Idle Point he was five years old and too young to know any better.

He was seventeen now. He'd spent summers in Florida, Arizona, Paris, London, Los Angeles, Hawaii, Montana, and that was just for starters. If his father hadn't had a second heart attack in May, Noah would have been on a ranch in Colorado right now instead of heading over to the animal hospital to pick up his mother's brand-new furball.

Some welcome home. He wasn't in the house five minutes before Mary Weston sent him out to play driver for a mutt. Not that he had anything against mutts. He'd spent most of his childhood praying for a dog of his own. He would have settled for anything—a cat, a hamster, a ferret—but a dog was special. There had always been some reason why he couldn't have one. His father's allergies. His mother's concerns for the help. The fact that by the time he was six years old he really didn't live there anyway.

He didn't like thinking about those first few years at St. Luke's Boarding School in Portsmouth. Back then he'd been smaller than the other students and scared of his own shadow, a mama's boy who didn't know his butt from a hole in the ground. He'd spent grades one through three getting the crap beat out of him until he finally got smart and learned how to fight back.

Maybe he'd learned too well.

He'd started the year on probation for being caught shoplifting from the school bookstore. "You have an unlimited account," the headmaster had said to him during one of those intense, we're-in-this-together chats he hated. "You don't need to steal." The headmaster had fixed him with a stern look. "You don't have anything to say for yourself?"

"Nope," said Noah. He didn't have anything to say the time he disappeared for a weekend or the time he was caught driving the science teacher's car up and down the main drag.

He'd been grounded, forced to work cleanup in the dining hall, threatened with expulsion. Nothing worked. All it took was another check from the Chase bank, and life at St. Luke's went back to what passed as normal among snotty rich kids just like him.

This time, though, he had struck pay dirt. That party outside of town would go down in Portsmouth history.

So would the arrests.

They knew how to manipulate the system at St. Luke's. Cover up. Erase. Expunge. Until you finally pushed so hard that even St. Luke's of the Bottomless Benefactor Slush Fund had enough of you. Plenty of time to think about how to tell his parents he'd been asked not to return to St. Luke's. He had all summer to do that.

It still bugged the shit out of him that his mother had finally decided to bring a dog into the house after all the years of telling him he couldn't even have a pet hamster. When he was little, he'd wanted a dog even more than he'd wanted to play quarterback for the Patriots. "No," she would say. "Your father doesn't want pets in the house." Noah cried and pleaded and made a pain in the ass of himself, but she wouldn't budge, not even that time with the kittens. His father's wishes were law around there. Since when did his mother stand up to the old man, anyway?

Not that it mattered. He was only temporary around there, if he had anything to say about it. Hell, he'd been only temporary around there most of his life. Why else would they have shipped him off to boarding school when he still had his baby teeth? He'd give it a few weeks, let his old man settle back into his routine, maybe wait until he started showing up at the *Gazette* a few days a week, then Noah would tell them that he was heading west to finish up what was left of the summer on that Colorado ranch before they found out he'd been kicked out of school. They couldn't stop him. He was seventeen, almost a man. They'd have to give in. He wanted something different, a place where nobody gave a damn that he lived in the big house on the hill, where nobody cared that his father's great-great-grandfather had founded the town and built it in his image.

He followed the winding road out of the heart of town. The place was old, tired, dead, even though they didn't seem to know it yet. Nobody in Idle Point ever did anything that hadn't been done before. They took pride in that fact. Ask them why, and they said, "Because that's the way it's always been." If he had a buck for every time he heard that phrase . . .

He rolled past lobster pounds, fish shacks, two marinas, the bank, the high school, the post office, and a store that seemed to sell nothing but lobster buoys without seeing any of them. Most of the buildings were weathered to the same bleached gray color by the relentless wind off the ocean. Saltboxes and colonials and glorified sheds lined both sides of the road. Most of the large houses on Main Street near the water boasted No Vacancy signs. Hard to believe that tourists from New York and Boston and points beyond paid big bucks to crash in a room with no bathroom, no telephone, and no cable TV in a nowhere town. They flocked to Idle Point and other coastal towns from May to November, pretending they'd love to shrug off their urban lives and get back to basics. "I'd take a lobster roll over pâté any day," he'd heard a well-manicured matron say one day at the lunch counter next to the *Gazette*.

Like hell. He'd been around those types now for years, both at boarding school and now at prep school, and he knew they wouldn't make it halfway through the first Maine winter before they went slip-sliding back to the big city in their spotless four-wheel drives. Not that he blamed them. He wasn't sure he could make it through this week.

No matter how hard she tried, Gracie had trouble imagining Ruth Chase with a pet. A perfectly groomed poodle maybe, or an aloof Siamese who rarely deigned to notice anyone's existence but her own, but definitely not this big-footed, slobbery Lab-Sheepdog mix Ruth had fallen in love with during one of the animal hospital's Adopt-A-Pet weekends. Gracie had been the one who let Wiley out of his cage to interact with Ruth, and she'd seen the two of them bond like old friends with her very own eyes.

Ruth had cooed over Wiley, telling him what a wonderful dog he was, how handsome and brave and strong, and Wiley had lapped up every last word. Even harder than imagining Ruth with this huge ball of fur was imagining Simon Chase allowing it to happen.

"You must be on his payroll," she mumbled as she finished combing out the last tangle in the dog's wildly abundant coat. The office was closed for lunch, and she had used the time to finish grooming him.

"You say something, Gracie?" Martin, Dr. Jim's technician, asked over his shoulder while he examined a slide.

"I was trying to imagine old Wiley here planting a big wet one on Simon Chase."

Martin laughed out loud.

"I'm not joking," she said, inspecting Wiley's shimmering coat with satisfaction. "Can you imagine Wiley here having free rein at the Chase house? It boggles the mind."

"Mrs. Chase loves that dog." Martin removed one slide, placed it in its special container, then reached for another one. "Rumor has it she told Simon she'd leave him if he said one word against Wiley."

"I doubt that," Gracie said, giving Wiley a hug before she helped him down from the grooming table. "Ruth doesn't look like the kind of woman who gets her way very often." The image of Ruth Chase standing up to her powerful husband was almost laughable.

Still, Gracie had to admit that Ruth Chase had always been very kind to her. When Gracie was a little girl, she'd had a crush on the lovely older woman and for a while she had fantasized that Mrs. Chase would invite her to come live with them in the big house on the hill, which was a bigger fantasy than anything Alice and the Mad Hatter had ever dreamed up.

"I'd better get up front," she said, snapping a lead to

Wiley's collar. The office reopened in ten minutes, and she was the receptionist this week.

"Why don't you leave him back here with me," Martin suggested.

"Thanks," Gracie said, "but he's good company. Besides, it's good for a dog to see how the simple people live."

Martin was still laughing as Wiley led her down the hall to the waiting room. A guy stood near the window with his back toward her. He was tall and lean, dressed in the Idle Point summer uniform of cut-offs, T-shirt, and deck shoes. Wiley tugged hard at the leash, but she held him back.

"Excuse me," she said. "May I help you?" *You might want to start by telling me how you got in here.*

"The door was open," he said as if he'd read her mind. "I figured I'd—" His words stopped cold as he turned around. "Gracie?"

Oh, God, he was the most beautiful human being she'd ever seen. He gleamed with an almost golden light.

"Gracie Taylor?"

Gracie's entire world turned upside down as she realized who he was. "Noah?" Suddenly she was five and a half years old on the first day of kindergarten, and he was her guardian angel. He was more beautiful than she'd remembered. "What are you doing here?"

He gestured toward Wiley. "Car service." His beautiful blue eyes twinkled as he said it, and Gracie was afraid her heart would tear through her chest and tumble to the floor at his feet. Was it possible to fall in love at first sight twice with the same boy?

She knelt down and nuzzled Wiley. "Can you believe it?" she asked. "I never thought I'd see the day the Chases—" She caught herself just in time. "I'm sorry. I didn't mean to—"

"Hey, don't apologize," Noah said, bending down to scratch Wiley behind the left ear. "I'm a Chase, and I can't believe it either."

She nuzzled Wiley again. Her face felt hot, and she was afraid she was blushing. She never blushed, not even the time she tripped and fell up the stairs in front of half the student body during assembly. This wasn't like her at all.

Wiley looked up at Noah with something approaching adoration, and they both laughed.

She looked at Noah over Wiley's ruff of fur. "You like dogs?"

"Love 'em." He grinned as Wiley leaned into a scratch. "When I was a kid I wanted a houseful of 'em."

"Me, too," said Gracie. "I used to look at that big house of yours and try to figure out just how many dogs and cats I could fit inside."

"You work here." He said it as a statement, not a question.

"Official dogsbody," she said, then wished she hadn't tried to be funny. What if he didn't get the reference? She didn't want to believe he was anything but perfect. Please, please, don't let him look at her with a blank expression on his face. He was already beautiful. Would it be too much to ask for him to be smart as well?

The sparkle in his eyes grew brighter, and she knew that he knew exactly what she meant. Her heart, already overflowing with emotion, attached itself firmly to her sleeve.

"Part-time dogsbody or full-time?" he asked.

"Full-time during the summer, part-time when school's open." She leaned back on her heels and went for broke. "I'm saving up for college," she said, "and time's running out." *You might as well know it all, Noah. I'm plain and smart and poor. A real triple threat.*

He didn't even blink. Instead, he leaned forward and said, "Where do you want to go?"

She listed her top three choices. "They all have great veterinary programs, but I'd have to win a scholarship in order to be able to afford any of them."

"Do you have the grades?"

She nodded, feeling undeniably proud. "Senior year's gonna be tough. It's make-or-break time for me."

He didn't say anything, and she wondered if she'd bored him to tears with her goody-goody plans for the future. Guys hated that kind of thing. She should have steered the conversation to music or movies. Something fun and normal and meaningless. She'd never done very well with meaningless.

"So which college are you planning on?" she asked, looking to shift the focus to him. "I'll bet you can have your pick of any one of them."

"Not if they check out my SAT scores," he said. "The only way I'll get into a decent school is if my old man's checkbook opens the door."

"That's been known to happen."

"He'd better be able to pay off the headmaster at St. Luke's, too."

"Uh-oh," she said. "You're in trouble."

"A-yup," he said, mimicking his father's Down East tones, "and I'll be up shit creek when my parents find out."

"Your secret's safe with me."

"I know it is," he said.

She leaned forward to adjust Wiley's collar as Noah leaned forward to scratch him behind his other ear. His fingertips accidentally brushed the top of Gracie's head, and her breath caught sharply in her throat. She prayed he hadn't heard the sound. She would die of embarrassment. You'd think she'd never been this close to a guy

before . . . close enough to catch the scent of soap and
sunshine on his skin . . . close enough to feel the warmth
of his body. His touch was light, gentle, a whisper of a
touch. She understood why Wiley was looking up at him
with something close to adoration. Given half the chance,
she would happily do the same thing for the rest of her
life or longer.

Noah hadn't thought about Gracie in years. Whatever
memory he had of her was of a sad-eyed, skinny little girl
who knew how to read and write before the rest of them
could tie their shoes. She was still skinny and still smart,
but the sad look in her eyes had been replaced by determination. She was going places. You only had to spend
five minutes with her to know that she had her life
planned out to the last detail.

She was busting her ass so she could go to college and
make something of herself, while the rest of her pals
screwed around on Hidden Island. No wonder she'd given
him such a peculiar look when he told her he'd been
kicked out of St. Luke's. She probably thought he was a
real loser, one of those rich kids who end up pissing away
their trust funds before they turn twenty-five. He had a
kind of sixth sense when it came to people, and he felt
the change in her attitude right away. She'd been interested in him right up until that moment, and then it all
disappeared, and he'd felt as if someone had turned off
the sun.

She'd been brisk and efficient with him, writing up a
receipt for Wiley's care, scheduling his next appointment
for shots, telling him to say hello to his mother and be
sure to mention how Wiley needed to be thoroughly
brushed every day. That was it. No flirting. No attempt to
make him stay a little longer. She almost seemed relieved
to see him go.

He glanced over at Wiley. "I think she likes you better than she likes me," he said to the dog.

Wiley wagged his tail, but he didn't argue the point.

Gramma Del didn't leave her small cottage very often these days. Ever since the Chases had told her they no longer needed her services, she'd been in a slow but steady decline. Not even Gracie, who couldn't bear the thought of a world without her grandmother in it, could deny what was happening, and she made it her business to see that Gramma Del ate properly, had regular medical checkups, saw her friends as often as she liked.

It wasn't as if Gracie could rely on Ben to see to it that his mother was taken care of properly. Oh, her father was a lot better than he used to be, but his was still an all-or-nothing personality, which meant when he wasn't drinking, he was off getting married. She'd lost count after the fourth wife and eighth fiancée. Sometimes she wanted to haul off and hit him in the head with one of the two-by-fours leaning up against the tool shed, anything to get him to notice she was alive, but she knew it was a lost cause. He was never cruel to her, not in any overt way. He didn't beat her like Mary Ann's father did, or touch her in the night like Sarah's father. Sometimes she thought that what he did hurt her more than any physical beating ever could: He looked right through her as if she was nothing but smoke and mirrors. As if she wasn't his flesh and blood at all.

"Gramma." She tapped on the door and inched it open. "Are you awake?" It was more a formality than anything else, a way to preserve what remained of Del's independence.

"*Wheel of Fortune*'s about to start," Gramma Del said. "Don't think you can start any conversations with me until I see what Vanna's wearing tonight."

"I brought over some supper." Gracie lifted the lid on the casserole she carried. "Mac and cheese. I thought I'd make you a little salad and—"

A commercial for an auto repair shop flickered on, and Del tore her eyes from the television set. "You going to eat with me?"

Gracie shook her head. "I grabbed a lobstah roll around four o'clock."

"Who made the macaroni?"

"I did." She bit back a laugh at the look on her grandmother's face. "I used your recipe."

"Well, then," said Del as Vanna floated onto the screen, "maybe I'll try just a little."

Gracie took the casserole into the kitchen where she fixed a tray for her grandmother, then poured herself a glass of iced tea. She carried everything back into the tiny living room and helped Gramma Del sit up straighter in her recliner. Once her grandmother started eating, Gracie sprawled on the floor next to her and offered up a running commentary on Vanna's hair and gown and shoes that soon had Gramma Del laughing despite herself.

When the show ended, Del switched off the power and turned to Gracie. "Spit it out, missy."

Gracie leaned on her elbows and looked up at her grandmother. "What makes you think there's something to spit out?"

"You learn something about human nature in eighty-two years of living, Graciela, and I can see you're about ready to pop."

Gracie had never been able to keep anything from her grandmother. "Noah Chase is back in town."

Gramma Del's smile thinned until her mouth was nothing more than a thin line of Maine granite. "Passing through, no doubt, same as every year."

"I don't think so," Gracie said slowly. "I think they're

all staying in town this year on account of Mr. Chase's heart attack."

"None of our business," Del said. "They live their lives, we live ours."

Gracie swallowed. "He came into Dr. Jim's to pick up Mrs. Chase's new dog."

Gramma Del was paying close attention to her now.

"He's not for you, Graciela." Kindness softened the stern warning. "Better you know that now."

"I don't know what you're talking about, Gramma. I was just passing on some town gossip."

"Look at me, missy. Let me see your face."

"Don't be silly." Gracie pushed her grandmother's hand away.

"Graciela."

"Okay, okay." She forced a laugh, trying to make a joke of Gramma Del's demand. "Here's my face." Gracie turned toward her and crossed her eyes. "Are you satisfied now?"

Gramma Del caught her face between her hands. To Gracie's horror, she realized her grandmother's eyes were filled with tears. "There isn't a man on this planet who's worth your dreams, Graciela."

"Gramma!"

"Listen to me!" Gramma Del's hands trembled as they held her face captive between them. "You can be anything you want to be if you hold tight to your dreams."

"Gramma, I haven't had a date in months. I'm working around the clock with Dr. Jim. I get up, go to work, come home again, all because I'm focused on a dream. If you think I'm going to let anything come between me and my future, then you don't know your granddaughter."

It was the first time Gracie ever lied to her grandmother, but it wouldn't be the last.

FIVE

He's an old man, Noah realized as his father paced the book-lined study the next morning. When he'd gone off to school in September, his father had been tall and strong, a man in the latter years of his prime. Now, nine months and two heart attacks later, everything had changed. Simon looked as gray and weathered as the town. He walked as if each step required major effort. Only his voice, that deep rich baritone, retained the power Noah remembered.

". . . a disappointment," his father was saying. "Your mother and I expect more from you than this juvenile act of rebellion. . . ."

Noah tuned out. He knew the drill. He'd heard it a million times before. It didn't change anything. It didn't mean his father wanted to know one damn thing about his life.

"There are responsibilities that come with being a Chase . . . expect excellence . . . you're very lucky to be part . . . how do we explain . . . you've disappointed me, Noah . . . hurt your mother . . . think about the future. . . ."

When Noah was a little boy, he would have given his pitching arm to be the focus of his old man's undivided attention. His father was a busy man, a pillar of the community, owner and editor of the best newspaper in all of New England. He had responsibilities that went far beyond what happened at home. He didn't have time to spend listening to the problems of his small son.

Still, Simon Chase had been Noah's idol, more than Superman or Batman or even Carleton Fisk. He didn't want to be a ballplayer or action hero. He wanted to be a newspaperman just like his father. He wanted to stand up for what he believed in and, with his words, make others stand up for it, too.

His father had that power. With just black type on white paper, Simon Chase moved mountains. His influence in Idle Point was legendary and, thanks to a Pulitzer Prize in 1979, that influence had been felt around the world, if only briefly.

The staff at the *Gazette* loved Simon. Noah's chest used to burst with pride each time he saw the way the editors and reporters gathered around his father when he spoke. They hung on his every word. They jumped when he barked out an order. They loved him and they respected him. "He's a great man, your father," Wendell Banning had told Noah after the heart attack at Christmastime when they all thought they were going to lose Simon. "If you turn out to be half the man your father is, you'll be better than most."

Noah didn't deny that when it came to the *Gazette* his father was a great man, but the wide-eyed hero worship of his childhood had given way to bitter acceptance of the fact that he and Simon would never be close. Not in the way he had dreamed about as a little boy.

Simon stopped pacing in front of Noah and looked down at him. "And what do you have to say for yourself?"

Noah shrugged. "Not much." Even less than his father would be willing to hear.

"What are your plans for the summer?"

Okay. Now's your chance. Take a deep breath and go for it. "I'm supposed to start work in Colorado the end of next week."

"Those were your plans before you were expelled from St. Luke's. What are your new plans?"

"I don't have any new plans."

"Then I recommend you come up with some by this time tomorrow."

"What's wrong with Colorado?" He knew he was pushing it, but he didn't care. It wasn't as if Simon had any idea what was going on in his life.

"Out of the question."

"Why?"

"Because I said so."

"Great reason," Noah muttered, slouching lower in his chair.

"I'll thank you to watch yourself, son. As long as you live under my roof, you'll do as I tell you."

Noah couldn't help it. He laughed in his father's face. "I haven't lived under your roof since I was six years old."

Simon looked stricken. "You're my son. This is your home."

"The hell it is." Noah was on his feet, facing down his father in a way he'd never done before. "That cell at St. Luke's was more my home than this place will ever be."

"Don't talk like a fool."

"You think I wanted to be there all by myself? I was scared shitless. I cried myself to sleep that first year."

"You got over it."

"Why did I have to? This house is a fucking hotel, and you didn't have room for me."

"I won't tolerate that language while you're under my roof."

"Don't sweat it, Pop," he said. "I'm never under your roof for long."

The early years had been everything Simon could have wished for. The long, arid desert of his barren marriage had suddenly blossomed with the boy's unexpected arrival, and for the first time their house felt like a home. So many disappointments along the way. So many mistakes, so many secrets tucked away in dark corners of the heart. He could still remember the crushing weight of regret, of a grief so black and desperate he thought it would swallow him whole. For a while, not even the explosion of light and hope that was their son seemed enough to save him. He was more like Ben Taylor than he cared to admit.

Through it all there was Ruth. Steadfast, resolute, more constant than the tides. He had pushed her far away once, and she had chosen a path neither one had ever imagined. Who was he to say what was right and wrong? He had never been sure if she forgave him his transgressions or merely found a way to live with them. In truth, he had never asked. She loved him. She always had. And because she loved him, she had come back.

Once, not that long ago, he had been willing to give up everything for love, too. His self-respect. His sense of honor. His work. His family. Everything he held dear. He would have walked away and never looked back, not even for the sake of the son he had waited so long to welcome into his life.

Ruth appeared in the doorway. Her gentle face looked drawn with worry.

"Is everything all right?" she asked. There was nothing jarring about Ruth, nothing loud or vulgar. She was a lady to her marrow. "I heard Noah roar down the driveway."

He told her what had transpired between them. He and Ruth had been together almost forty years. She knew how to read between the lines. *He used to love me, Ruthie. He used to look up to me. What happened? Where did it all go so wrong? Why do I keep pushing him away?*

"The trip to Colorado would do him good," she said, patting him on the left forearm. "Work off some of those high spirits."

"I'm not going to reward him for being expelled from St. Luke's."

"Hard work is scarcely a reward," she pointed out.

"No," he said. "Is a summer at home such an inhuman punishment?"

"He was looking forward to working on that ranch."

"He can work here."

"You know that isn't the same, Simon. His friends will be on the ranch."

"His future is here in Idle Point."

Ruth sighed. "There's time enough for that," she said gently.

"It's time now, Ruth," he said. "It's time our son came home."

Ruth couldn't shake the sense of foreboding that settled across her shoulders. Simon went upstairs to rest while she wandered through the house, unable to settle down to her correspondence or her reading or anything else. Twice their new cook Greta asked if she could fix Ruth a pot of tea, but both times she had brushed off the poor woman with the merest shake of her head. Her mind was elsewhere.

For over ten years she had dreamed of having her son home to stay, only to discover that the reality of it filled her with unease.

Gracie.

Mona Taylor's sad-eyed daughter. Who would ever have imagined that plain, brown-haired girl would catch the eye of Ruth's golden son? He had been filled with talk of Gracie last night as mother and son sat together on the front porch. How hard she worked, how capable she was, how smart, how funny. There was a quality of innocence about Noah as he spoke of Mona's girl that struck terror in Ruth's heart.

Life wouldn't be that cruel.

She had always harbored a deep affection for Gracie. She could still remember the feel of that tiny, fragile hand in hers on those afternoon walks home from kindergarten. Del had been working for the Chases back then, and with Ben Taylor being the way he was, Gracie had needed a place to stay until her grandmother was ready to leave for home. How Ruth had loved seeing Gracie bent over a coloring book at the kitchen table while Noah built a skyscraper at her feet. Sometimes Ruth pretended they were both her children, and the feeling of joy in her heart was so intense that it stole her breath away.

More and more, the young people were striking out from Idle Point to make their living in Boston or Hartford or maybe even New York. The *Gazette* was losing subscribers, and Simon seemed distracted and worried, which meant Ruth saw very little of her husband. When she wasn't volunteering at the hospital, she was often at the school, overseeing one of the Chase family's many bequests. She used to find Gracie curled in a wing chair near the window, engrossed in Dr. Seuss or one of the many Golden Books available. She had felt awkward around Gracie after that incident with the Christmas sweater, unsure just how much the little girl knew about the situation between Simon and Ben, so more often than not she disappeared back into the shadows without saying hello.

But how Gracie's face lit up each time she saw Ruth. The poor little thing had been starving for a woman's touch. For a mother. Ben had gone off and gotten himself married again right after that terrible Christmas; he and Nora Fahey had moved up the coast to pursue a job possibility for Ben, leaving Gracie home with her Gramma Del. Ruth and Del had worked out a way to care for Gracie but still keep her presence in the Chase home a secret from Simon.

Sometimes Ruth felt as though she was drowning in secrets.

She thought about the monthly letter she posted like clockwork, a letter filled with love and pride and more guilt than she could sometimes bear.

Be grateful for what you have, Ruth.

How often had she cautioned herself over the years? Give thanks. Be satisfied. Be grateful for the blessings she had been given and not mourn the blessings she had been denied. She was a fortunate woman. She lived well and without worry in the big house on the hill. She had friends who cared for her, charity work that fulfilled her, a son whose existence was a miracle.

And she still had Simon.

He loved Noah more than the boy realized. Noah was the reason Simon got up in the morning, the reason he kept the *Gazette* running. Noah gave meaning to every breath he took. When Simon had had that first heart attack at Christmastime, it was Noah who made him fight his way back when it seemed as if the end was at hand. What they were experiencing now was classic father-son behavior. Two male lions fighting for dominance. One, an aging patriarch; the other, a fierce young hunter. What they both needed was space and time for it all to work itself out naturally.

Nothing good would come of forcing the boy to remain in Idle Point this summer. Nothing good would come of forcing him to work at the *Gazette*. Simon was wrong in this, and she would wait a few days for the situation to

cool down, then tell him exactly that. There would still
be plenty of time to get Noah to Colorado.

The truth was, Ruth wouldn't rest until he was gone.

Everyone was either still asleep or at work, Noah thought
as he drove down the main drag and headed out toward
the highway. The only person he'd seen was Laquita Adams coming out of the old motor court next to Eb's Stop
and Pump. He'd heard the stories about Laquita when he
was home for Christmas, but he hadn't wanted to believe
them. The sight of her in last night's clothes and last
night's makeup as she stumbled toward her car gave him
an unsettled feeling in the pit of his stomach.

He remembered her as a round-faced girl with pretty,
dark hair and a soft manner. Smart, but quiet about it. All
caught up with her houseful of brothers and sisters, most
of whom seemed to be in her care one way or the other.
They said her parents were kind people but forgetful.
Once a baby was out of diapers, they turned all of their
attentions to the next one in line. "Wonder what they'd
do if they didn't have Laquita around?" Don had said the
other night when they met up with each other near the
bowling alley.

It looked to Noah like they didn't have Laquita around
all the time, not if she spent the night with Rick from the
hardware store. What the hell was she thinking? The guy
was old enough to be her father.

He caught up with Don near the bowling alley and
linked up with a crowd of almost-familiar faces. Don had
pretty much caught him up with who'd been doing what
around town. It sounded as if Laquita slept with anybody
who asked, which was her business even if it was wreck-
ing her reputation. Funny thing, Noah worrying about
someone's reputation. He'd been going out of his way to
trash his own rep since the day he first left Idle Point.

Tim and Joe were working at the supermarket. Terri and Joann fried burgers beneath the golden arches, while Ethan took orders over at Patsy's Luncheonette. They all acted as though they were glad to see Noah again, but it was clear they viewed him as an outsider, even though he'd been born there same as they had. He couldn't blame them. He didn't feel much of a connection himself.

Don's parents owned a fishing boat, and Don went out with his father every morning during summer vacation. He told Noah he could go with them. All he had to do was be down at the docks by four A.M. Noah liked him, mainly because Don didn't seem to care that Noah was Simon's son. He liked Noah despite that fact. Don didn't sweat the small stuff, like whose father did what for a living. He worked hard and played hard and figured everyone else did the same. "We go over to Hidden Island just about every night," he had told Noah as they walked toward their cars after the bowling alley closed. "Bring a six-pack with you, and you're in."

Noah grinned as he considered the idea. It would piss off his father big time. His son and heir chugging beer with the locals on Hidden Island, the most notorious makeout spot between here and Kittery. The only thing that would piss him off more than that would be if Noah found himself a minimum-wage job right there in town. A job that wasn't at the *Gazette*.

No doubt about it. That would be a first-class ticket out of there.

He could pump gas for Eb at the Stop and Pump or maybe bag groceries for the summer people at the new Food Basket at the corner of Main and Dock Streets. He could caddy for the old farts at the club or, even better, shovel dog shit like Gracie. That appealed to him. Not the dog shit part, but he liked Dr. Jim, and being around Gracie didn't sound half bad.

Besides, give it two weeks, and he'd be on his way to Colorado.

Gracie jumped at the sound of Dr. Jim's voice.

"What is with you, young lady?" he asked as she bent down to retrieve the syringe she'd dropped. "You're more nervous than Jasper Dawson's hound the day he was fixed."

"Just clumsy, I guess." She disposed of the syringe in the special receptacle, then reached for a new one. The Siamese on the table in front of her meowed nervously. "I'm sorry, Lady," she said, bending down and kissing the cat on top of its head. "You should be glad Dr. Jim's giving you the injection."

"If I didn't know better," said Dr. Jim as he took the new syringe from her, "I'd think you had a boy on your mind."

She laughed, but it didn't sound quite as convincing as she might have hoped. "Who has time?" she countered. "You run me ragged around here."

Gracie whispered soothingly to the protesting cat while Dr. Jim quickly administered the shot.

"The Chases' boy has certainly grown up, hasn't he?"

Gracie gathered up Lady in her arms and feigned temporary deafness.

"I hear all the girls in town are buzzing now that he's back."

"I'm glad they have time to buzz," Gracie snapped. "I have more important things on my mind." She quickly turned away so he wouldn't see that she was blushing the color of the Idle Point Volunteer Fire Department's one and only engine. "I'm going to put Lady back in her cage."

She hurried toward the back of the building where the boarding kennels were located. If Dr. Jim knew that Noah

Chase had called her at work a little while ago and asked
her to meet him for lunch, she'd never hear the end of it.
He'd probably think it was a date or something stupid like
that and blow it all out of proportion. It wasn't a date,
she told herself. Dates called you a few days in advance.
They came to your house and picked you up and met your
family. They didn't call you at 10:22 on a Wednesday
morning and say, "Why don't we grab a lobstah roll at
Andy's and sit out on the rocks?" The sound of Maine
was still there in his voice, and it made her smile.

"I don't care if it's a date or not," she told Lady as she
made the animal comfortable, then locked the cage se-
curely. She was going to have lunch with Noah. That was
all that was important.

She was on her feet and heading for the door at the
stroke of noon. "Lock up for me, Martin?" she asked the
lab technician. "I have an errand to run."

Her hands shook as she applied eye shadow and mas-
cara in the car. She ran a brush through her hair, wishing
she were blond and blue-eyed and beautiful. Why hadn't
she worn something more appealing than her favorite pair
of threadbare jeans and a green tank top? Her sneakers
looked terrible, worn and stained. She kicked them off.
She didn't have much going for her, but she did have nice
feet. She fumbled around in the glove compartment and
pulled out a bottle of hot pink nail polish. Maybe she
could dazzle him with her pedicure. She wondered if there
was time to race home and change, then decided against
it. No matter what she did, she wasn't about to transform
herself into the type of girl who could attract someone
like Noah. It just wasn't going to happen.

She'd been in her element at Dr. Jim's office. She drew
her strength from animals, caring for them, learning what
made them tick. People were more problematic by far.

Take her out of the animal hospital and put her in Noah's world, and she'd be in big trouble.

"It's not a date," she told herself as she started the car.

"It's not a date," she repeated as she zoomed toward Andy's Dockside Shack, Home of the World's Best Lobster Roll.

"It's not a date," she whispered as she pulled into a parking spot.

Then she saw him, and once again she was lost.

The first thing Noah noticed when Gracie climbed out of her car was her smile. She had beautiful teeth, perfect and even and white, and her smile was wide and genuine. He'd seen the other kind and he knew the difference.

The second thing he noticed was her body. She was long and lean and graceful, strong and still feminine. He liked the way her waist curved in and her hips flared out and the way her legs seemed to go on forever. Her hair was a deep rich brown—he hadn't realized how beautiful it was yesterday when he saw her in the office—and it shimmered with red and gold highlights in the sun. Her breasts were small and round, and they jiggled softly with each step. He felt every step deep in the pit of his belly, an awareness that shook him right down to his shoes.

She wasn't the most beautiful girl he'd ever seen, but she did something to him no girl had ever done before: She made him feel unsure of himself, as if he'd have to try harder somehow to make her happy. As if making her happy was the only thing in the world worth doing.

Then he caught himself.

This isn't a date, moron. You just want to ask her about a job.

Somehow he seemed to have forgotten that fact in the time it took for her to walk from her car to where he stood leaning against the side of Andy's Shack.

"Sorry I'm late," she said as she approached. "Mrs. Daggett showed up with one of her Siamese and . . ." Her words dissolved into soft laughter, and Noah found himself laughing with her even though he didn't get the joke.

She wasn't like anyone he'd ever known. Her jeans were patched, her feet were bare, but her toenails were polished a glossy hot pink. She smelled of soap and shampoo and faintly of Siamese, and the combination dazzled him.

"I ordered you a lobstah roll," he said, wincing at the way he said lobster. They used to tease him at St. Luke's about that. "I figured you'd be short on time."

"Great," she said, smiling up at him as if a lobster roll was the best thing going. "Lemonade, too?"

"If you want."

"A big one," she said, "with lots of ice."

He grinned. "Anything else?"

"Not right now, but you never know."

Joey Anderson, whose mother taught at Idle Point Elementary, had Noah's order waiting for him. "You're with Gracie Taylor?" he asked as he rang up the bill.

Noah grunted something noncommittal and handed Joey a ten-dollar bill.

"Gracie's a good kid," Joey said, "but real serious about things. If you're looking for a good time, why don't you row over to Hidden Island one night. The whole crowd's there. Just make sure you—"

"Bring a six-pack," Noah said, pocketing the change. "Don told me."

"Hey, Joey." Gracie joined them. She reached for the drinks and some paper napkins. "How're you doing?"

"Could use some days off, that's for sure." He grinned at Gracie, and Noah found himself moving a step closer to her. "Any chance you'll be at Joann's party tomorrow night?"

Gracie shook her head. "I'm on late shift tomorrow, but I'll be thinking about you."

"You're invited, too," Joey said to Noah. "You can bring someone if you want." He looked from Gracie to Noah, then shrugged. "Or not. Whatever."

If the invitation made Gracie uncomfortable, she gave no sign of it.

Noah followed Gracie across the parking lot and out onto the beach. The tide was low, exposing the rounded backs of rocks that had been around long before the Chases or anyone else discovered Idle Point. It was what he liked most about the beach; the fact that it belonged to nobody but itself.

"Be careful," Gracie called over her shoulder. "The rocks are slippery."

"Yeah," he said. "I've noticed." Twice he'd almost landed on his ass.

Not Gracie. Her bare feet gripped the rocks as she walked, as if she was born to it. A brisk wind was blowing in from the ocean, and her slender body bent into it like a willow. No missteps, no awkwardness. She didn't spill a drop of lemonade. He wanted to stop in his tracks and just watch her move. The idea made him feel hot with embarrassment and something else, something deeply unsettling that he couldn't identify. Or maybe he didn't want to. He never thought things like that. A girl was pretty or not. She had a great bod or she didn't. She was fun to be around or a total drag. He'd never wanted to stop time so he could watch a girl walk in the sunshine.

Gracie found them a spot on a boulder halfway between Andy's Shack and the water.

"Here?" Noah asked. He didn't sound very enthusiastic about it.

"Sure," she said, settling down on the leeward side. "If

we're quiet and don't disturb them, the seagulls will land near us and crack open clams and mussels while we eat."

"That's a good thing?"

She grinned up at him. "I think so." Funny how she felt more sure of herself here on the beach than she'd felt just minutes ago in the parking lot. "I love low tide," she said as he sat down next to her. "It's like watching the ocean reveal all of her secrets."

"All I see is dead fish."

"I see dead fish, too, but there's so much more if you know where to look." She caught herself and shook her head. "Sorry. Like you really want to know my thoughts on low tide at Idle Point."

"Maybe I do," he said, and there was something in his tone of voice that made her heartbeat leap forward. "I don't know a whole lot about low tide at Idle Point."

His voice was deep, and the sound of it made her feel the way she did on nights when the moon was high. A little wild. A little crazy. Not at all like her careful, cautious self. She'd never felt this way before, and it scared her. She'd seen enough of life to know what kind of trouble a girl could get into if she let herself follow her emotions. Her father was like that, making decisions spurred by demons she'd never understood. She'd watched him bring home one wife after another, searching in vain for the happiness he'd known with her mother.

But she wasn't her father. Her feet were planted firmly on the rocky shoreline of Idle Point. She wasn't about to let her life take her by surprise. She had plans for her future, and she knew how to make her dreams come true. She also knew she should take a giant step away from Noah Chase right now, but she couldn't move. Or maybe it was that she wouldn't move. Not while the boy she'd loved since she was five and a half years old was only inches away from her.

He asked questions about the docks and the fishing, and she found herself telling him more than he ever wanted to know about the history of lighthouses. He even remembered Sam the Cat, then laughed when Gracie told him her official name was now Samantha the Dowager Queen of Idle Point.

"You love it here," he said.

"It's my home."

"It's my home, too," he said, "but I don't feel much of anything for it."

"Big surprise." She took a sip of lemonade. "You haven't really lived here since we were in kindergarten."

"Remember when you used to come home with me after school? I wanted to show you my stuff, but—"

"Your father wouldn't let you." She bit off a piece of lobster roll and chewed slowly.

"You knew about that?"

"Gramma Del told me. I kept bugging her about why I couldn't see your electric train set." She kicked his ankle lightly. "Don't look so embarrassed. It's not like it was a big secret or anything."

"I never could figure it out. I mean, it's not like my old man is that big a snob."

Gracie laughed. "I'm not so sure about that."

"I had some of the other kids over and—" He muttered an oath. "Sorry, Gracie. I didn't mean to hurt you."

"Old news," she said. "I don't know what their problem is, but my family doesn't like yours any better than your family likes mine." Who cared what they thought, anyway? It all seemed as far away and unimportant as the price of tea in China. The only thing that mattered was that Noah was back in Idle Point, sitting right here beside her on a sunny afternoon in June.

They watched quietly as a seagull landed a few feet away from them and began to hammer at a clam with his

long, sharp beak. When that didn't work, the gull picked
up the clam and flew a lazy circle around the spot before
dropping the clam onto the rocks below. The clamshell
shattered open, and the bird returned to enjoy his feast.

Gracie laughed softly as another seagull tried to steal
the bounty but was scared away in a flurry of squawking
and ruffled feathers. "Gramma Del used to take me down
to the beach when I was little. We'd walk along the shore,
and she'd teach me the names of the birds and the different shellfish."

"She taught me the phases of the moon," Noah said,
"and all about the tides. The house isn't the same without
Del."

"She doesn't think we should be friends." She regretted
the words the second she uttered them.

"I thought she liked me." He sounded hurt, and Gracie
couldn't stop herself from placing her hand on his forearm.

"She used to," Gracie said. "She thinks you might be
trouble."

"She might be right."

"And she might be wrong."

"Don't bet on it."

He looked so sad when he said those words that Gracie
felt compelled to explain. "Gramma Del worries. She just
doesn't want me to spend time with any guy."

"Neither do I."

His words hung in the air between them. He looked
down to where her fingers rested lightly against his skin.
She thought about moving her hand away but didn't. The
breeze off the ocean was sweet and soft against her bare
arms and legs. They stayed locked in position for what
seemed like forever, and then Noah leaned closer to Gracie and Gracie moved nearer to Noah and the lemonades
and lobster rolls and lighthouses were all forgotten.

He kissed her the way she had dreamed of being kissed, with strength and tenderness and a yearning that matched her own. Her lips parted slightly. He touched his tongue to hers, sweetly . . . so sweetly that she felt herself melt against him even though she hadn't moved an inch.

The kiss lasted only a few seconds, but those seconds changed their lives forever.

S I X

Gracie had never lied to Gramma Del before in her life, but there was no other choice. She couldn't possibly tell Gramma that she was seeing Ruth Chase's son. The merest mention of the Chases upset her grandmother so much that Gracie worried about her heart. Besides, she was seventeen now and entitled to a life that belonged to her alone. The days of sharing everything were gone, and Gracie's happiness was laced with a bittersweet sense of regret.

Noah's plan to work at the animal hospital went by the boards when Simon stepped in and made it clear that Noah's summer would be spent learning the newspaper business from the ground up. In a way, Gracie was glad. She couldn't think when Noah was around. Something happened inside her brain every time she saw him or spoke with him or even knew he was somewhere in the vicinity. Her heart beat faster. Her hands trembled. Her concentration flew out the window like Old Man Horvath's runaway budgie. She fit all the other bits and pieces of her life into the spaces between Noah's kisses.

There was a lot of talk about Noah around town. Everyone had a story to tell. He'd been spied in the backseat of Laquita Adams's Toyota. Somebody else claimed to have seen him with the principal's daughter out near the football field. Partying on Hidden Island, sneaking down to Portland, getting wasted at work when his father wasn't looking. They could talk all they wanted to, because it didn't matter to Gracie. She knew the real Noah.

"Sit down, missy," Gramma Del said one evening in mid-July when Gracie was particularly eager to run to Noah's arms. "You eat so fast you'll make yourself sick."

"Sorry," Gracie said, chastened. She tried not to glance over at the anniversary clock on the credenza. "I'm starving!"

Gracie ate dinner every night with Gramma Del unless Dr. Jim kept her late at the animal hospital. Gramma Del was in frail health, but her spirit was as strong as ever. She kept busy knitting scarves and mittens for the church's winter carnival and playing cards with her friends, women she'd grown up with right there in Idle Point more than eighty years ago. Del's friends took good care of her. They even kept a close eye on Gracie, much to her chagrin. Suddenly Gracie's blameless life had become a crazy quilt of white lies and half-truths. She hated sneaking around, but if that was the only way she could be with Noah, then that was what she'd do.

At least she didn't have to worry about what Ben thought. Her father and his wife du jour were working for a shipbuilding firm up near Calais on the Canadian border. He'd been good about sending home money each month, which meant he wasn't drinking at the moment. Gracie was learning not to expect too much of her father. Gone were the days when she would bring home bouquets of A's and academic awards and wait, almost dancing with excitement, for her father to suddenly realize what a gem of a daughter he had. Of course that never happened. Ben remained as remote from Gracie as he ever had, but at least now it didn't hurt quite as much as it used to.

She was finally coming to terms with the fact that she would never have the happy family of her dreams. "You're not responsible for your dad's failings," her high school guidance counselor had said to her last year when Ben didn't drive down to see Gracie awarded with the New England Merit Students Award of Excellence. "Don't waste your time trying to straighten up his life. Spend your time learning how to live yours to the fullest. Perfection isn't possible, Gracie, but excellence is."

She thought of those words every time she found herself envying someone for the things she didn't have. Sometimes it even helped.

"Marie outdid herself with this casserole," Gramma said, reaching for the salt.

"It tastes just like yours," Gracie pointed out. She pushed the salt just out of reach.

"That's because she finally followed my recipe." Gramma Del knew she was the best cook in Idle Point, and she wasn't above reminding people every chance she got. "I don't know what took that woman so long."

They both laughed at Sam the Cat, who meowed for her own serving of mac and cheese.

Gracie cherished her time with her grandmother. Maybe she didn't have a normal family, but no girl had ever had a better protector than Gramma Del. For as long as she could remember, Del had been the one person she could count on. Gramma Del was the one who'd taken Gracie with her to an Al-Anon meeting in the church basement a few years ago, where Gracie began to learn that she wasn't to blame for her father's unhappiness or his drinking or his string of bad marriages. Del had put aside her pride and sat there with her granddaughter, even though that kind of public display went against everything she believed in. Gracie doubted she could ever repay her grandmother for that gift.

If only she could tell Gramma Del about Noah. That would make life almost perfect. There were times when she thought she would die if she couldn't share her happiness with someone. She knew she couldn't tell her father. The memory of the night of the kindergarten Christmas play was still too vivid for her to be able to pretend he would understand. She would never forget the look of surprise, then resignation, on Mrs. Chase's face when Daddy threw the sweater at her. Whatever bad blood there was between him and the Chases, it still ran deep and hot. She'd asked him once a few years ago about that night, but he'd looked at her with a blank expression on his face and said, "Graciela, I don't know what you're talking about," and she let it go at that. Her father had huge black holes in his memory. She didn't know if they were the result of booze or convenience, and she didn't much suppose that it mattered. Either way the truth was lost.

So many secrets. So many forbidden topics. They were hidden upstairs in the attic, buried in the basement, stashed in closets and under mattresses and behind locked doors. Don't ask questions. Whatever you do, keep family business inside these four walls. When she was a little girl, she used to pepper Gramma Del with questions about her mother. Was she pretty? Do I look like her? What did she sound like? Did she love me? Did she sing to me? Would she like me if she met me today? Gramma Del's answers grew shorter and less forthcoming until one day she sat Gracie on her lap and said, "Maybe it's time we let your mother rest, child, and talked about other things." She never answered another of Gracie's questions again, and, after a time, Gracie stopped asking. But she never stopped wondering.

Oh, she knew bits and pieces of the story. Idle Point was a small town, and people talked. Maybe not as much as Gracie would have liked, but enough for her to piece together part of the picture. They always said, "Poor Ben," when they talked about her mother. Said it with troubled eyes and tight lips, then turned away from Ben and Mona's child as if they regretted saying even that much. "He loved your mother more than a man should love a woman," Gramma Del had said once in a rare moment of indiscretion. Gracie clung to that scrap of insight, examined it from every angle, in every light. The notion of loving too much seemed wildly romantic, like a real-life *Wuthering Heights* with Heathcliff crying out his anguish to the windswept moors.

Am I like my mother, Gramma? Will I love one man deeply and forever? Or am I like your son? Tell me, Gramma. Tell me what she was like. Did she love Daddy as much as he loved her? Did she whisper his name when she died? Did she love me the way Mrs. Chase loves Noah? After all those years of waiting, did I make her happy?

If only she could tell Gramma Del about Noah and how amazing it was to be loved in return. Of all the dreams she'd ever dreamed since childhood, this was the one she'd never believed would come true.

He's so wonderful, Gramma. You loved him when he was a little boy. I know you'd love him just as much now. You're not working for the Chases anymore. What difference does it make if I see their son? He's so good to me, Gramma. He's handsome and kind and he makes me feel like the princess in a fairy tale, except I know our story will have a happy ending.

But she didn't say it. Gramma Del was engrossed in *Wheel of Fortune* and, no matter how hard she tried, Gracie couldn't seem to find the words.

• • •

Idle Point was a typical small town. News traveled fast, and usually it ended up being dissected at the coffee shop next door to the *Gazette*. When Noah was little, the men used to gather at Nate's Barber Shop, but when Nate went unisex, the men moved down the block to the coffee shop in a show of male solidarity. Times changed, and nowadays the band of happy gossipers included men and women. The only requirements were a love of caffeine and a juicy story to share.

Simon used to take Noah for pancakes at Patsy's Luncheonette every Saturday morning before he was sent away to boarding school. Ruth would brush Noah's hair and dress him in a soft flannel shirt and jeans, then wave good-bye to the two of them as they drove off down the road. Noah had loved the way all the men stopped talking when he and Simon entered the room.

"The boy can't stay away from your blueberry pancakes, Patsy," Simon said every single time as the place erupted in laughter. They all knew the truth. Simon was there to show off his son, his boy, the apple of his eye, the one who would carry on his name.

As he grew up, Noah began to notice that there was more than simple pride involved in his father's eagerness to show him off. There was a sharp edge to his father's pride, a certain belligerence that he'd been too young to recognize before, almost as if Simon were daring Idle Point to contradict him. Noah asked his mother about it once, but she'd told him he was imagining things. "We waited a long time for you, Noah," she said. "You can't blame him if he's sometimes a tad heavy-handed."

He accepted her explanation, but he never forgot the expression in her eyes as she turned away. He didn't want to know what made her look so sad. And he didn't want to know why his father had never loved him.

Noah's return generated a fair share of interest, and before long it seemed as if the entire town knew what he was going to do before he did it. The guys at the *Gazette* teased him about prep school and his rich-boy haircut and the girlfriends they were sure he had by the dozen. If he talked to one of the typists, his father's pals nudged each other and exchanged winks. If he looked tired in the morning, they ribbed him about having had a big night before. They took breaks and lunches together at Patsy's same as ever, and the fact that Noah never joined them didn't escape their notice.

Or Simon's.

They'd asked Noah to join them for lunch that afternoon, but he'd been halfway to his car, and his mind was already consumed by thoughts of Gracie. He'd brushed them off with a shake of his head and kept on walking. It wasn't a big deal. At least it hadn't seemed so to him, but it looked like he was wrong. Simon began reading him the riot act as soon as they sat down to dinner that evening.

"They're good men," his father said to him. "They're the ones you'll need in your corner when you take over the *Gazette*."

"I don't need them in my corner," he said, "because I'm never going to take over the *Gazette*."

"You say that now, but you'll change your mind."

"I'm not going to be trapped in this place the rest of my life." He wanted to chart his own course, not follow in his father's footsteps.

"You'll do what I tell you to do," his father had said, anger tightening the corners of his mouth.

"You can't tell me how to live my life."

"Many sacrifices have been made for you. I—"

"Simon." His mother touched Simon's forearm with her hand. "There's no need for this."

He had never seen his father look at his mother with such fury. "Maybe it's time he learned what was sacrificed so that he could—"

"That's enough!" Fear laced her words, a fear so real Noah could almost smell it in the room.

Suddenly he wanted to get as far away from there as fast as he could.

"Where do you think you're going?" his father had called out as he kicked back his chair and stood up.

"Out."

"Dinner isn't over."

"Stay," his mother urged. "Have some dessert."

"Don't wait up for me," he said. "I'll be late."

Five minutes later, he was racing down the road toward the lighthouse and Gracie.

Noah always parked just around the bend where the road split, making sure his tiny sports car was hidden deep in the shadows thrown by the lighthouse. Gracie slipped her ancient Mustang into the space between his car and the fence and darted swiftly across the rocks to where he waited for her on a slender strip of sand. He was lying on his back on the faded blue blanket they called their own, hands linked behind his head, looking up at the stars.

Gracie threw herself down on the blanket next to him and kissed him. "I'm sorry I'm so late," she said as she snuggled down into his embrace, "but Gramma felt like talking and . . ." Her words trailed off. She didn't want to talk about what lay ahead. "I'm glad I'm here."

He pulled her closer. His body was warm and hard and strong, and she melted against it, amazed as always by the way they fit together.

"I was afraid you weren't going to make it," Noah said after they'd kissed a few times, deep delicious kisses that made her restless and hungry inside.

"Nothing could keep me away from you," she said, even though she knew you were never supposed to tell a boy how much you cared. "The worst nor'easter in the world wouldn't keep me away."

He looked at her strangely for what seemed like forever. His beautiful blue eyes looked dark with shadows.

"What?" she asked, forcing a little laugh. "Why are you looking at me like that?" You would think he had never seen her before, the way his gaze roamed across her face. Like he was memorizing every inch of it.

He trailed his index finger down over her right cheekbone to her lips. Nobody had ever looked at her that way before, as if he wanted to disappear into her soul.

"I love you, Gracie."

She stopped breathing while the words flashed and sparkled in the air before her, brighter than Venus and Vega overhead. "I'm dreaming," she whispered. "Say it again."

He did, more softly this time, and then he tilted her chin until she was looking directly into his eyes, same as he had the first time he'd kissed her, and in that instant she knew that he meant every word. For the rest of her life she would remember this moment when all of the stars in the summer sky swooped down from the heavens and lifted her higher and higher until she was sure she could reach out and touch the moon.

"Gracie." His voice was low, urgent, wonderfully uncertain. "Don't keep me hanging . . ."

"I love you." She knew she would never say those words to another man, not as long as she lived. "I've loved you from the very beginning."

His eyes glowed with pleasure. "Yeah?"

She kissed his chin, his cheek, his neck. "Yeah." She kissed his mouth, feeling shy and wild. "You told me to hang up my sweater in the coat closet so Mrs. Cavanaugh wouldn't get mad at me, and I decided right then and there that you were my guardian angel."

"I don't remember that."

"I do," she said. "You even held a seat for me, and because you liked me, the other kids decided it was okay for them to like me, too. I'll never forget that."

"You wore a red sweater," he said slowly as it all came back to him, "with a tiny gold cross around your neck." He fingered the delicate chain that disappeared beneath her blouse and found a gold cross dangling from it. "This isn't the same one, is it?"

"Same one." The tiny filigreed cross was all Gracie had of her mother. She never took it off.

He trailed his finger against the curve of her breast. "Your skin is still warm from the sun."

"Impossible." She shivered at his gentle touch. "I worked inside all day." He pressed his mouth to the base of her throat, and the world seemed to spin around her. "In the air-conditioning."

His hand slid under her shirt, his long fingers tracing the line of her rib cage. "Warm and soft."

"We shouldn't . . ." His touch was magical, impossible to resist. "What if someone sees us . . ."

"Nobody will see us." They'd been coming there every night for almost two months, and nobody in town had any idea.

It was a big step, the biggest step she'd ever taken, and the consequences could change her life forever.

"I'm scared, Noah," she whispered, pressing her forehead against his shoulder and closing her eyes.

"So am I."

She frowned at him. "Don't make fun of me. I'm serious."

"Here," he said, taking her hand in his. "Feel." He placed her hand over his heart. "See? Scared as hell."

"I scare you?"

"Right now you do."

She drew in a deep breath, then placed his hand in the center of her breastbone so he could feel the answering beat of her own heart.

"I want it to be perfect for you," he said.

"I don't want to disappoint you," she said. "I never—"

"I know," he said. "That's why I'm scared."

She had a million questions she wanted to ask him. Who and what and where and how many times, but the answers held too much power. She was better off not knowing. The world was filled with beautiful girls who knew how to have fun without talking it to death. Girls who didn't plan their every move or worry about the consequences. Why couldn't she be one of them? Instead, she'd been born plain and smart, careful and wordy. "Poor you," she said softly. "You could do so much better. You could be over on Hidden Island with the others and—"

He grabbed her by the shoulders. "Don't say that." His voice was flinty with anger. "You're the best thing that's ever happened to me." His words poured over her like honey. She was more than he'd ever dreamed of. . . . She made him feel he could accomplish anything. . . . She made him want to be better than he was. She was dazzled by his words, drunk on them.

"I wish I was beautiful," she said. "I wish I knew how to make you happy. I don't—"

He stopped her with a kiss. His mouth was hot and sweet, and she wanted to drink him in like champagne. She'd never had champagne, but she knew it couldn't compare to Noah's kisses.

Gracie was so fragile in his arms, so delicately made that Noah was afraid he'd hurt her. His hands felt big and awkward as he slid her denim skirt up over her hips then removed her panties. She looked so beautiful, so incredibly vulnerable and trusting as she lay there in the moonlight that tears sprang to his eyes, and he buried his face in her thick brown hair and struggled to regain control.

It wasn't that he'd never been with a girl before. He hadn't been kicked out of St. Luke's for being a choirboy. There were lots of girls in Portsmouth looking to have a good time with no strings attached, and his weekends were a blur of keg parties and one-night stands. He was smart enough to always use a rubber, but beyond that, he didn't much give a damn about anything but beer and good times.

Nothing had prepared him for Gracie and the way she made him feel.

He felt clumsy around her, like one of those guys who try so hard to impress but keep stumbling over their own feet. She'd breached all of his defenses before he had even realized what was happening. She'd awakened dreams in him that he'd almost forgotten. He had wanted to be a journalist once a long time ago, a foreign correspondent who moved from city to city, calling every place and no place home. He told her about Paris and how one day he would live there and write the way Hemingway did in *A Moveable Feast*. They would know him at the café, and his table would always be waiting, the one out there on the sidewalk where he could watch the parade. He would eat garlicky oysters and wash them down with crisp white wine, and the words he wrote would be clear and true. Gracie believed in him and in his dreams, the same way he believed in hers. She didn't know that without her by his side, Paris would be just another city.

He'd never met anyone like her, anyone he'd wanted more to impress or understood less about how to do it. His parents loved him for the simple fact of his existence.

They loved him because they had created him. Gracie loved him for who he was. Nobody had ever done that before. He had been loved for the way he looked, the family he came from, the money he had in his trust fund. Gracie loved him for his dreams. There was no cruelty in Gracie, no cunning. She asked for nothing from anyone but herself. When he saw how hard she worked toward her goals, he felt ashamed to have done so little with all that he had been given.

She ran her hands down his spine, her touch tentative at first, then more assured. He sucked in a deep breath and tried to think of anything but the sweet smell of her body beneath his. Her fingertips traced the swell of his shoulders, tiptoed down his spine, then quickly moved back up to his shoulders as if she'd sensed he was close to losing it.

The ocean roared inside his head. His muscles tensed as if he were readying himself for battle. His senses took over, burning away words, burning away everything but the need to be inside her body, to feel her holding him tightly within her. He couldn't have stopped now if he wanted to.

He was hard as a rock, harder than he'd ever been before, and she gasped as he began to move against her, a gentle thrusting motion that came close to bringing him to climax. Knowing that he was the first, the only guy, to be with her this way made him feel he must have done something pretty great in another life in order to be so lucky. No matter what else happened in their lives, no matter where they ended up, he would always be there in a corner of her memory.

A part of her heart would belong to him forever.

Gracie cried afterward. Noah had warned her that it would hurt for a moment, and he'd been right, but that wasn't the reason for her tears. She was so filled with emotion, so overcome by the power of love, that she had to cry or dance or shout out her happiness to the sleeping world. Everything around her had changed. *She* had changed. All of the rough edges, the aching sadness that had been with her for as long as she could remember, the sense that she would always be alone—all of it had vanished, and in its place was contentment. She felt connected to the world in a way she'd never known before. The air smelled sweeter. The stars twinkled more brightly. All because Noah loved her. She never would have believed her own skinny and forgettable body was capable of experiencing such wonder.

"I'm sorry," he was murmuring against her breast. "I didn't mean to hurt you that much. Next time it will—"

She cupped his beloved face between her hands. "I love you," she said, then laughed through her tears. "I love you I love you I love you I love you—"

Once again he silenced her with a kiss. "It will be better next time, Gracie. I swear to you."

"It couldn't be better. This was perfect, wonderful, amazing . . ." She rained kisses on his head and neck and shoulders. "Why isn't everyone doing this all the time? How does anything ever get done in this world when you could be making love?"

He tried to tell her that sometimes, with some people, it was nothing more than sex, but she didn't believe him. How could that be? Two bodies coming together then breaking apart. No magic. No wonder. Nothing more than a quick release. She tried to imagine the act without that soaring sense of joy but couldn't. She knew there would never be a time when the touch of his hand would be anything short of miraculous.

"I'm glad it was you," she whispered. "I'm glad you were the one."

"There's only you, Gracie. From now on . . . I'll never love anyone but you."

"You can't know that. We're so young. . . . What if you meet someone this year or when you go to college"—she smiled—"or Paris . . . Anything can happen."

"I love you, Gracie," he said again. "Nothing will change that."

"You can't be sure. People fall in and out of love all the time. They don't mean for it to happen, but it does, just the same." All she had to do was look at her own father to know that was true.

"It won't happen to us. This is forever." He chucked her under the chin. "Hey, aren't you the one who's supposed to be saying that?"

"Oh, Noah," she said, "I'm so happy that it scares me."

"Better get used to being happy," he said, "because that's how it's gonna be from now on."

The last of her defenses shattered. "Promise me nothing will ever come between us," she begged as the unknowable future hovered all around them. "Promise me it will always be like this."

"I promise," he said, and because she was young and in love, she believed him.

It wasn't like Ruth Chase to drive around so late at night. For the most part, Ruth was a homebody who rarely ventured out after dark unless she was going to a social function with Simon, and it had been a long time since her husband had wanted to go anywhere at all.

The doctors said that depression often followed a heart attack and that Ruth shouldn't be surprised if Simon seemed despondent as the weeks wore on. June melted into July; suddenly it was mid-August, and she found she couldn't remember the last time she had seen her husband smile. He didn't go into the office, even though the doctors said he could. He didn't read or sail or watch television. He refused to drive over to Patsy's for breakfast or go to the club with Ruth. He sat instead in the library and stared in the direction of the window. Conversation was limited to monosyllables. Ruth tried everything she could think of in order to rouse him from his melancholia, but to no avail.

"We can talk about antidepressants at his next appointment," the doctor told Ruth. "His body has been through an ordeal. Heart attacks cause psychological trauma as well as physical. Simon's a strong man. Let's see how he does on his own a little longer."

Simon's depression made an odd counterpoint to Noah's obvious happiness. Her son glowed with it.

"Who is she?" Ruth had asked that morning over breakfast. "She must be very special to keep you out so late every night."

He colored slightly and looked down at his stack of hotcakes. He offered no names, no details, and a knot of something very close to fear formed in the pit of Ruth's stomach. It lingered with her, growing stronger as the day wore on.

It was with her at the hospital where she worked as a volunteer. At the beauty salon. At the post office and even at Eb's Stop and Pump.

"Why don't we go over to the club tonight?" she suggested to Simon and Noah at dinner. There were times she felt that the sound of her voice was the only thing keeping their family together. Nobody else made an effort. "They're having a jazz quartet and dancing. It would do us all good to get out together for an evening."

Simon shook his head. Noah said he had other plans.

"Go with your mother," Simon ordered. "She needs to get out."

"Could we do it another night?" Noah ignored his father and directed the question to her.

"That's fine," she said, eager to forestall more unpleasantness. "We'll check our calendars."

"What's so important that you can't spend time with your mother?" Simon persisted. He loved his son. She knew that as well as she knew her own name. Why did he feel the need to bark orders at the boy?

"Please, Simon." Ruth managed to keep her voice calm and even. "I'm not even positive the quartet will be there tonight. We'll do it another time."

Unfortunately, her husband wasn't finished with the boy. "I phoned the headmaster at St. Luke's this morning," he said, reaching for his coffee cup. "After some bargaining, I managed to convince him to take Noah back so he can graduate with his class."

"I'm not going," Noah said. "I thought I'd finish out high school at I. P. High."

"Yes," said Ruth carefully. "Remember, we had that discussion, dear, about how nice it would be to have Noah around for a while before he goes off to college and out into the world." Simon's health was precarious. It was time for some fence-mending before it was too late.

"I made the decision for St. Luke's."

"Why didn't you ask me?" Noah demanded. "It's my life. Don't I have any rights in this?"

His father leveled him with a stern look. "No," he said. "When it comes to ruining your life, you have no rights at all. I know what's best for you."

"You know what's best for *you*," Noah countered, "and that's the *Gazette*."

"Do you know how many jobs would be lost if the *Gazette* went under? Think about it. Half the families in town would end up living in trailers like those Adams hippies near the river. Sometimes you have to make personal sacrifices for the greater good—"

"Bullshit!" Noah kicked back his chair and stood up. "Just because your life didn't go the way you wanted it to doesn't mean you can use my life to make up the difference."

Simon's face went from pink to scarlet. Noah's aim had been true. Ruth rose from her chair and stepped around to his side of the table. "He didn't mean it," she said as the front door slammed behind their son. "He's young. He'll come around. He doesn't know what he's talking about. . . . He couldn't."

Simon looked up at her and didn't say a word.

She'd wandered the house after dinner, too restless to settle down. Simon took a sedative and went upstairs to bed, and the house seemed almost unnaturally quiet.

Finally, a little after ten o'clock, she told Simon she was going out to pick up some Advil at the convenience store on the outskirts of town and climbed behind the wheel of their Chrysler New Yorker. She drove slowly past the *Gazette*'s offices, waving to some of the employees who were sitting outside in the warm night air. Patsy's Luncheonette was closed. Patsy's had been the favorite meeting place back when she and Simon were in high school. She still remembered the hush that had fallen over the crowd every time Mona Webb walked in the door, with her shiny dark curls and ruby lips and big wide smile.

Almost forty years had elapsed since high school, but it all still seemed clear and vibrant to Ruth. She had never hated Mona for her gift of effortless beauty. It would have been like hating the sunrise. Mona was lush where Ruth was spare; the sun to Ruth's moon. How could she blame them for loving Mona when there had been a time when she would have sold her soul to be Mona for just one

day? She wanted to know how it felt to be the focus of
attention everywhere you went. She wanted to know how
it felt to be the love of a man's life.

She forced her attention back to her driving. Over the
years, she'd learned how to compartmentalize her emotions, how to file away the dark and frightening memories
in some dusty cabinet where they couldn't hurt her. The
best way to navigate your way through life was to stick
to the main roads. You could never lose your way on the
main roads.

Simon loved her. She had no doubt in her mind about
that. She was a good and loyal wife, a fine mother, a
concerned citizen. She never embarrassed him. She ran
his house efficiently. She kept his life running smoothly.
She had been there at his side during the good times and
the bad, and she knew he recognized that and appreciated
it enough to accept her one fall from grace. That had been
a time long ago when it had all been in doubt, when it
seemed as if the life she cherished would be taken from
her, but somehow they had weathered that storm.

They were partners, she and Simon, life partners, and
nothing would ever change that.

So why on earth did she feel so uneasy, as if a
nor'easter were brewing in the center of her chest?

She'd lied to Simon about the Advil. She had enough
Advil and Tylenol to ease every aching joint in Idle Point.
She had come out in search of her son. Something didn't
feel right to her, and she couldn't put it to rest. All summer long the bits and pieces of the puzzle had worried
her, but it wasn't until tonight that she forced herself to
see. It seemed odd to her that he hadn't brought home
any friends to use the pool or watch the big screen TV in
the den. She knew how hard it must be for him, trapped
all summer in a town he barely remembered. You would

think she'd know more about what he'd been up to than the simple fact of his employment at the *Gazette*.

He's practically a grown man, Ruth. He's been living his own life at school for over ten years now. Isn't it a little late to start hovering over him like an aging mother hen?

She prayed he wasn't spending time with that Laquita, the eldest of the Adamses' eleven children. Laquita was a wild child who was frequently seen exiting the only motel in town at daybreak. One of the local beauty salon gossips had mentioned to Ruth that she'd seen Noah's car and Laquita's van out near the motel late one night, but Ruth had laughed it off as a case of mistaken identity. It didn't take ESP to know the poor girl was heading for big trouble, and Ruth was selfish enough to want her son to be far away when it happened.

She had been so caught up in caring for Simon and seeing to his myriad needs that it seemed she'd blinked and discovered her golden-haired little boy was almost a grown man. She knew so little about him. His life had been lived behind the walls of St. Luke's, and she had no knowledge of the forces that had shaped him once he left home. How she regretted the loss of those years.

At the time, she had believed she had no choice. She had been so grateful that Simon stayed, so grateful for Noah, so grateful that from sorrow she had found joy, that she had accepted the conditions of her happiness without question.

She stopped at a traffic sign at the corner of Main Street and Beach Road a few hundred yards from the lighthouse. The absurdity of her situation suddenly hit her square in the face. What on earth was she doing out there, driving around in search of her son and his mystery girlfriend? What difference did it make? He was only seventeen years old. Little more than a child in the eyes of the world.

Certainly too young to be making life decisions—or even thinking about them.

Wiley pressed a wet, cold nose against her shoulder, and she started in surprise. "You're right," she said to the dog. "This is ridiculous." Next month Noah would be back at St. Luke's for his senior year, thanks to another generous donation to the school's dormitory fund. After that there would be college, then graduate school, and then he would take his father's place at the *Gazette*. The summer he was seventeen would be nothing more than a memory.

She checked the road and was about to execute a U-turn when Wiley nudged her again then barked three times. Each bark was more insistent than the one before it. Ruth turned toward the lighthouse and saw a tiny sports car parked in the shadows near the fence. What was Noah doing out here by the lighthouse? She hushed Wiley and peered into the darkness as two figures stepped back into the shadows. She looked more closely and noticed the beat-up old Mustang tucked in between Noah's flashy car and the fence. She knew that car. She had seen it many times in the parking lot of the animal hospital.

Her son and Mona's daughter. The thought made her dizzy, and she rested her forehead against the steering wheel and closed her eyes. This couldn't be happening. Out of all the combinations possible, that those two young people should find each other was the most terrible joke of all. There was no future for them. Surely they must know that. Simon wouldn't allow it and, she was certain, neither would Ben Taylor. There was too much history between the families. Those two children were doomed before they even started. She should get out of her car right this minute, march over to them, and tell them it had to stop before someone got hurt. Love had fangs and sharp claws. She was sure they didn't know that yet, but they would in time.

Ruth's eyes filled as she remembered Gracie as a little girl, the tiny hand placed so trustingly in hers, the look of joy on Gracie's face when she saw her Christmas present. Ruth would never forget that moment. The sweater was such a small gift in the greater scheme of things; that it could give a child so much pleasure caused Ruth physical pain. She had loved having Gracie at their house every afternoon and she had been very angry with Simon for a very long time after he put a stop to it. The child had never been any trouble at all. So much had been denied Gracie—and so much of it had been Ruth's own fault.

Gracie was a hardworking young woman. Ruth kept up with her academic awards through beauty shop gossip. Noah could benefit from being around someone as disciplined and motivated as Gracie. Summer was almost over. In a few weeks Noah would be back in Portsmouth at St. Luke's, and Gracie would be engrossed in her studies. Their romance would be nothing but a sweet memory.

Once long ago Ruth had bent fate to suit her own purposes, and the results had been tragic. She wouldn't make that mistake again.

SEVEN

‿‿◦◦◦⌒◦◦‿

The gods were kind for the next few years, and they
watched out for Noah and Gracie. What started out as a
summer romance grew into something much deeper and
infinitely more important than either had expected or
maybe even wanted, but it happened just the same.

There was nothing Gracie couldn't say to Noah, no
thought too dark or too silly to share with him. She even
shared her worries, and they were considerable. Noah took
life as it came, but Gracie was a worrier by nature. She
worried about Gramma Del, about her father, about every
animal—big or small—that came under her care. She
worried that she would be a failure as a vet. She worried
that her emotions would keep elbowing their way into
situations where they didn't belong and cloud her judg-
ment. She had been penalized harshly by one of her pro-
fessors for weeping during a particularly difficult
consultation. Gracie had apologized and promised to keep
her emotions under tighter control, but sometimes she
worried that she was sacrificing humanity for efficiency.
Noah teased her sometimes and said that worrying was
her hobby. She never laughed when he said that, because
she suspected he might be right.

Gracie was Noah's anchor, his home in all the ways that mattered. He never told her that, though. At least not with words. His feelings for Gracie ran so deep that he couldn't begin to gather them together in any one portion of his heart. Nothing that happened to him had any meaning until he shared it with her. He fell asleep at night thinking about her. She was his first morning thought. Gracie was strong where he was uncertain. She knew the where and when and how of her life; all he knew was that he loved her. She was all that he needed. He loved that she was so serious. Making Gracie laugh made him feel as if he had conquered both Everest and Denali on a single day.

He called Gracie at the University of Pennsylvania a few times a week. Her voice, her laughter, carried him through. He would have chucked everything—school and family and all of his dreams—to be with her in Philly if she'd given him the slightest encouragement, but she never did. Not his Gracie.

He blew off his studies and spent much of his time skiing or surfing out on the Cape. He couldn't remember the last time he'd handed in a paper or shown up for a test. The stack of letters from various department heads were probably meant to enlighten him on that score. He didn't know why he kept fucking up, what made him throw roadblocks in his own way. A counselor had told Noah that it was his way of striking out at Simon, that denying his father's dreams was Noah's way of gaining control, but the whole idea had made Noah angry, and he'd walked out with twenty minutes left in the session. He was good at walking out on conversations that got under his skin. Why the hell did they believe that his every move reflected his relationship with Simon? He was more than his father's son. A hell of a lot more.

Gracie was the only one who never made him feel angry or unsettled. Her dreams for him were even better than his own. She believed he could do anything he set his mind to doing, and when he was with her, he believed it, too. What she thought about him mattered more than he'd ever realized. He wanted to be her hero in every way.

The sound of Noah's voice on the phone filled Gracie's heart with a kind of happiness unknown to her before that first blissful summer. She couldn't afford to phone him very often, but she wrote to him every day, long stream-of-consciousness letters that touched on everything from the injured dog she had been unable to save to how many children they would have after they married. They weren't officially engaged yet—that would mean coming clean to their families, and neither one of them was ready for that—but the commitment was rock-solid, just the same.

Gracie applied herself to her schoolwork with the kind of intense dedication she brought to every endeavor. Nothing in her life came easy; she accepted that fact as one of the givens. In a way, she was glad that Noah was far away in Boston because she would never have been able to concentrate with him close at hand. Noah was one of the lucky ones. He learned quickly with little effort. Gracie had to bite her tongue on more than one occasion when he talked about blowing off the whole thing and getting a job down there in Philadelphia. "Rich boy talk," she'd called it once. After seeing the look on Noah's face, she never said that again, but the thought lingered.

Still, she knew she was right. Only someone born into privilege could toss aside his education, secure in the knowledge that he could pick it up again any time he liked. When you were on scholarship, you didn't have that luxury.

Sometimes Noah drove down from Boston for the weekend, and Gracie found herself torn between her love for him and her need to work. She'd set herself a rigorous schedule that included starting her premed courses a year early, but that all depended upon her ability to maintain top-notch grades. And since even full scholarships didn't cover every need, she worked part-time as a waitress at a nearby coffee shop.

Noah teased her about her work ethic. She tried not to look askance at his casual attitude toward education, but she couldn't help herself. He'd been given so many gifts. Parents who loved him. A beautiful home. Every opportunity money and privilege could buy. She couldn't be blamed for feeling the tiniest bit jealous every now and again, could she? Sometimes it seemed to Gracie as if he had turned his back on everything she'd ever dreamed of.

They saw the world through very different eyes, yet back home in the shadow of the lighthouse, their differences fell away. Lying together in the sand in a wash of moonlight, they understood each other in a way impossible for anyone outside their magic circle of two.

And it was magic. No other explanation for the intensity of their connection was possible. Their bodies knew each other intimately. Some nights as she lay there in Noah's arms, Gracie found it impossible to tell where she ended and he began. She loved the way her hand looked against his bare chest, the sight of his fingers as he traced the line of her thigh. She had always felt competent, but he made her feel beautiful as well. They fit together so perfectly that Gracie was sure they had been made for each other. They didn't need anyone else. Their time together was so precious, what they felt for each other was so intense, that there wasn't room for anything else.

The most amazing thing of all was that nobody knew about them. Idle Point was a small town, and small towns were notorious for gossip. Both the Chases and the Taylors had been the subject of much discussion over the years, but somehow Noah and Gracie remained just beneath the town's radar. Laquita Adams had seen them once coming out of a motel two towns over, but since Laquita was there with a married teacher, she had no room to talk. Gracie and Laquita exchanged embarrassed hellos each time they met, but neither one acknowledged the incident.

Much of the old crowd had scattered. Don was working on a fishing boat out of Key West for the summer. Joe and Tim were traveling through Texas. Joann was in summer school in New York; Terri was working as a counselor at a resort in Boothbay Harbor. Everyone, it seemed, was someplace other than Idle Point.

Noah complained about the sameness of Idle Point, but Gracie took comfort from that very fact. All around her things were changing at the speed of light, and the fact that Idle Point remained as immutable as its rocky coastline gave her a sense of security and history that only Gramma Del had ever provided. She loved knowing that the bank had stood at the corner of Main and Promontory Point since the turn of the last century, and that it would still be standing there at the turn of the next.

Gracie had always believed that Gramma Del would be with them at the turn of the next century, too. It fell to Ben to tell her otherwise the day she arrived home for the summer between her junior and senior year.

"Your grandmother isn't doing well," her father told her. Ben had divorced and moved back to Idle Point the previous winter. He made ends meet by working as a handyman at the church. Gracie would have bet her old Mustang that he had been hired as a favor to Gramma Del. "The doctor says it could be any time."

Gracie had been expecting this for months, but hearing it from her father made it all suddenly real. Ben had been sober for a while now, but the weight of his troubles had taken their toll. Gracie realized with a start that he had grown old when she wasn't looking. His dark brown hair had faded to gray, and there were lines and wrinkles where they had never been before. The handsome father she had loved so much now lived only in her memory, along with her dreams of a perfect family.

How long had it been since they had last lived together as a family, anyway? She couldn't remember. She wasn't even sure it mattered. Like it or not, this small and imperfect union of souls was her blood. A lifetime of disappointment wasn't enough to make her forget how much she loved Ben or how much she wished he loved her back. Next to Gramma Del, he was the only other person on this earth who shared her blood, and that connection wasn't something she took lightly.

"I'll need some help on Wednesday nights," he said, almost apologetically. "They shifted the AA meeting time for the summer, and your Gramma's church friends can't—"

Gracie raised her hand to stop him. "Of course I'll help," she said, and he thanked her. They sounded like two polite strangers on line at the bank, and it almost broke her heart. *I'm doing really well in school, Pop. I aced all of my finals, and they're letting me start premed in September instead of waiting another year. Did you know they ran a little story on me in the* Philadelphia Inquirer *last month? I'm one of the top three students in my class, Pop, and the only one holding down a job while maintaining the grades. Are you proud of me? Do you think my mother would be proud? I'm standing right here in front of you. Why don't you look at me? You're sober now. Why can't you hear me?*

"Your father does the best he can with what he's got," Gramma Del said last night, "and if it's not enough for you, there's nothing anybody can do about it." Gramma

Del still clung to life with a stubbornness and determination that defined courage.

"Sometimes he acts like he doesn't even know me," Gracie said, trying to make her grandmother understand what she was feeling. "I went to hug him, and he took a step back."

"Don't be looking to change the man," she cautioned. "You can't make things perfect, no matter how hard you try."

But Gracie was obsessed with the changes in her father. Maybe if he'd been falling-down-drunk she wouldn't have felt this way, but to see him sober and responsible made her yearn for everything she'd missed over the years.

"If he would just sit down and talk with me," she said to Noah one night in mid-August. "There are so many questions I want to ask him about my mother and—"

Noah kissed her quiet. "Maybe he doesn't want to answer those questions, Gracie. It's taken him a long time to get over your mom's death."

"That's right," she said, "and I'll *never* get over it if I can't even talk about her with him."

"Leave him alone. He's doing great for the first time in years. Don't mess with it."

She glared at him. "You sound like Gramma Del."

"Thanks," he said. "She's one of my favorite people."

Gracie pushed him away and sat up with her back against an outcropping of rocks near the base of the lighthouse. It was one of those dark and hazy late-summer nights that reminded you of why lighthouses were still so important. There was something comforting about the sweeping circle of light. "I wish—" She stopped herself.

"You wish what?"

She shook her head. "Just another ridiculous thought."

"Tell me."

"No," she said firmly. "It's impossible."

"Is it about your Gramma Del?"

He knew her so well. He had this way of shining light into the darkest, most secret corners of her heart.

"I want her to know about us," she blurted out. "She's going to die, Noah, and I don't want her to go before telling her about us. I can't keep this from her any longer." Lying didn't come easily to her. She had done it, and done it well, the last few years, but she owed her grandmother the truth.

"That's not a good idea, Gracie. You know how she feels about my family."

"But she always loved you, Noah, I know she did, and she respected your mother. I want her to know how I feel about you. I want her to meet you the way you are now, see how wonderful you are—" She blinked away tears. "If she sees your face, it will all come back to her, all of those good feelings. I know she'll be happy for us, Noah. I'm sure of it."

"Gracie, I—"

She reached for his hand. "I want her blessing, Noah."

The only thing Noah was sure of was that they were making a mistake, but in the end he gave in because he loved Gracie and he respected her grandmother. He didn't want to be the one who stood between the two women and closure as the clock ticked down. He stood up, knocked sand from the back of his jeans, then said, "C'mon."

Gracie looked up at him. "Now?"

"No time better." Or worse, for that matter. He reached for her hand and helped her to her feet. "We'll take your car. No point letting the whole town in on it."

Gracie threw her arms around his neck and showered him with kisses. "You won't regret this," she said as they walked toward her beat-up Mustang. "We'll get her blessing, Noah. We'll finally have family in our corner."

He hadn't realized that meant so much to her. He didn't need his parents' approval to love Gracie. Their approval didn't change a thing. He had managed to scrape by without it since he was five years old. Sure, life would be a hell of a lot easier if he'd fallen in love with someone from the list of rich girls from the right side of the tracks, but he didn't need easy. He needed Gracie, and suddenly he had the feeling she was slipping away.

"We could run away," he said as they neared the docks and the house where she'd grown up. "Keep driving and see where we end up."

She glanced across at him. "You don't mean that."

"Yeah," he said. "I think I do." He swiveled in his seat until he faced her. "Just keep driving, Gracie."

She laughed uneasily. "I'll run out of gas before we reach Portland."

"I have money." He dug into his pockets and withdrew a fistful of credit cards. "I have enough plastic to float us for a year." He motioned for her to pull over to the side of the road, and she did. "We'll go to New York," he said, "or Paris or San Francisco. You name the place, and it's yours."

The look in her eyes was shadowy, intense. He took that as encouragement.

"Noah, that's crazy. We have school to think of. Jobs. Our futures. We can't go running off."

"Give me one reason why not."

"My scholarship." She drummed the steering wheel with her right thumb. "Maybe you can afford to take off whenever you feel like it, but I can't. If I lose that scholarship, Noah, I lose everything."

"Take a hiatus."

"I'll lose momentum."

"We'll get married," he said. "I'll support you."

She started to laugh. "Doing what? You're a student too, Noah."

He waved the credit cards at her and she made a face. "I have savings," he said. "Trust funds. Books I can hock. We can make it work, Gracie. Hell, we really could go to Paris."

"We could stay here in Idle Point."

"Paris has the Eiffel Tower."

"Idle Point has the lighthouse."

"Marry me, Gracie," he said again, taking her hands between his. A sense of urgency was building inside him, almost a sense of desperation. "We could do it this weekend, just drive down to Portland and get a license, pick a judge somewhere, and do it."

"Noah!" She sounded breathless and pleased but not quite as enthusiastic as he would have hoped. "Where is this coming from? We can't just run off and get married like that."

"We'll elope. We've loved each other for a long time, Gracie. This will make it official."

She hesitated, and in that moment of slight hesitation, Noah felt his world begin to shift and change forever.

"Noah, I—"

"Forget it," he said, leaning back in the passenger seat. "You're right. It wouldn't work."

"I never said it wouldn't work."

"Listen, if you have to think about it, it isn't right."

"But you're asking me to change all my plans on a moment's notice. I'm not a rich man's daughter. I can't turn away from a scholarship. I might not get a second chance."

Her words hurt. She didn't mean them to. He knew she was trying to make him understand how much school meant to her. He shouldn't have said anything about marriage. There was something elusive at the core of Gracie's personality. The more he pushed, the more she withdrew. He must've been nuts to think she'd toss everything aside to run away with him. School meant everything to her. Hell, she wouldn't even cut class to see a movie.

No matter how hard he tried, he would never be able to understand how it felt to worry about money. If he never worked a day in his life, he would still be okay. It wasn't something he thought about down at school, but with Gracie it was a major issue. "We'd better get moving if you want to talk to Del before she goes to bed."

She brushed his words aside. "You know I love you, Noah. I've loved you since we were five years old. It's just that I—"

The sound hit them first. A piercing wail that made the hairs on the back of your neck stand straight up. Gracie looked at him, her eyes wide, and before he could say a word, they were hit with the lights. An ambulance and a squad car were bearing down on them full speed. Gracie fumbled for the stick shift, but Noah stopped her.

"Wait," he cautioned. "They're not coming for us. Let them pass."

"They're heading toward the docks," she said. He could see that her hands were trembling.

"Probably some drunk fell into the water," Noah said, then cursed himself. "You know what I mean, Gracie." He didn't mean it as a cheap shot against her father.

She shook her head. "It's Gramma Del. I can feel it."

"Maybe it's a car crash," he said. "They haven't repaired the streetlights yet past Bigelow's. Somebody probably rammed into the fence near Fogarty's farm and—"

"No," she said, starting to cry. "It's Gramma Del, and she's gone."

After a good meeting Ben always felt he could whip his weight in polar bears. If you'd told him five years ago that he'd be spilling his guts in front of a bunch of other drunks almost every night, he would have laughed in your face and reached for another whiskey, but damned if that wasn't exactly what he was doing.

Too bad this hadn't been a good meeting. They had probed too deeply tonight. Or maybe he was feeling too exposed. Questions seemed to carry a sting; comments were thick with innuendo. When the group leader mentioned they were negotiating with Simon Chase's *Gazette* for meeting space in the basement, it was all Ben could do to keep from telling them all to fuck themselves and walking out.

What he wanted was to get drunk.

He'd been attending meetings over near Boothbay for almost six months now, and he'd been dry for seven. One day at a time. That's what they said. One painful, uneasy day at a time. Just keep stringing those days together and don't take anything for granted. There were no guarantees. Nobody could promise you that you would never take another drink. That part was up to you.

The first time he'd walked into a meeting he'd been shocked by the familiar faces all around him. He knew Bill Minelli and Richie Cohan liked their booze, but he hadn't figured it was a problem for either one of them. They were happy drunks, hail-fellow-well-met types whose presence turned good bars into great ones. Mitzi Baines and her married sister Tabitha were there, too. They sat together on the far side of the room and tried hard to be invisible. Mitzi taught second grade at Idle Point Elementary, while Tabitha worked as an office assistant at the *Gazette*. Mr. Hennessey from the bank shocked the hell out of him when he walked into the room and greeted everybody like long-lost friends. Hennessey? He looked like the kind of guy who slept in a suit and tie, real buttoned-down, always in control. Not a pathetic drunk like Ben himself.

There was something about finding out that some of the best people in town had the same problems as you that made your problems seem less insurmountable. Looking at the world through clear eyes took a hell of a lot of getting used to. You needed all the help you could get. Without booze to dull the sharp edges of your mistakes, those mistakes cut into your every waking hour. His hatred of Simon Chase had always been clear and sharp to him, even through the murk of whiskey and wine. It had survived both blackouts and sobriety intact. How it must have amused the bastard to have Del working for him. His enemy brought so low that his mother had to cook for the man who destroyed his family. That's what booze did to you. Wrecked your pride, humbled your family, made you forget why you were put on the earth.

But it was all coming back to him now. Every day he regained a new piece of his past. Sometimes the memories crashed over him like waves during a nor'easter, and all he could do was wait them out. He had done everything possible to blot out the memory of the early years with Mona, the good years, but they came back to him unexpectedly, in detail he'd thought lost to time. He wasn't her first choice but he had done right by her. He had loved her enough to accept whatever she could offer him and not ask for more. She had made her peace with it, and they had been happy together, at least for a while. Nobody could tell him otherwise. They were going to have a big family, sons to carry on his name, daughters to care for them in their old age. The old house by the docks would rock with love and laughter. They were going to be together for the rest of their lives.

So many dreams.

The years passed, and the dreams of a house filled with

children were put aside. They grew apart, and just when it had seemed as if saying good-bye was the only thing they could do that made any sense, Mona came to him and told him she was pregnant, and the world came alive again.

He should have known happiness like that was never meant to last.

It hurt, thinking about those years. His heart felt raw and pummeled inside his chest, and he found himself longing for the solace of booze. Sweet fire that filled all the empty places in his soul. He wasn't that far from Bigelow's. One drink wouldn't hurt. He could handle just one. A little emotional anesthesia to dull the sharp fangs of regret. You couldn't be expected to go through your life just letting the world beat up on you without a little something to soften the punches.

You're a drunk, friend. An alcoholic. You don't know the meaning of just one drink. One drink, one bottle—before you know it, you'll wake up, and it'll be next week and you'll be pissing away everything you did these last seven months. You came home to put things right. Don't fuck it up now.

Sometimes the little voices in your head were all that stood between you and oblivion.

Still, he was making progress. He was determined to stay sober, stay single, stay in Idle Point. If he could manage those three things, maybe then he would be able to undo some of the damage he'd done to his mother and Gracie over the years. Especially Gracie. She deserved so much more than he'd been willing to give her. What the hell kind of man hated a child for living? That's what he had done. He had spent the last twenty years hating Gracie because she had lived and Mona had died.

She was a good kid. Smart and bright and generous. He should be proud of her, but that would imply he had

had something to do with the way she'd turned out.
Everybody in Idle Point knew that was about as far from
the truth as you could get. His mother got all the credit
for that. Gracie worked hard, and she didn't ask for anything from him, which had always suited him down to the
ground. It wasn't fair that a child should bear the burden
of anger and regret, but that was what had happened.

He thanked God as he turned off Main that there was
still time to make amends, that he was still young enough
to change or at least to make another attempt. He thought
of the past six sober months as a gift to his mother, although Del would never acknowledge them. Her disappointment in him ran too deep, almost as deep as his own.
Grief had pulled him under for a very long time; it had
blinded him to what remained. When had grief turned into
anger? He wondered about the moment when sorrow and
rage became one, when he began drinking to remember
as well as to forget.

It was all a blur. Missing days of his life. Missing
weeks. Huge bloody chunks of his heart ripped from his
chest and lost. Forever. Del remained constant, the rock
upon which his family depended. Because of Del, Gracie
would make something of herself in this uncertain world.
Gracie would survive because Del taught her how.

"Gracie." Noah stood in the doorway to Gramma Del's
bedroom. "They need to come in now."

"No." Gracie hugged herself tight and closed her eyes.
She was sitting on the floor next to her grandmother's
bed. She had been sitting there for the last two hours.
"Tell them to go away. I need more time."

"The man from Walker's Funeral Home is here. They
want to take care of your grandmother."

Noah's bare feet scratched softly against Gramma's
pine floor as he walked toward her. *Don't you go tracking*

sand into my nice clean house, Graciela! Wash those feet before you come in here.

"Brush off your feet," she said. "Gramma is very fussy about her floors."

Noah crouched down next to her and put his arm around her shoulders. "Let them do what they need to do, Gracie. I'll be here with you."

"No!" She pushed him away. "She's sleeping. She took too much of her medications. They could wake her up if they just tried harder."

"They did try." He sounded so tired, so sad. She wanted to clap her hands over her ears to block out the sorrowful sound of his voice. "Your grandmother is gone, baby, and they need to take care of her now. You know that. It's time to let her go."

"I can't," she said, tears streaming down her cheeks. "What am I going to do without her?" Noah held her as she cried. Gently he led her out into the yard so she wouldn't see or hear what was going on in Gramma's room.

"Here," he said, taking off his shirt. "Put this on. The mosquitoes are biting."

The cotton shirt was warm and soft, and it smelled like him. "Thanks," she managed. She shivered. "It's cold out tonight."

He led her down toward the docks as the car from Walker's backed up to the front door. She didn't want to think about Gramma Del angled across her narrow bed with the phone dangling from her hand. If she thought about it for even a minute, she would fall apart. Gramma Del was the only reason her father had come back to Idle Point after his last divorce. He had arrived home minutes after Noah and Gracie, in time to see Gracie crying in Noah's arms, to see the grim expressions on the faces of the cops and emergency crew. Too late, always too late.

She had turned to her father to comfort and to be comforted, but he had looked through her as if she were made of glass. Now there would be nothing holding the family together. He wouldn't stay for Gracie. He never had. Years and years of promises. *Next month, Gracie. You can come up here to live with us next month.* Next month. Next year. Next decade. He moved from town to town, job to job, wife to wife, and never, not once in all that time, did he make room for his daughter.

Why would he start now? Gramma Del was dead. His last tie to Idle Point was severed. He would probably sell the two tiny houses and move someplace warm, and Gracie would come home from school each summer to a rented room and no family.

The thought filled her with such dread that she could barely speak. She didn't want to become one of those people who lived alone and volunteered to work holidays so the folks with real families could be home with their loved ones.

"Hold me," she whispered to Noah as the hearse from Walker's crunched its way toward the main road. *Hold me and don't ever let me go.*

She moved against him, desperate to be held, to be made love to until she couldn't think of anything but the way his body fit with hers, couldn't feel anything but the way the heat gathered deep in the pit of her stomach every time he touched her.

"I need you," she said, then in words shockingly blunt with need she told him how and why. She needed to know she wasn't alone.

He couldn't help himself. He knew they were taking a chance, that making love on the dock behind her house was asking for trouble, but she was so hungry, so needy, so warm and wet with desire, so beautiful to him in the moonlight that his brain shut down and desire took over.

He was never sure where he stood with Gracie. No matter
what she said, no matter how many times she showed him
how much she loved him, he always sensed there was a
part of her that remained beyond his reach.

Tonight all of her barriers were down. She was naked
in every way possible. Her long slender limbs gleamed in
the moonlight. She straddled him, eyes closed, body
arched like a bow, and moved in ways that surprised them
both. He came almost immediately, but she didn't seem
to notice. She continued to move against him, hungry for
sensation, and he rolled her onto her back then buried
himself between her thighs. She cried out when he found
her with his lips and tongue, tasting her, letting her taste
them. The sounds she made when she climaxed came
from the deepest part of her soul. And then she cried. He
shielded her with his body and held her as she wept. She
begged him not to stop holding her, and he swore he
would be there until the stars fell. She was his. He believed it finally. This was more than sex, more than making love. This was communion, a sacrament of the flesh.
Nothing would ever separate them now.

And that was how everyone in Idle Point found out about
Noah and Gracie.

Pete Walker, the funeral parlor owner's son, happened
to be working that night as a lifter, and he saw Noah and
Gracie on the dock behind her Gramma's cottage. He
wasn't sure, but it looked like Noah was pulling on his
jeans, and Gracie had the look of a girl who'd had herself
a good time. He was friends with Jake Horowitz whose
brother Paul worked at the newsroom, and gossip being
what it is, the news hit Simon Chase's breakfast table
along with his copy of the *Gazette*.

Nothing short of Mona's death had ever hit him harder.
Not even his third heart attack, the one that had almost

killed him, caused the gut-deep pain this news did.

He was, at heart, a moral man. He had lived his life by a strict moral code. He believed in the God of his parents and their parents, a just God who set standards that were meant to be upheld.

He was known as a good man. That was what they called him. A good man. He paid his employees handsomely for their hard work. He was there to listen to their problems. When you worked for Simon Chase, you knew you had a job for life. Do your job well, keep your nose clean, and you would never need to look elsewhere for employment. He rewarded loyalty in kind.

He was wealthy and well respected. He had a fine wife, a beautiful home, friends to listen to his stories.

One small slip, one tiny fall from grace, and it had almost come tumbling down.

It had taken him years to rebuild his marriage. Even now, so long after the fall, he sometimes caught Ruth when she didn't know he was looking, and he saw in her eyes all that he had done.

The saddest thing of all was that he would do it again in a heartbeat for the chance to spend his life with Mona Webb Taylor. The madness was never far from the surface, simmering in his blood despite the years, despite her death. That madness was his punishment.

He greeted his son with icy calm that hid the emotion inside. "You're not to see her again," he said as he passed Noah the carafe of orange juice.

Noah's skin reddened. "See who?" he mumbled through a mouthful of toasted English muffin.

"The Taylor girl. She is off limits to you."

"Who said I'm seeing Gracie Taylor?"

Too quick, my boy, thought Simon. *Too defensive.* If he had had any doubts about the veracity of the rumor, they were dispelled by Noah's response. The knife inside his heart twisted a little deeper. "We're not here to debate the issue, son. I am telling you that you are to stay away from Gracie Taylor. It's over."

Noah's embarrassment turned to anger. "I love her," he said. Simon was impressed with his passion. It surprised him that Gracie Taylor inspired that degree of heat. She was more Mona's daughter than he had suspected. He also admired Noah's honesty. He expected neither passion nor honesty. He most certainly hadn't expected a declaration of love, but there it was, the monster in the closet. "There's no way in hell I'm staying away from her."

"That isn't what I was hoping to hear."

"Stay out of my life," Noah warned. "I'm not a kid anymore. You can't control me."

"As long as you live under my roof and accept my money, you'll do as I say."

"You can shove your money for all I care."

Simon spread a thin layer of margarine on his toast. "So easy to say. So difficult to do."

"Watch me," Noah said. "You'll choke on those words."

Perhaps, thought Simon as his son stormed from the room, *but it would be a small price to pay if it got Gracie Taylor out of their lives for good.* Noah would come around. Life was long, and the choices were many. Very few young men fell irrevocably in love before they reached their majority. It had happened that way for Simon, but he hadn't known how to handle the gift and let it slip through his fingers. By the time he realized his mistake, it was too late for them all.

I understand more than you know, son. I know how it feels when your heart doesn't start beating each day until you see her face or hear her voice. I know how it feels when she's taken away from you and your world goes black . . .

He would do anything for his son, move heaven and earth to give him only the best the world had to offer. He would sacrifice his remaining years on earth to see to it that Noah's happiness was ensured. He would even bear his son's wrath if that was necessary. But there was one thing he wouldn't do, not even for his boy. He would never allow Gracie Taylor to become part of his family.

EIGHT

"We're so sorry, dear." Mary Townsend clasped Gracie to her pillowy bosom and hugged her tight. "Cordelia was the finest churchwoman I've ever known."

Gracie tried to pull away, but Mrs. Townsend's grip was one of iron. "Thank you," she murmured over the top of the woman's helmet of dyed red hair. "Gramma appreciated all you did for her over the last few years."

"It was the least we could do," Mrs. Townsend said, releasing Gracie from her grasp. "Cordelia was always the first one to pitch in when others needed help."

Cordelia. The sound of her grandmother's Christian name startled Gracie. She knew Gramma Del, but she would never know Cordelia. All of Gramma's secrets and stories were gone now and with them so much of Gracie's history.

The woman took her place in the tightly knit circle of church members standing near the doorway. Mary Townsend, Celia Grove, every female in the Daugherty family, Diane Heston and her great-granddaughters—the list was endless. Many of them were white-haired and in need of canes and walkers. They were the ones who had grown up with Gramma Del, who sat beside her in grade school, who shared joys and sorrows with her over the years. There was a sense of tribal ritual about the gathering, as if they gathered strength from the familiar stories, the old jokes.

She wished she could take comfort in memory, but right now the grief was too fresh, too new. Her grandmother was only two days dead. The sight of her cottage with the lights off and the windows locked broke Gracie's heart. Without Gramma Del, it no longer seemed like home.

Her father had taken off as soon as the EMTs told him Gramma was gone. She and Noah had walked out on the docks while the men from the funeral parlor attended to their business. By the time they returned to the house, Ben was gone, and he hadn't been heard from since.

Gracie wished she cared. She wished she could find it within herself to find him and tell him it was okay, that she would be the one now to shoulder his burdens, but she couldn't do it. Something inside her had shut down with Gramma Del's death, and she found herself filled with anger every time she thought about Ben. She wanted to slap his face until her hand hurt. She wanted to scream at him until her throat was raw and hoarse. She wanted to tell him that this was all wrong, this topsy-turvy family of theirs. He was the parent. He should be there to comfort *her*. He should be telling her that things would be all right, that he would take care of her, that she would never have to worry about keeping a roof over her head or food on the table. He should have done that when she was a little girl, when the world was a dark and scary place without a mother to love her.

Children were adaptable creatures. They could get used to almost anything but the absence of love.

When she was in kindergarten, she used to lie awake

at night imagining how it would be if she lived with the Adamses down near the river. They had so many children, all ages and sizes. What difference could one more make? She'd pictured herself slipping in through one of the bedroom windows and curling up next to Laquita, maybe, or one of her sisters, burrowing under a big puffy quilt just like she belonged there. In the morning she would line up with her toothbrush and wait her turn to use the bathroom. By the time she trooped into the kitchen for cereal, she would be one of the gang.

How she had longed for family, for brothers and sisters. For a mother to love her no matter what. For a father who didn't look away every time she came into the room. Without Gramma Del, she didn't know how she would have survived.

Ruth Chase finished buttoning her jacket, then surveyed herself in her bedroom mirror. Old, she thought. There was no other way to put it. She looked old and tired and sad beyond description. "Oh, Del," she said to her reflection. "You always said black wasn't my color, and you were right."

Del Taylor had never been one to withhold her opinions. How Ruth missed those long-ago afternoons around the kitchen table, trading town gossip while Del chopped onions for supper and Gracie did her homework. With Noah away at boarding school, the big house seemed empty to Ruth, and she had relied on Del to bring it to life.

Had she ever told Del how much she loved her? Ruth couldn't remember. Their bond had been strong, but so were their differences. Ruth wore a yoke of guilt that would never be lessened, and each time she saw Del and Gracie, it grew a little heavier.

She had been down in Boston for a few days, catching

up on shopping with her sister Laura and had only found out about Del's death on her return late last night. She hadn't been prepared for the rush of bittersweet memories the news unleashed.

In two hours the doors to the Catholic church would open wide, and the casket containing the mortal remains of Cordelia Taylor would be carried down the aisle to the foot of the altar where a priest would intone a prayer in celebration of her life. In three hours they would gather together at the small graveyard to bid their final good-byes to a woman who had worked harder for her family than anyone Ruth had ever known. Gracie was living testament to all of Del's hard work, a glowing example of achievement and grace. The deck had surely been stacked against the girl, but Del had helped her to find the strength and discipline to succeed. There wasn't a soul in Idle Point who didn't believe Gracie was going to make them all proud one day, Ruth included.

How she wished she had said these things to Del.

She had been right to ignore that moonlight encounter she had spied between Noah and Gracie a few years ago. Whatever else it had been, it hadn't been permanent, and for that she was grateful. Not that she would have minded Noah being interested in a smart girl like Gracie. She couldn't imagine a better young woman for her son. If only Gracie weren't Mona's child . . . Even now, so many years after her death, Mona Taylor still had the power to destroy Ruth's life.

As she turned away from the mirror, Simon entered the room.

"Have you seen my reading glasses?" he asked. He was wearing his cotton pajamas and a light robe, and his hair was still uncombed.

"Shouldn't you be getting dressed?" she asked, trying to squelch the note of alarm in her voice.

"To read the *Gazette*?"

"To attend Del's funeral." *Don't let him hear how annoyed you are. That will only set him off.* Simon hadn't been himself since the heart attack, and she worried about adding to his stress level.

He was rummaging through a stack of books and magazines on his nightstand. "We sent flowers, didn't we?"

"Of course we did, but—"

"That's enough."

"She worked for us for almost twenty years, Simon. We should be there for the service."

"Absolutely not."

"Simon, we owe it to Del to be there for her granddaughter."

"And what about her son? How do you think Ben Taylor would like it if we showed up at his mother's funeral?"

"From what I hear, that shouldn't be a problem. Ben Taylor hasn't been seen since the night Del passed away."

"We're not going."

"I'm afraid I am, Simon."

"I forbid it."

"Forbid?" Her voice escalated the slightest bit, just enough to be noticed. "In forty years I don't believe you have ever forbidden me to do anything."

"I mean it, Ruth. I will not have you attending that woman's funeral."

"The child needs to know that those who loved her grandmother are there for her."

"She isn't our problem, Ruth." Simon turned toward the door. "And she isn't a child any longer."

The cops found Ben sleeping off a two-day drunk halfway between Idle Point and Boothbay Harbor. The manager of a McDonald's reported an old man slumped behind the wheel of a Jeep Cherokee in their parking lot at closing time, and of course it was Ben Taylor. Who else would you expect to find the night before his mother's funeral?

They took him into the station and tossed him in the drunk tank for a couple hours until the stink of puke and unwashed flesh got to him and he began to sober up. One of the rookies took pity on him and let him use the shower in the back, and by dawn Ben looked almost respectable again. He only had one regret. He wished they'd let him rot in his own vomit back there in the parking lot.

Disappointment burned like acid in his veins, displacing even sorrow. He was a coward, a worthless piece of shit who didn't deserve to take up space in this world. He had failed and failed and failed again, failed until it was practically an art form. The only thing he was grateful for was that Del would never know about this. She had died believing he was sober for good.

"We took in your car," the rookie told him after he was dressed and ready to go. "Two-hundred-fifty-dollar fine. We take Visa and MasterCard."

"Do you take IOUs?"

The kid didn't have much of a sense of humor, but he did have a heart. "Listen," he said, "I go off duty in a half hour. Why don't I drive you to the church for your mother's funeral, and we'll settle up the fine later."

Ben looked at him for a long while before he spoke. "Thank you," he said over the throbbing pain behind his eyes. "I appreciate it."

As it turned out, they were too late for the services. Ben almost wept with relief. He was hung over, bereft, incapable of facing Graciela. "Listen," he said to the young cop. "I'll walk home from here."

Instead the rookie, in an act of kindness Ben didn't deserve or even want, said, "No problem. I'll drive you to the cemetery instead."

•   •   •

Gramma Del, you should see the flowers! They must have raided florists from here to Bangor and back again. Roses everywhere you look, the cream-colored ones and those yellows you love. And the freesia! I wish you could smell the air right now, so sweet and fresh. So many people loved you, Gramma, but you knew that, didn't you? And you knew I loved you most of all.

The cemetery was jammed with mourners, rows and rows of people, every single one of them there to honor Gramma Del. The crowd from Patsy's, the school, church, the *Gazette*, everyone at the animal hospital, including Dr. Jim, her friends from high school. Even Noah's mother had made a brief appearance at the church, just long enough to give Gracie a swift hug in the vestibule before she disappeared. Gracie didn't ask any questions. She was merely grateful that Mrs. Chase had shown up at all. It was more than her father had done.

The crew from Walker's Funeral Home had told her that her father left right after she and Noah walked out onto the dock. He had taken one look at the hearse, then turned and bolted. There had been random sightings over the last two days, always at a bar or tavern, but beyond that, nothing. She knew what that meant. Her father's boozing had formed the pattern of her days. She told herself she wasn't disappointed, that this was no more than she had learned to expect from her father, but it was all a lie.

This time she thought he was going to make it. He had been sober for almost six months. He went to work each day at the church, helping to rebuild the rectory inside and out. She knew it was a struggle, but he'd been hanging onto sobriety for the first time she could remember. When she told Gramma Del how excited she was for him, Gramma had only nodded and continued watching *Wheel of Fortune*.

Anger filled her chest. She was angry for all the lost years, for the little girl who had looked up to a father who couldn't see her through the haze of booze. She was angry for Gramma Del who deserved so much more from her son than she had ever received. If Ben had dared to show up, she would have—

She heard him before she saw him. He must have bumped into one of the other mourners because his "Excuse me" seemed to shatter the stillness of the cemetery like the sound of glass breaking beneath a sledge. She looked up at Noah. His gaze was riveted to a spot slightly behind her and to the right, and she turned around, knowing what she was about to see.

Ben walked slowly toward her. She saw nothing but her father; heard nothing but the slide of grass beneath his shoes. He wore dark pants with bent creases, a white shirt, and a navy blue tie. His eyes were red-rimmed and glassy. The corners of his mouth were turned down in sorrow. From forty feet away she could see the splotchy skin and the broken veins spidering his cheeks and nose. That he had the nerve to show up at Gramma Del's graveside after a two-day drunk pushed Gracie over the edge.

"Get out," she said as he came closer.

He stopped for a moment, then took another step forward. "Graciela, I'm sorry."

"Get out," she repeated, dimly aware of Noah by her side.

"I have a right to be here," her father said.

"You gave up your right to be here when you got back in your car and hauled ass the night Gramma died."

"I made a mistake."

"You've made lots of them."

"You're right. Let me make up for it. Your grandmother deserves a proper good-bye."

"You should have thought of that when you missed her funeral mass."

"Gracie, I'm sorry. I—" His words stopped cold as he focused in on Noah. "You're the Chase boy, aren't you?"

Noah nodded and shifted his weight from his left foot to his right. "Noah," he said and extended his right hand.

Ben ignored it. "You're not welcome here," Ben said in a voice loud enough to be heard in Cape Cod. "Get the hell out before I have you thrown out."

Noah's face reddened, but he stood his ground. "I'd like to pay my respects to Mrs. Taylor and to Gracie," he said, his voice steady and calm. For the first time, Gracie saw him not as the boy she had always loved, but as a man.

"Your parents didn't think they had to come around. Why should you?" Ben was in his face, jabbing at Noah's chest with an angry forefinger.

"Mrs. Taylor was always kind to me. I figure it's the least I could do for her."

"Get out," Ben said, jabbing Noah again. "We don't need anything from you or from your family."

"Please!" Gracie stepped between them. She was shaking so violently she thought she would collapse. "He's here for Gramma Del. Don't take that away from her because you hold some stupid grudge against the Chases."

"Don't go poking your nose where you don't belong, Graciela." Ben stumbled over his words in a stink of Pepsodent and Johnnie Walker Red. "You don't know what came before."

"I don't care what came before. All I know is that you're drunk and—"

She should have seen it coming. He telegraphed his movements every step of the way, but she was out of her head with rage and pain and couldn't see beyond the red mist swirling around her head.

The crowd fell silent. The crack of Ben's hand against her face seemed to echo in her head, driving out all thought. They were staring at her, the churchwomen, dockworkers, the crowd from Patsy's and the *Gazette*. Oh, God, her friends from high school were knotted together, faces pale and wondering. *This never happened before. . . . I swear it. Don't look at me like that!*

Next to her, Noah sprang to life. He grabbed Ben by the lapels and lifted him off his feet, and Gracie feared he was going to kill the man.

"He's not worth it," she said in a voice so cool and controlled she barely recognized it as her own. "Let him go. He's nothing but an old drunk."

She turned and started walking away with as much dignity as she could muster, given the circumstances. Her exit line would have been more effective if she hadn't broken down into tears on the last word, but she made her point. She hurried across the grass, past the mausoleums and the office, across the parking lot toward her car with Noah close behind.

"Gracie!" He grabbed her before she reached the Mustang. "Are you hurt?"

She wiped her eyes with the back of her hand and laughed. "He couldn't hurt me if he tried. There's nothing he could do that could possibly hurt me."

"Let me see your face."

She pulled away. "I'm fine."

"Your cheek is red."

"It's nothing."

"He knows about us, Gracie. That's what this was all about."

"Don't be ridiculous."

"They all know." He told her about the confrontation with his father.

"I don't understand any of this. Why does your father

hate me?" she demanded of Noah. "What did we ever do to any of them?" Bits and pieces of memory floated just out of reach.

"Why does your father hate me?" Noah asked. "None of it makes any sense."

"I asked Gramma Del at least a dozen times, and she refused to answer."

"All I know is that our parents used to be friends and—"

"What?" She felt like somebody had turned her world upside down. "Say that again! What are you talking about?" Their parents, friends? Impossible.

"They were friends. They all hung out in the same crowd. Your mother dated my father," he said, "way back in high school."

"That's ridiculous."

"No, it's not. I started thinking there had to be a connection. They all grew up here. They're all the same age. There's only one high school." He'd slipped into Simon's library while his father was napping and dug up the Idle Point High School yearbook for the class of 1952. "Your mother and my father. Simon Chase and Mona Webb, king and queen of the senior prom." He paused for a moment as if he couldn't believe it either. "The couple most likely to say 'I do.' "

Gracie tried to imagine her beautiful young mother with dour old Simon Chase. The image made her shiver. "What happened?" she asked. "Why didn't they get married? Who broke it off?"

"I don't know," Noah said.

"Maybe my mother jilted your father. That could explain why he hates my family so much." Gracie's parents married three months before Noah's parents did.

"It wouldn't explain why your father hates my family."

"My father's a drunk. Don't expect anything he does

to make sense." She leaned her head against Noah's shoulder and closed her eyes. Her mother and Simon Chase. She tried to wrap her brain around the concept, but it was impossible. The world seemed dark and puzzling to her, with secrets hidden everywhere like land mines. They were talking about events from over forty years ago. Why should old grudges and jealousies determine what happened to her and Noah? It didn't make any sense. "We should have kept driving," she whispered. "We should have run away when we had the chance."

"It's not too late, Gracie. All you have to do is say yes."

She opened her eyes and looked at him. He was the love of her life. He had been since they were five years old. He would still be the love of her life when she breathed her last. *I wanted to tell you, Gramma Del. I know you would have understood once you met Noah again.* School would always be there, but a chance for this kind of happiness came only once, if you were lucky. He was, after all, her only true family.

Laquita Adams grabbed Ben Taylor by the arm. "You need to sit down," she said quietly, leading him toward a chair near where the priest was standing with his open prayer book. "Put your head down and breathe deeply."

He was ashen. She reached for his hands. No surprise. They were cold and clammy. The man was seconds away from falling flat on his face. The damn chair was near the head of the casket. Not a good idea. He was already in emotional overload.

"Cheyenne!" she called to her sister. "Grab that chair and bring it over here."

What was wrong with everyone? They were standing there like statues. Couldn't they see the man was in trouble, or did a year of nursing training give you exceptional eyesight as well as the ability to give painless injections?

Cheyenne shoved the chair behind Ben's knees, and he slumped down onto the seat.

"Head between your knees," Laquita ordered. "Big deep breaths. You'll be fine."

Cheyenne poked her in the side. "He slapped Gracie."

"I know," Laquita said as she kept a steadying hand on the back of Ben's neck. "He'll answer for that when he feels a little better." *Are you worth saving, Ben Taylor? Am I making a big mistake here?*

She had never seen anyone look more lost or alone than he did as he stood there next to his mother's casket and watched his daughter walk away. Nobody talked to him. They gathered in small groups, scattered around like mushrooms on the forest floor, and they did nothing. Say what you would about the man—and there was plenty that could be said—but that was his mother dead in that casket. A person might drink to block out the pain, but Laquita knew the pain always found a way. She couldn't have turned away from him if she tried.

"You don't have to do this," Ben said in a voice thick with despair.

"Sure I do." She kept her hand firmly on his head. "I'm in nursing school. I need the practice."

Ben grunted something, but she paid no attention. Activity swirled around her. Pained glances. Clucks of disapproval. Familiar whispers. The usual responses when they saw her with a man. She couldn't blame them. She had given them plenty to cluck and whisper about over the years. Not that she was apologizing for anything, because she wasn't. She made her choices, continued to make them, and they were nobody's business but her own.

"Where's Gracie?" Ben asked. "I want to see Gracie."

"She's gone," Laquita said quietly. "Did you really think she'd stay around after you slapped her?"

His moan of anguish tore at her heart. "I have to find her . . . apologize—"

"That will have to wait. She's not here, and you're in no shape to go traipsing off looking for her. Besides, I don't think she wants to see your face right about now."

He twisted away from her and squinted in her general direction. "Who the hell are you, anyway?"

"Laquita Adams," she said calmly. "Oldest of Rachel and Darnell's eleven kids."

"You mean the hippie family by the river?"

She sighed. She would have to move to Timbuktu in order to escape it. "We like to think of ourselves as homesteaders."

"Homesteaders," he repeated. "And I'm a social drinker."

She couldn't help it. She laughed. Not loudly, not enough to draw any more attention to herself, but she laughed. Maybe her instincts weren't wrong after all. There just might be something there worth saving.

NINE

Three days after Gramma Del's funeral, Gracie and Noah drove down to Portland to apply for their marriage license. They brought their birth certificates and driver's licenses with them, then waited patiently on line while other happy couples went through the process ahead of them. When it was their turn, they filled out the forms, paid the fee, then waited for the clerk to hand over their future.

"There's a forty-eight-hour waiting period." The clerk took a second look at their application then put it aside. "Best of luck, folks."

"You can still change your mind," Noah said as they stepped out into the sunshine. "That's only a license, not a marriage certificate."

"I'll never change my mind about you," Gracie said, then kissed him right there on the top step to prove it.

Three office workers on break burst into applause. Noah grabbed Gracie's hand, and they dashed down the steps in search of a lobster shack where they could have a cheap lunch. They needed every cent they could find to fund their plane fare to Paris.

The funny thing was that she believed in him. No matter how many times he screwed up, she went on believing.

Even he couldn't manage that. Gracie would have to believe hard enough for both of them.

They ordered lunch at a lobster shack near the docks. "Almost as good as they make back home," Gracie said, which made Noah laugh. She thought everything was better at Idle Point. Their haddock and chips were served on paper plates that they carried over to a wooden picnic table. Businessmen in suits wolfed down lobster rolls, leaning forward so they wouldn't spill mayonnaise on their fancy clothing. A trio of young women in shorts and halter tops eyed the men as they waited for their sandwiches. They were probably the same age as Noah and Gracie, but they looked so much younger. Neither one of them had ever been young quite like that.

They ate quietly, both overcome by the significance of the piece of paper tucked away in Gracie's huge leather tote bag.

Gracie had walked through the last few days suspended somewhere between terror and elation. In the blink of an eye, her dreams of a happy family had vanished, and she was forced to see her life for what it really was. Gramma Del was gone. Ben didn't give a damn if his daughter lived or died. He loved a bottle of booze more than he loved his own flesh and blood. Idle Point no longer seemed like home. School couldn't fill the empty, jagged hole inside her heart.

Only Noah could do that.

She had loved him for so long. She couldn't remember a time when he hadn't been part of her life. He knew all of her secrets. He understood her dreams. He believed in her the way nobody but Gramma Del ever had. They wouldn't end up being one of those couples whose dreams withered and died in the face of day-to-day reality. They wouldn't let that happen. There was room enough in this world for both of their dreams. They were young and they had time to make them all come true. How could you go wrong if you followed your heart?

"You're not paying attention, Chase," Joe from Production said with a note of exasperation in his voice. "You type in the slug lines the way I showed you; the codes fill in automatically."

It was only the tenth time Joe had told Noah how to key in his story.

"Sorry," Noah said. "I've got it now."

"What the hell's with you, anyway? Your body's here, but your brain is sure as hell someplace else."

"One of those days," Noah mumbled, pretending great interest in the words on his screen. He was finding it tough to care about the thirty-second Annual Labor Day Weekend Festival hosted by the Kiwanis Club when in less than six hours he and Gracie would be getting married.

They had it planned down to the minute. Some of Gracie's old high school friends were throwing a beach party to celebrate the start of her first year in veterinary school. Gracie managed somehow to be a popular loner, a trick Noah had never quite understood. While their friends built the barbecue pit and carted the cases of beer down to the beach, he and Gracie would be on their way to get married.

Gracie would meet him out at the edge of town at five o'clock in the motel parking lot out past the lighthouse. Together they would drive north to a little Unitarian church where a minister named Bo, brother of Noah's B. U. roommate, would perform the ceremony as a favor.

She was giving up so much to be with him that it scared the hell out of Noah. She had made his dreams come true. Now all he had to do was figure out a way to return that favor every day for the rest of her life.

• • •

Gracie finished packing her bags around three o'clock. She had stuffed her favorite books into the corners of her backpack and along the bottom of her suitcase, layered with photos of Gramma Del and her mother Mona. She wanted to take nothing of Ben with her to her new life. The memories were more than enough.

He was gone again, most likely off on another drunk. She hadn't seen him since that moment when he'd slapped her at the cemetery and the last shred of compassion she felt for him disappeared. There was something to be said for closure. She believed now that there was no hope for them to ever be more than strangers to each other. He would never, could never, be the father she'd longed for all her life.

She had thought she would feel enormous sadness saying good-bye to the only home she had ever known, but she didn't. She felt nothing at all. Not happiness. Not relief. Not even a bittersweet sense of regret. Without Gramma Del, it was nothing but a house, and she couldn't wait to be gone. She tried not to think about school and her scholarship and all of the plans she had made to come back to Idle Point and work with Dr. Jim as his partner. She told herself it would all work out the way it was meant to. All that mattered was being with Noah.

Sam the Cat meowed and twined herself between Gracie's ankles. Sam was going on fifteen years old. Her eyesight was dimming with age. Her old bones ached on cold mornings. Sam the Cat had been Gramma Del's companion the last few years while Gracie was at school, spending long sunny afternoons curled up next to Del on the feather bed by the window. Gracie was horrified to realize she had forgotten all about her old friend.

"Oh, Sammy!" She bent down to pick up the cat and cradled her close. "I've been so caught up in my own life I forgot all about you."

She couldn't leave the poor cat alone in the house with only Ben to depend on for food and water. She couldn't board Sam at the animal hospital without a lot of explanation and a fair amount of guilt. She just plain couldn't leave Sam.

"So how do you feel about Paris?" she asked. "I don't know if you'll like the cat food over there, but I guess we can figure it out as we go along." She had never been good at being impulsive or spontaneous. It unnerved her that Sam had somehow slipped through the cracks. That kind of thing never happened to Gracie. She loved detailed master plans that included backup plans, contingency plans to the backup plans, and additional plans for any and all emergencies that might crop up along the way.

She checked Gramma Del's pantry and found an even dozen cans of cat food plus two boxes of dry food. They used to keep the cat carrier in the tool shed, but that was before Ben took the shed over for his tools and other equipment. She rummaged through Gramma's two closets then ran back across to the main house to check the basement. She had barely let herself in the front door when she heard the sound of a car approaching. She knew it wouldn't be Noah. Oh, God, please don't let it be her father. She wasn't looking for a confrontation with him. All she wanted was to walk away from the mess he'd made of his own life and build something fine and wonderful and lasting with Noah.

She parted the yellow and orange curtains and peered out the kitchen window. A shiny silvery gray Lincoln Town Car was pulling into the driveway next to her Mustang. The contrast between the cars was laughable. She knew only one person who drove a car like that.

She could actually hear her heartbeat pulsing in her ears, at the base of her throat, deep inside her chest. She tried to pull in a deep breath, but she was trembling so hard it was almost impossible. A coincidence, that's all it was. Simon Chase couldn't possibly know about the elopement. She and Noah had gone to great lengths to keep their plans secret. Not even the almighty owner of the *Gazette* could have ferreted out the truth.

Noah! What if something had happened to Noah, some terrible accident like the one that had killed her mother, and Simon was here to tell her about it? What was wrong with her? She was letting her imagination run wild when all she had to do was open the front door and ask him what he wanted.

"Good afternoon, Graciela." Simon was tall and spare with a thick head of snowy white hair that sparkled in the sunlight. She looked into his brown eyes but couldn't see any of Noah's goodness reflected back.

She tried that deep breath one more time. *You're as good as any of them, Graciela, and don't you forget that.* "What can I do for you, Mr. Chase?"

"I was sorry to learn of Cordelia's passing."

"Thank you."

"She was a good woman."

"Yes," Gracie said, "she was."

"Did you get our flowers?"

"We did," she said. "I mailed a thank-you note this morning." *My manners are impeccable, Mr. Chase. My grandmother, your cook, saw to that.*

"Aren't you going to invite me in?"

Not if I can help it. "Do you need to use the phone?" *I'll bring it out to you.*

"I would like to talk with you, Graciela, and I'm afraid the hot sun is too intense for me these days." An allusion, no doubt, to his heart attacks and compromised health.

"Please." She stepped aside. "Come in."

He nodded, but his expression never altered. For a man

suffering from the heat, he seemed cool and perfectly controlled.

"Please sit down," she said, gesturing toward the couch with the pale blue sheet tossed over it to hide the tears. "Would you care for some iced tea? Pepsi? Lemonade?"

"Water would be fine."

Water. Leave it to him to ask for water, the one thing she hadn't offered. "Be right back."

Seconds later she returned with a glass of ice water. She wasn't about to give him a chance to go poking around in there alone.

"Here you go."

"Thank you." He took one sip then placed the glass on the coffee table in front of him. "Please sit, Graciela."

"I'd rather stand."

"I would feel more comfortable if you sat down while we talk."

That's exactly why I want to stand. She hesitated, then sat on the arm of the chair across from him. Sam the Cat strolled into the room. Sam was very friendly by nature, but she gave Simon Chase a wide berth. *Smart cat,* Gracie thought. There was nothing warm or comfortable about Noah's father. He was the stranger in her house, yet he somehow made her feel as if she was the one who didn't belong.

She folded her hands in her lap so he wouldn't notice that she was trembling. "What is it you want to talk about?" It was almost three-thirty. She had a million things to do before she met Noah at the outskirts of town.

"You haven't had an easy life, have you, Graciela."

She frowned at him. "Is that a question?"

"Perhaps," he said, "but I would say it is a fact. Life hasn't been particularly kind to you."

"I have no complaints." Her throat felt tight. She had to force the words past her lips.

"No, you never did complain, did you? That's an admirable trait."

"My grandmother taught me how to stay focused."

He nodded. "Cordelia was a remarkable woman."

Gracie shifted position. "Is this going somewhere, Mr. Chase, because if not, maybe we could—"

"I know about the wedding."

Simon's words hit her harder than her father's slap. Her world telescoped down to the sound of those words. Everything else faded to black. It occurred to her that he might be bluffing, that he had a suspicion but nothing concrete, and he was simply trying to trick her into betraying her own secret.

She said nothing. Let him spell it out for her.

"I have friends in Portland," he said. "One of them called me this morning. Do you know which department she works in?"

Gracie still said nothing.

He leaned forward and reached into the breast pocket of his navy blazer. She watched as he withdrew a sheet of paper and unfolded it.

"I have a copy of a marriage license," he said, "for Graciela Marie Taylor and Noah Marlow Chase, two-day waiting period, valid for ninety days in the state of Maine."

"I love Noah," she said quietly. What else was there to say to a man she barely knew who was about to become her father-in-law?

His expression seemed equal parts sorrow and dislike. She wasn't sure which part worried her more.

"This is, of course, a terrible mistake."

"We don't think so."

"You're both very young." He gestured with large, elegant hands, tanned from the sun and spotted by age. "Much too young to marry."

"We disagree."

"Of course you would," he said, favoring her with a smile. "That is why I'm here, Graciela, to explain it to you."

She stood up. "I think you should go now."

He stayed seated. "I have more to say."

"I'm sorry, Mr. Chase, but I don't want to hear it. If you have something to say, you should say it to Noah and me together."

"You're an intelligent young woman," he said. "You seem to have your life planned out."

"I'm ambitious, if that's what you mean."

"My son isn't."

"I know that."

"If you two run off and get married, I'll cut him off without a cent."

She forced a laugh. "Look around you, Mr. Chase. Being poor is hardly something new for me."

"It would be something new for Noah."

"I think you underestimate him, Mr. Chase."

"You don't sound confident."

"You should go now. I don't want to have this conversation."

"Neither do I, Graciela, but it's necessary."

She watched as he again reached into the inside pocket of his blazer. This time he withdrew an envelope.

"Here," he said. "This is for you." Her name was written across the front in thick black ink.

She wrapped her arms around her chest. "No, thank you."

"Ten thousand dollars," he said. "In cash."

"A wedding gift?"

"You have a sense of humor. A thank-you for calling off the wedding."

"You're trying to buy me off."

"Yes," he said, "I am. Take the money and go back to school. I'll take care of the rest."

"And what about Noah?" she asked. "Doesn't he have a say in this?"

"Not in this. This, Graciela, is between you and me."

She took a step back. She hadn't meant to; that step betrayed too much. She had the sense of being at the edge of a cliff and the only way was down.

"I really think you should leave now."

"I haven't finished what I came here to say."

"Yes, you have, Mr. Chase. I shouldn't have let you say as much as you did."

He was sweating. My God, the cool, calm Yankee patriarch had broken into a sweat around his hairline. Somehow that scared Gracie more than anything he had said so far.

"There are things you don't know about the past."

"I know everything I need to know."

"You don't know about your mother."

Her breath caught. "Noah told me you dated my mother in high school."

"I loved her." His voice sounded different, softer, and laced with pain. For a moment he almost sounded human to Gracie.

"D-did she love you?"

He smiled, but the smile wasn't meant for Gracie. It was meant for someone long gone, never forgotten. It was meant for the love of his life. He didn't have to say a word for Gracie to know that and more, and she turned away.

"She loved me," he said, his words finding her as she walked toward the kitchen. "She loved me the way a man dreams of being loved: heart, soul, and mind." His footsteps followed her. "Is that the way you love my son?

Would you follow him anywhere, do anything, be all that he needed you to be?"

"Yes," she whispered, keeping her back turned to him.

"I see Mona in you," he said. "Your walk, the way you carry yourself."

"I look nothing like her."

"I didn't say you did. Your mother was beautiful—"

"Thanks," she snapped. "How kind of you to remind me."

"You have your own charm, Graciela. More subtle, perhaps, but it's there."

The need to slap back at him was undeniable. "She left you, didn't she? She fell in love with my father and dumped you." She felt dizzy, disoriented, as if bits and pieces of her essential self were being torn from her.

"That's not how it happened."

"Yes, it is. That's exactly how it happened." She spun around. She wanted him to see her face, to be reminded in some small way of the woman who had walked out on him. "She didn't love you anymore, and she left you for my father."

"She didn't leave me, Graciela. I left her."

"That doesn't make sense. You loved her. You said so yourself. Why would you leave her?"

"Because I was young." He braced himself against the kitchen table, fingers splayed against the scarred wood. His left arm trembled slightly. She could see every spot, every vein, every bone clearly. "I wanted more than she could give me. . . . She was like quicksilver, your mother. . . . She was so beautiful, and the men . . . God, how they followed her, sniffing like hounds. I was always looking over my shoulder, watching . . . wondering. I needed a solid foundation, a woman I could lean on while I rebuilt the *Gazette*."

"So you married Ruth."

"I married Ruth," he said, "but I never once stopped loving your mother."

The story was taking shape in front of Gracie, cryptic comments from Gramma Del, Ben's despair, Simon's anger that had seemed so hard to understand.

"But my mother didn't love you anymore, did she? She loved my father."

"She loved me."

"No!" The water was running in the sink. Why hadn't she turned it off? "That's not true. You're lying. She loved my father, and he loved her. They were happy together."

He rode over her words. "We found each other again. Our marriages were both barren. We were both lonely and then suddenly we weren't. The love we'd had as teenagers was still there, still burning . . ."

"Shut up!" Gracie screamed. She kicked at the chair in front of her, knocking it on its side with a crash.

". . . we decided to run off together. We were still young, barely forty. We still had many years ahead of us. We would divorce our spouses. I would sell off the *Gazette* to one of the conglomerates hammering at my door. Then we would disappear from Idle Point forever." Paris, he said. London. Rome and Florence and Cairo and Tokyo. He would show her the world.

"I don't want to know anymore," Gracie cried. All of her pretty stories were being smashed under his heel. "Please stop—"

"We had it all worked out. I would leave Ruth and Noah well provided for. She would let Ben down as gently as she could, and you—"

"No! Please . . ."

"—would be with us."

She tried to leave the room, but he stepped in front of her, blocking her way. They were almost the same height. Both tall, both lean, both brown-eyed.

"Do you understand now, Graciela?"

She pushed against his chest, but he didn't budge. "I don't care about anything you have to say. It's old news. It doesn't matter anymore."

"We were going to be together, the three of us. That's where she was going the day she died. We were going to be a family."

"She wouldn't do that. She would never have taken me away from my father." Ben hadn't been drinking then. They had been a happy family.

"She wasn't taking you away from your father, Graciela; she was taking you to him." He forced her to meet his eyes. "I am your father."

Done, Simon thought, as he left Gracie behind. He had seen her dreams crumble with his own eyes.

He waited for the elation, but so far there was none. Where was the sense of payback he had sought for so long? That Mona had died and her daughter lived . . . unfair . . . more than unfair . . . unthinkable . . . she had ruined everything, the girl had . . . better she had never been born . . . that's why Mona stayed with that drunk she'd married . . . for the child . . . for that plain and forgettable child . . .

Hot. Why was it so hot in the car? He fiddled with the air-conditioning. Beads of sweat dripped down his temples and down his cheeks. His shirt stuck to his back. He hated the heat . . . felt better when it was cold out . . . brisk, he called it . . . heat made him queasy . . . dizzy . . . hard to focus on the road . . . pull over for a minute . . . maybe call Ruth . . . the car phone . . . it's somewhere . . . that's what he should do . . . catch his breath . . . catch his breath . . . catch . . .

• • •

Keep moving, Gracie. Don't stop. Put your bags in the trunk. Leave the house keys on the kitchen table with the letter for Ben. Now you know why he drinks, why he does everything short of putting a gun to his head in order to stop the memories. Of course you can't tell him that. You can't tell anyone anything at all because if you do you'll be forced to believe it, and right now that's more than you can take. Isn't it enough that your heart is breaking and there's nothing anyone can do to make it whole again?

Don't think.

If you think, you'll go crazy. If you think, you'll start crying, and you'll never stop.

Forget all the sweet stories. Forget the mother you thought you knew. The mother you dreamed about. The father who broke your heart. Don't think about his pain, because if you let it seep into your skin, you'll never be free of it. Forget everything that made you who you are, because it is all a lie.

Write a letter to Noah. You can leave it here on the kitchen table because you know he will come looking for you. You wrestle with each word, but what can you say now that could possibly matter? Let him go. Don't burden him with questions. Tell him it's you, all your fault, that you thought you could do it, but you couldn't leave everything behind, school and work and all your dreams of a future to call your own. Tell him that you wish him Paris and sidewalk cafés and garlicky wine-soaked lunches with Hemingway's ghost. Tell him you wish it could have been different, but maybe you had been a fool to ever believe it would end any other way.

And then just tell him good-bye.

Five o'clock came and went.

Five-fifteen.

Quarter to six.

By six o'clock, Noah was convinced something had happened to Gracie, and he climbed back behind the wheel of his sports car and started toward her house. Damn it. Why hadn't he pushed the issue and picked her up at home the way he'd wanted to in the first place? What if Ben had come home, drunk and pathetic, and begged her to stay and help him? She didn't need that. She shouldn't have to deal with it. Or maybe that old car of hers had finally fallen apart, and she was stuck in the driveway, hoping he would show up.

The roads were clear. It was the lazy end of summer when everyone moved more slowly than usual. Tourists stayed at the beach past sundown. Townies headed over to Hidden Island or one of the other secret spots. He'd never fit in with either group, a stranger in both camps, which was a lot like the way he felt at home. More like a visitor than a real member of the family.

But that didn't matter anymore now that he had Gracie. She was his family, his home. She made him want to be more than he thought possible, if only to make her half as proud of him as he was of all she had achieved.

He was about to turn off the main road and head toward the docks and Gracie's house when he recognized his father's Town Car angled onto the grass on the opposite side of the street. Simon's head rested against the driver's window. The engine was still running. A knot formed in the pit of Noah's gut.

Screw it. You should be on your way to your wedding right now. You didn't see anything.

Noah made it to the corner before his conscience kicked in. He made a U-turn and pulled to a stop just behind the Lincoln. He beeped the horn. No response. Okay, maybe his old man was napping. Simon was on a lot of medication these days, and those things all had side effects that could drop a horse. He'd make sure Simon was okay, then move on. He owed his father that much.

"Dad." He rapped twice on the window. "Dad, are you okay?"

No response.

He rapped again. "Say something, Dad! Open the door."

Still nothing.

"Shit." He tried the door. It was locked. He ran around to the passenger's side, tried that, but it was locked as well. Simon looked dead white. A sheen of sweat glistened on his sunken cheeks. "Oh, Jesus . . ."

There wasn't a soul in sight. No pay phones. Simon's car phone rested on the passenger seat, but what good did that do him with the door and windows locked tight. Gracie's house was less than three minutes away. He could call the cops from there, make sure they brought out an ambulance. He could do that much for his father. Gracie would understand. She would do the same. He knew that. Shit. Her house seemed so far away. What if his father died? Don't think about that. That wasn't going to happen. It couldn't happen. He'd call the cops, the cops would call out the ambulances, and they'd make Simon better. It had happened before. It was happening now. They'd deal with it.

But what if Simon died while he was getting help? He had to do something now. He knew CPR. He'd do what he could, then get help. There was no time to waste. He glanced around for a rock or heavy branch then opted for a scissor kick that smashed the passenger-side window. A second later he was in the car next to his father, unbuttoning the man's shirt, clearing an airway, calling for help. Time slowed down to a crawl as he worked in a vacuum of fear and silence.

"No."

He jumped at the sound of Simon's voice.

"It's okay. I'm here. An ambulance is on its way."

"No!" Louder this time, more frantic. He pushed at Noah with flailing hands.

"They'll help you," Noah said, trying to calm him. "You're going to be okay."

"Graciela . . ."

"What?" Noah leaned closer so he could hear his father's words. "Say it again."

"Graciela . . . no . . . no . . ."

"Don't talk," Noah said. "Rest." They could argue this ten years from now while the grandchildren were playing outside.

"Gone . . . finally . . . gone."

"Listen!" The siren's wail grew closer. "The ambulance will be here any second."

". . . her fault . . . she ruined everything . . ."

A chill ran up Noah's spine. "Ruined what? Dad, what are you talking about?"

Simon's eyes closed. His breathing stilled.

"Come on," Noah muttered. "Come on, damn it." Where the hell were the cops? The ambulance should've been there by now. His father was dying right in front of his eyes, and there wasn't a damn thing Noah could do to help him.

"Goddamn it, Dad." He pumped his father's chest in a desperate attempt to save him, but it was too late. It had been too late the day Noah was born.

"I'm really sorry, Noah," said Pete Winthrop, son of the old police chief. "The EMT staff said you did everything you could."

Noah felt drained. Beyond tears. Beyond sorrow. The weight of things left unsaid was crushing. He wished Gracie was there with him. He needed her more than he'd ever needed her before. He wanted to see her face, touch her hand, reassure himself that the future they'd dreamed of was still within reach.

"Noah."

Noah started. "Sorry." He forced himself to pay attention. "What did you say?"

"You'll want to tell your mother before she finds out some other way."

"Oh, Jesus." He felt like crying. His mother's world revolved around Simon. What would she do without him? "Yeah, I'll tell her." He had to find Gracie. His mother liked Gracie, and he knew Gracie thought highly of her in return. He couldn't do this alone. He wanted to climb behind the wheel of his sports car and break the speed of sound getting the hell out of there. He was good at running away from things he didn't like. That was one of the first things you learn when you're six years old and far away from home and everyone you love.

He had to find Gracie. Gracie would know how to handle this. She would know the right way to tell his mother.

"Noah." Pete Winthrop's voice broke into his thoughts. "You okay to drive?"

He nodded. "Yeah. I'm fine."

Pete stepped closer. "You don't look so good."

He pushed past him, trying to get to his car. He had to get out of there. He had to find Gracie. He'd stop by her house. It was late. Hours past when they were supposed to meet. Gracie was logical. Clear-headed. She would go home and wait for a phone call, wait for him to show up. He had to get to her. This would all make sense when he saw her again, when he held her in his arms.

Minutes later, he whipped into her driveway. Her car was nowhere in sight, but that didn't mean anything. Maybe she called Gabe's Cab Service and got a lift. Maybe she'd left her car back there in the parking lot with a note for him under her windshield wiper. Maybe if he kept moving it would all start to make sense.

His heart beat so fast and hard that it hurt. Jesus, what the hell was going on? He banged on the door. No answer. He tried the door. It was unlocked. He stepped into the front room. "Gracie!" He moved toward the hallway. "Mr. Taylor?" His footsteps sounded like cannon fire. The rooms were clean and neat. There were no signs of life anywhere, not even Sam the Cat. He stepped into the tiny kitchen. The dishes were washed and put away. The floor sparkled. He noticed wet streaks in the white tiles. He glanced at the kitchen table. Sugar bowl in the center. Creamer next to it. Salt and pepper shaker. Two envelopes, one with his name on it.

He opened the envelope and pulled out a folded sheet of typing paper. Gracie's handwriting—formal and precise—angled across the page. She was sorry . . . she loved him but . . . school . . . the future . . . sorry . . . so very sorry . . .

He stood there in the middle of the quiet kitchen for a long time, and then when the world reassembled itself around him, he walked out of the house, away from Idle Point, away from Maine, away from the world he'd known, away from the life he'd dreamed about, the girl he loved and the lies she had told, and it would be eight years before he looked back.

TEN

---ↄ◉⌥ↄ---

New York City, eight years later

It had occurred to Gracie more than once over the last week that she just might be crazy to even think about returning to Idle Point for her father's wedding. She didn't usually attend Ben's weddings—he'd had so many of them, after all, and not one of them had lasted—but it wasn't every day your father married the girl who used to sit behind you in English class back in high school.

Maybe if he hadn't called her on the day the hospital put her on suspension, she might have begged off and sent the happy couple a potted plant and her best wishes but, as luck would have it, he'd caught her as she walked in the door to her apartment with her arms piled high with files and Rolodex cards and an old cat named Pyewacket who didn't seem all that pleased to be there.

"Graciela," Ben had said in his flat Maine accent, "this is your father."

"Hello, Dad," she'd said, ignoring the little tug of emotion the sound of her given name aroused. Nobody but Ben called her Graciela. You wouldn't think such a simple thing could still hold such power over her heart, but it did. He was her father, not Simon Chase, no matter that her DNA might say otherwise.

They had come a very long way since the terrible day of Gramma Del's funeral. He never knew that Simon had come calling. The note she had left him said nothing more than, "Went back to school a week early. Gracie." She had been shocked to learn months later that Simon had died that very afternoon not far from her house. Shocked but not saddened. All she felt was a deep regret that she would never be able to ask the many questions that had plagued her ever since.

A few hours earlier, and her life and Noah's would have been entirely different. Then again, that was part of the fantasy, wasn't it? If what Simon had told her was true—and she had no reason to believe otherwise—her future with Noah had been doomed from the start.

She only thought about that every other day.

Her newfound relationship with her father had started slowly with Hallmark greetings and an occasional picture postcard of the Idle Point lighthouse or the Lobster Shack with the blue and white buoys hanging from the weathered shingles. From there it progressed to phone calls on Sundays when the rates were low. To her amazement, Gracie had found herself looking forward to those calls. He was her only family, and it mattered to her. Three years ago, he drove down to Manhattan to see where she was working, and she took him to all of the tourist spots, including the Empire State Building, the Statue of Liberty, and Central Park, and her eyes actually filled with tears when it was time to say good-bye.

She told herself that she was being a sucker and that if she'd learned anything in life, it was the fact that you couldn't trust anyone but yourself, but there was still no denying that Ben Taylor was a different man these days. He had been faithfully attending AA meetings for over seven years, and Gracie had endured a painful telephone conversation where he apologized for his transgressions and vowed to make amends. *I know the whole story,* she wanted to tell him. *I know about my mother and Simon Chase. I know what she did to you . . . what they both did to you. I know I'm not really your biological daughter. . . .* They both knew that nothing he could do would ever be enough to erase the years of neglect. If only she knew how to tell him that she understood more than he could imagine.

Funny the way things sometimes worked out. Simon Chase had destroyed her future with Noah on that long-ago afternoon, but his revelation had made it possible for her to understand Ben in a way she had never before been able to do. Simon had given her the gift of compassion. So much about her life made sense now to Gracie. The way Ben had kept her at arm's length from him. His reluctance to talk about her mother. The deep hatred between him and Simon. The cloud of bitterness and despair that seemed to surround him.

She wondered sometimes if he knew the truth or only suspected. It wasn't something she could bring herself to ask him. Her mother and Simon Chase were long dead. Gramma Del was gone. Her father—and that was who he was to her; Simon's words would never change that—was finally making some sense of his imperfect life. What could be gained by derailing him now? Let the past stay where it was, buried beneath old newspapers and discarded photographs where it belonged.

Over the years she had grown very good at burying the past.

That night he told her the trees were long past peak. She told him it was cold and rainy, but not that she had just been suspended from the hospital. She kept her life just out of his reach. Some habits were difficult to break.

He asked for Gramma Del's macaroni and cheese recipe. She waited while he found a pencil then recited it to him from memory. Then he hit her with the reason for his call.

"I'm getting married again, Graciela."

"Congratulations," she said, sifting through the stack of mail on her hall table while Pyewacket sniffed the closet door with great suspicion. It wasn't as if she hadn't heard those words a few times before, but she was still a little surprised. He had, after all, been single for over nine years. "Anyone I know?"

"Darnell and Rachel's daughter Laquita."

A copy of *Cat Fancy* slid to the floor at her feet. "Laquita *Adams*?" she asked, aware that her voice had climbed an octave and a half.

"Ay-up," he said, never more the New Englander than when put on the spot.

She moved the phone away from her ear and stared at it the way they did on bad *Nick at Nite* sitcoms. *Please tell me there are two Laquita Adamses in Idle Point.* "Not the same Laquita I went to school with." The quiet little girl who lived down by the river. The quiet big girl who knew every motel between Idle Point and Boston.

"The same," he said to the sound of profound silence from Gracie. "Two weeks from yesterday at the old church near the harbor."

Gracie's silence deepened. She wanted to say something, but the thought of her father marrying Laquita had struck her dumb with shock.

Her father cleared his throat, a noise like rocks scraping over concrete. "I'd like you to be there."

She leaned against the wall. She must be oxygen deprived. The room seemed to spin around her axis. "Would you say that again, please, Dad?"

"The wedding," he said, and she knew the effort each word required. "Will you come?" He knew she had a big, important job down there in New York City and more responsibilities on her shoulders than half the men in Idle Point, but he and Laquita would be glad to put her up for a few days, even longer if that was what she wanted. It would mean a lot to both of them if she could be there. The next thing Gracie knew, she heard herself saying yes to everything he suggested. The wedding, the visit, everything.

She regretted it the second she hung up the phone. She hadn't been back to Idle Point since the day she walked out on Noah and their dreams of happily-ever-after. Going back would only remind her of everything she had lost, all the things that could never be.

"I must be crazy," she told Pyewacket as she pulled Sam the Cat's old bed down from the hall closet and rummaged around for suitable food and water dishes. She had missed having a cat around the house. You could tell a cat things and be fairly sure they would never end up on the front page of the *National Enquirer*. "I don't want to go back home. I'll meet them one day in Boston and wish them well." The whole thing was too strange to even contemplate. She knew that Laquita attended AA meetings with her father and that they had some kind of mutual support team going between them, but she had never in a million years imagined anything like this. What do you say to a new stepmother who used to swipe your crayons in kindergarten?

Still, Ben had sounded solid and happy, and knowing what she now knew about his life, she couldn't help praying this all worked out for him. He was pushing seventy. There wasn't much time left for the happy home he'd been searching for since Gracie's mother died. Gracie only wished he could have found that home when she was young enough for it to matter. Funny how the little things hurt so much. The Christmases and New Year's Eves when she worked so her colleagues could be home with their families. The Thanksgiving dinners spent with friends who took pity on her. The birthdays that came and went without anyone knowing that the years were stacking up faster and faster, and she wasn't any closer to having a family of her own than she had been the day she left Noah behind.

She fed Pyewacket, made a makeshift litter box, then settled down for the night. Tomorrow morning was time enough to call her father and beg off on the wedding invitation.

She woke up the next morning with the sun shining and Pye purring against her chest, and she put off the phone call for another day. And another. She kept putting it off and putting it off, and that was how Gracie came to be showing her former coworker Tina around the apartment one week later as she prepared to head back to Idle Point.

"The faucet in the bathroom is fluky," Gracie said as she walked down the hallway toward the living room. "Make sure you tap it twice after you turn it off, or you'll end up flooding the apartment downstairs."

Tina, a big-haired blonde with an outsized personality, nodded. "Gotcha. Turn off, tap twice. Roger that."

She glanced over her shoulder at her former assistant. "I told you that before, didn't I?"

"Three times," Tina said, snapping shut her notebook. "Not that I'm counting or anything."

"I mentioned the radio in the bedroom, didn't I? You have to—"

"Set it thirty-two minutes earlier than you want the alarm to go off." Tina hugged the dark green leather notebook to her ample chest and grinned. "I think that's covered on page seventy-six of *Taylor's Apartment-Sitting Manual*." She paused. "Volume one."

"Not funny," Gracie said, although she couldn't hold back a smile. "I'm just trying to make sure I've covered everything."

"Trust me," Tina said, "you've covered everything. I know more about your bathroom drain than I know about my blood pressure, cholesterol, and estrogen levels combined."

"It's an old building with an even older landlord who hates sublets, even short-term ones like this. You need to know the ropes, or it's off with our heads."

Tina pretended to bang her own fluffy blond head against the wall. "Please," the young woman begged, "I can't take anymore. This is the most beautiful apartment I've ever sublet, quirky faucet and all. I'm going to be so happy here, you may never get rid of me."

Gracie opened her mouth to say something, but Tina wouldn't let her.

"Just go already. Grab your cat, jump into your car, and hit the road before it gets any later. You're going home for Thanksgiving, girl. You should be happy!"

Gracie peered out the window, angling her head so she could see the sky. "Looks like rain." She poked her head back in. "Maybe I should wait until tomorrow."

"That's what you said yesterday."

"I hate driving in the rain."

"The forecast said sunny and clear through the weekend. You'll make it to Maine in record time."

"You sound like you're trying to get rid of me."

"I am," said Tina. "Greg from Admittting is coming over for dinner, and I wasn't planning on setting three places at the table, if you get my drift."

Gracie's eyes widened. "Greg with the gorgeous—"

"One and the same. If that's not the way to celebrate my first night without roommates, I don't know what is."

Tina cast a longing look in the general direction of the bedroom.

Tina and Greg, naked in her bed. Gracie's old four-poster wouldn't know itself. So far her only male visitors had been Ben and Jerry of ice cream fame and now Pyewacket.

"That does it," she said. "I'll find the cat and get out of your hair."

"Now that's music to my ears," Tina said. "I want to take a long bubble bath, give myself a pedicure. Maybe even a facial if you ever leave."

"Pye!" Gracie clicked her tongue against her teeth. She waited a moment then called out again.

"This isn't that big an apartment," Tina observed, "and Pyebucket—"

"Pyewacket."

"—whatever, isn't exactly the Kate Moss of felines."

"Pye isn't fat," Gracie snapped. "He's big-boned."

"Yeah," said Tina, "and I'm a natural blonde."

Tina trailed her from room to room, treating her to a running commentary on the dangers of Fancy Feast and Nine Lives and the wonders of the real, the natural, the tasteless.

"No wonder all of your cats ran away," Gracie said as she spied Pye's fluffy tail poking out from under the living room sofa. "They were starving."

"You should know better," Tina said reproachfully. "You're the vet. I'm just a lowly clerk."

"Unemployed vet," Gracie reminded her. "As of eight days, eleven hours, and thirty-three minutes ago."

Tina made a face. "Not to worry. It's just a suspension. Three months from now it'll all be forgotten."

"Don't bet your bonus check on it, Tina. I'm in big trouble, and it doesn't look like it's going away anytime soon."

"They said it was a three-month suspension, and that's all it will be." Tina did a good job of sounding sure of herself, but neither woman was fooled.

"They said it was a three-month suspension, and then they'd review the case. Big difference."

"Since when did you become a cynic?" Tina shot back. "How can they fire you for saving an animal's life? That's what you were trained to do. That's like bringing a brain surgeon up on charges because the patient lived."

Gracie got down on her hands and knees and peered under the sofa. "You know the deal, Tina. If the owner wants a sick or old animal euthanized, that's what we do. We can counsel, but we can't take matters into our own hands."

"It's so unfair."

"Tell me about it." When Pyewacket's owners brought him in to be put down, Gracie had tried to convince them that the elderly cat was still healthy and could be expected to live a few more happy, contented years. She had believed she was delivering good news and was shocked when, instead of praising her for delivering the stay of execution on their beloved cat, the Albrights had turned on Gracie as if she had singlehandedly brought down Western civilization.

The powers that be at the East Side Animal Hospital—a convenient walk from Bloomingdale's—sided with the Albrights. "They have the right to make this decision," the administrator told Gracie. "You know what's expected of you, Taylor."

The Albrights made their dry-eyed good-byes to Pyewacket and left Gracie to put him down. She told herself it was part of the job description, that she couldn't force others to live according to her expectations. She whispered to the cat, stroked him behind the ears, then prepared the injection. Pyewacket looked up at her, and maybe she was crazy, but she thought about her dear old companion Sam the Cat, about how she would have done anything to buy more time with him, and she knew there was no way she could do it. She disposed of the syringe, gathered up the aged cat, then walked out the door with him and straight into a three-month suspension.

The funny thing was, she didn't miss the place. That was the part that didn't make sense. She had a great position at the most prestigious private animal hospital on the East Coast. She earned a fabulous salary, worked bearable hours, and now that she was gone, she realized she didn't miss it one single bit. Walking out that door with Pyewacket in her arms, she'd felt the way she used to feel way back in Idle Point when she worked for Dr. Jim. Back then, it had been about the dogs and cats and birds and livestock who were brought to them for treatment. Dr. Jim had taught her to think first of the animal in her care and let everything else fall into place behind that. The poor man would never have made it through the "Growing a Business" module she had taken just before graduation or her introduction to big-city methodologies when she joined the East Side Animal Hospital. She wondered what he would think of the woman she had become.

There would be time enough to find out if she ever managed to corral Pyewacket and start for Idle Point. Pye gave her a run for her money, but in the end, Gracie won the battle and managed to place him in his carrier over his piteous yowls for mercy. "C'mon, Pyewacket, after all I've done for you . . ."

Tina clapped her hands over her triple-pierced ears. "You won't have any hearing left by the time you get out of the city."

Gracie latched the carrier door and double-locked it, then gathered up the rest of her things while Pye supplied the sound track for good-byes.

The two women looked at each other, then Tina dissolved in tears. "It won't be the same without you at the hospital," she said as they hugged good-bye. "You were the only real human being in that place."

Gracie laughed despite herself. "I'm a vet, Tina. How big a compliment is that?"

"You know what I mean," Tina said, wiping her eyes with the back of her hand. "Oh, hell." She gave Gracie a big hug. "I'm gonna miss you."

"I'd be happy to stay and have dinner with you and Greg."

Tina gave her a look. "I'm not gonna miss you that much."

Gracie picked up the cat carrier, her gigantic leather tote bag, and her car keys. She repeated the apartment instructions to Tina once again. Then, when she couldn't delay another second without risking bodily harm, she said good-bye.

"Safe trip," Tina said from the doorway. "I'll see you in two weeks."

"Maybe sooner," Gracie said. "Depends on how things go with my dad."

But Tina wasn't listening. She had already closed the door. Gracie heard the snap of locks shifting into place as Tina began to get ready for her night with Greg from Admitting.

"Okay, Pye," she said as she started for the elevator. "Looks like there's no turning back now."

Pyewacket wisely remained silent.

"We're going to miss you, Dr. Taylor." Jim, the weekend doorman, helped her load Pye and the rest of her bags into her Jeep. "Won't be the same around here without you."

"I'll only be gone a couple of weeks," Gracie said. "You won't even know I'm away."

"Nothing like going back home." Jim held the door while Gracie climbed behind the wheel. "I'm from Rockport myself. You eat some lobstah for me, okay?"

Gracie promised that she would and, moments later, she was headed north for home.

Idle Point

The white-haired woman in the iron-gray suit fixed him with a stern look meant to scare him into submission, then said, "I'm sorry, Noah, but she's a biter."

Noah, who had been thinking about how Mrs. Cavanaugh looked just as old today as she had more than twenty years ago when she taught his kindergarten class, leaned forward in his seat. "Would you mind saying that again?"

"I said, your daughter is a biter. We had two complaints about her this week. I'm afraid Sophie has become quite a disruption to the class."

"Sophie's a kicker, Mrs. Cavanaugh, not a biter." He knew that for a fact. He had a bruise on his left shin from the plane trip that was only now beginning to fade.

Mrs. Cavanaugh's expression darkened even more. "I was planning to address the kicking when we finished this part of the discussion. The biting issue is more urgent."

"She's having some trouble adjusting," he said, admiring his mastery of understatement. "The culture difference and all. Give her another few weeks and—"

"We can't tolerate a biter." Mrs. Cavanaugh cut him off neatly. "The other children have the right to attend class without fear for their personal safety."

"Aren't you exaggerating a little?" he asked, feeling his temper starting to rise. "She's only five years old."

"The patterns of childhood are the patterns of adulthood," Mrs. Cavanaugh intoned.

"What should I do?" he asked, at the end of his rope. "Lock her in the basement until she's twenty-one? The kid's been through a lot the past six months. She just needs some time to fit in." He knew exactly how she felt. Since returning to Idle Point to oversee the sale of the *Gazette*, he had felt like the proverbial fish out of water.

"I'm not trying to be harsh, Noah, but I am concerned both for the other students and for Sophie. The sooner we nip this problem in the bud, as it were, the sooner Sophie will be integrated into the student community."

"So is she suspended or isn't she?" Might as well cut through the bull and get to the heart of the matter.

"Yes," Mrs. Cavanaugh said after a long pause, "but only for two days. Please understand that if she so much as bares her teeth at a schoolmate again, I'll be forced to take even more decisive action."

Like what? he wondered. *Lethal injection? Electric chair?* Just how did you handle a little girl who had lost her mother, her home, and her country with one bang of a judge's gavel?

"Fine," he said, pushing back his chair and rising to his feet. "I appreciate your time."

Mrs. Cavanaugh creaked to a standing position. "I'm sorry to hear your mother is doing poorly," she said, offering him a gnarled hand to shake. "I thought she was recovering quite well. Please give her my regards."

Noah shook her hand, then left the room.

Sophie was sitting in the hallway just outside the door where he had left her. She was small-boned and petite like her mother, with a heart-shaped face and a tiny, pointed chin, but that was where the resemblance ended. Catherine was dark and languid and indolent. She moved with the flowing grace of a cougar stalking its prey. Sophie's hair was golden, the way his had been as a little boy, and she darted rather than walked. Her movements were sharp-edged and decisive. like a predatory bird. You could hear her coming two rooms away. She fought sleep and only gave in when exhaustion overcame sheer stubbornness. He was the same way. Sleep had always seemed to be a waste of time. The only time he had ever loved sleep was when he held Gracie in his arms and—

His brain clicked off. He knew how to stop those dangerous thoughts dead in their tracks. He had had years of practice, after all.

"Can we go now, Papa?" His little girl looked up at him with big blue eyes that would one day be a lethal weapon. His Sophie, a biter? Impossible.

"Sure," he said. "We can go now."

She held out her tiny hand to him, and his heart did a somersault inside his chest. It was all so new to him, so long denied, that he still had trouble recognizing it for what it was. *Love,* he thought. That was how love felt, the way he remembered it.

That was the way it had been with Gracie.

It was impossible to be in Idle Point and not think of her. She was around the bend at Dr. Jim's, looking fresh and competent the way she had that first afternoon. She was sitting at the end of the docks with her beautiful narrow feet dangling in the cool water. She was standing in the shadows of the lighthouse, near the school, in the kitchen of his mother's house, every damn place he looked.

He had known it would be that way. That was one of the reasons he had stayed away from Idle Point. How could you forget when reminders of what you had shared, the dreams you'd dreamed, waited around every corner?

At least the black anger was gone. That coiled rage had been with him for too long, laying waste to everything that stepped into his path. He couldn't remember exactly when the rage had turned to bitterness, when bitterness turned to a combination of sorrow and acceptance, but he thanked God that it had happened before Sophie came into his life. He didn't know much about bringing up a child. He was befuddled by the clothes and the tantrums and the great expanse of future unrolling in front of them. The only thing he was sure of was that she needed love and security in great measure. Steadiness. She had had damn little of it in her short life, and now it fell to him to prove to her that she had finally come home to stay.

He and Sophie stepped out into an overcast November afternoon. He used to wonder why gray days seemed to bring out the best of the autumn foliage, not that there was any left to speak of. The contrast, maybe, or some trick of the light. He had always meant to ask somebody about that. He should look it up in the library or surf the Internet. Parents needed to know these things. Next year Sophie would look up at him with those long-lashed blue eyes of hers and ask the same question, and he had to know the answer. That was what fathers did, wasn't it? They answered questions and paid the bills and caught spiders.

Sometimes he thought about his own father and tried to figure out where Simon had made his mistakes, but his memories were so caught up with adolescent loneliness and hero worship and anger that he didn't know where truth ended and fantasy began. His father loved him. His father was indifferent. His father controlled his every move. His father wouldn't have noticed if he'd vanished off the face of the earth. His father was proud of him. His father thought he was a failure. It was all true, and none of it, and he didn't know how to piece it all together.

"Your father did the best he could," was all his mother would say on the subject. "Never doubt that he loved you, Noah. Never, ever doubt that."

But he did. Now that he had a child of his own, he

understood how love should feel. Sophie's very existence had made him feel as if his chest was three sizes too small for the size of his heart. He knew that the thought of sending that tiny scrap of humanity out into the world alone was enough to bring him to his knees. Had he been that small at five years, that vulnerable? How in hell had his father been able to push him out of the nest a year later and send him off to St. Luke's?

He had been drifting before Sophie. She anchored him in time and space. Losing Gracie had been like losing an essential part of himself. Without her by his side, his dreams of Paris meant nothing at all. It was nothing more than a city by a river. He had been waiting for a sign from God, a bolt of lightning, something to wake him up and turn him in the right direction. He had never thought that sign would come in the form of a little girl with the face of an angel. He had spent the last eight years bumming his way through Europe, trying on different personae for size, pretending he hadn't left his broken heart in the hands of a serious young woman with better things to do than spend her life with him. He finished his degree in London, then found himself a job writing ad copy for an international publishing concern. He had learned all about deadlines during his summers at the *Gazette*, and he wrote quickly and well and was rewarded handsomely for that ability. If he ever had the sense that he could be doing more with his gifts than hawking the next best-selling how-to book, he did his best to push that thought from his mind before it had a chance to cause any trouble. If he ever missed that sense of community he had enjoyed on the staff of the *Gazette*, he refused to acknowledge the fact. He had discovered that you could have a fine life without ever breaking the surface. Gracie had been wrong about that. Not everyone needed to dive deep.

In the end, it was both the *Gazette* and Sophie that

brought him back to Idle Point. His mother Ruth was in failing health, and she wanted to sign over the management of the paper to him. Ruth had come into her own with Simon's death. She had surprised everyone in town when she took over the reins of the *Gazette* rather than sell it off to one of the conglomerates that had expressed more than a passing interest in the paper. She had quietly watched and learned a lot over the years, and her hand on the reins was sure and gentle. She understood that selling to one of the conglomerates would mean putting a lot of loyal employees out on the street, and she steadfastly refused to do it, thereby gaining the undying loyalty of her staff and the unending exasperation of her accountants.

Noah knew all of this because the accountants had told him so last month when he returned to Idle Point. He also knew that the *Gazette* was hemorrhaging money like a severed artery, and that if they didn't sell soon, there would be nothing left to sell. He had come home to introduce his mother to her granddaughter, to give Sophie a sense of family that had been missing in her young life. And, if he was being honest with himself, he came home because he had been everywhere else, and the emptiness was still deep inside his heart.

He wanted to see his daughter walk the streets he had walked as a kid. He wanted to see his mother's face when Ruth realized that Sophie's eyes were his eyes, were her eyes, were the eyes of who knew how many dead relatives reaching back into yesterday. And, damn it, he wanted the *Gazette* to stay in his family's hands. A year ago, none of this would have mattered to him. Now it meant everything.

ELEVEN

Gracie supposed there was a certain ironic symmetry to the fact that she ran out of gas thirty yards away from Eb's Stop and Pump. Of course, it wasn't Eb's any longer. Eb had died a few years ago while on a whale-watching trip out of P-town. She liked thinking of her old friend out there on the ocean with a pair of binoculars and a lot of curiosity. It made her feel good to know he was adventuring when his time came, but his loss was deeply felt.

The big red sign now read Gas-2-Go, and the smaller signs beneath it promised that milk, cigarettes, magazines, and coffee were all waiting inside to soothe the frazzled traveler. There was a car wash adjacent to the parking lot, a Jiffy Lube and, unless her eyes deceived her, the ramshackle motel behind Eb's gas station was now a sparkling Motel 6.

And that wasn't all. She had already noticed the brand-spanking-new condo that curved around the harbor, all preweathered siding and gingerbread trim with Hollywood-perfect rowboats bobbing in the calm waters that lapped against the owners-only pier. Unless she missed her guess, she'd bet there were more condos where that one came from.

Idle Point was bursting at the seams with prosperity, and she felt almost like a stranger as she sat there in her truck with the New York plates and her New York attitude and tried to take it all in. She wondered if this was how Noah had felt when he came home from St. Luke's each summer to a town that had changed just enough to keep him slightly off balance, not quite sure if he was a townie or a tourist or just passing through on his way to someplace else.

She reached over and scratched the top of Pye's head through the bars of the cat carrier. Pyewacket opened one lime green eye, yawned, then dived back inside a dream. *Lucky you*, she thought as she climbed out of the car and stretched. At least Pye's dreams couldn't break his heart. The worst that could happen was tuna for supper instead of mackerel.

Her limbs were stiff and sore from spending eight hours behind the wheel without a break. Once she had crossed the Triboro Bridge and headed north toward New England, she had simply kept on going. A smarter woman would have stopped for lunch in Massachusetts, walked around a little, read a magazine or two, then knocked off the rest of the drive up the coast to Idle Point.

Or then again, maybe a smarter woman wouldn't be there at all.

Everywhere she looked she saw ghosts. Old Eb, his eyes brimming with tears, as he wished her well. Gramma Del and her friends hosting the church bazaar in Fireman's Park across the street. Noah racing down Main Street in his flashy red sports car.

Noah.

Damn it. She had promised herself she wouldn't fall prey to memories, but now that she was standing there with the ocean breeze whipping all around her, so sharp and salty she could almost taste it, it was impossible to keep the past at bay. At least she wouldn't run into Noah while she was here. The last she'd heard, he was still in Europe somewhere, living the life he'd always dreamed about. The kind of life that, if she was being honest, had never appealed to Gracie. She would have followed him because she loved him, but she would have always longed for home. Idle Point was where she had wanted to be, where she had thought she would settle down and establish herself with Dr. Jim as the second-best vet in town.

You know you could turn around and drive back to New York right now. The voice followed her as she strode toward the man lounging in front of Gas-2-Go. *Who'd know? You're a stranger around here. Fill the gas tank, then run for your life.*

The man lounging near the air pumps looked over in her direction. He had dark hair, a slightly receding hairline, and a look of shock on his face. He looked vaguely familiar to Gracie. She stopped and looked at him closely as the years slid away. "Don?" she asked. "Don Hasty, is that you?"

"Gracie?" He stood up. "I'll be a son of a bitch! Gracie Taylor, you've finally come home!"

"You worry too much," Laquita said to Ben as he paced the small living room of the house by the docks. "Everything will go smoothly." She patted his arm with a gentle hand. "I promise you."

Ben felt that touch deep in his soul, but he still wasn't convinced. "It's a long time since Gracie's been home. A lot's changed."

Laquita smiled. "I'm the biggest change, Ben, and you've already told her we're getting married. The rest is window dressing."

He stopped pacing and sat down on the arm of the sofa Laquita had reupholstered last year. The fabric was pure creamy white with streaks of sunny yellow and pale green running through it. He couldn't quite remember what color the old fabric had been—spilled tea, maybe, or a nice shade of used coffee grounds. If you had told him ten years ago that he would be living with something so beautiful, he would've pegged you for the one with the drinking problem. He'd never cared much about the way he lived. Drunks never did. All a drunk cared about was the next bottle of Johnnie Walker.

Drunks didn't care about their kids, either. Drunks didn't show up for birthday parties or first communion or graduation. They didn't notice the awards or the scholarships or the hard work. They didn't notice when the sleeping infant in the baby blanket turned into an accomplished young woman with sad eyes. They sure as hell didn't notice when that young woman stopped coming home. Not while they were drinking. He would still be a drunk if it weren't for Laquita. He'd still be peeing in his pants, sleeping in his own vomit, wondering why his daughter didn't love him the way a father ought to be loved.

"I saw what you did in Ma's cottage," he said. "It looks swell."

"Better than swell," Laquita said with a smile. "It's looking wicked good."

"I think Graciela will be comfortable there." He had cleaned the place from ceiling to basement, and then Laquita had performed some magic with paint and paper and fabric until the little cottage looked like a home for the first time since Del died.

"I think she'll love it. We all need our own space, especially while we're getting used to being a family." Laquita reached for the coat she kept on the peg near the door, then slid her arms into the sleeves. "She knows the cottage belongs to her?"

Ben nodded. "She never much cared."

"Can't say that I blame her," Laquita said as she moved into his arms for a hug. "This wasn't a happy place when she lived here."

He winced again. He wanted to correct Laquita, try to put a different spin on her words, but he knew she wouldn't allow it. Honesty was part of recovery. Brutal honesty about your own failings was crucial to rebuilding your life. Laquita never blinked when she faced her own demons, and she refused to allow him to blink when he faced his. It was one of the countless things he loved about her.

"I'm sorry I have to leave," she said as he walked with her to the front door. "I never thought I'd be called in for night shift this week, but with Tammy being sick and my vacation coming up and everything—"

"She'll understand. You're a nurse. You go when you're needed."

"Apologize to Gracie for me, will you, Ben? I left her a note but—"

He kissed her. "Don't worry. Just drive safely. Those wet leaves are—"

"Slippery as ice. I grew up here, remember? I know all about wet leaves." She said it kindly, but she said it as a reminder that she was a grown woman, his equal in all the ways that mattered.

He stood in the doorway and watched while she warmed up her car then backed slowly out of the driveway. She beeped her horn twice, waved, then disappeared down the road. He stayed there until her taillights faded into the dusk, then went back inside to make himself a cup of coffee and wait for his daughter to come home.

Laquita's smile didn't falter until she made the turn onto Sheltered Rock Road. She held it, wide and true and unwavering, for exactly that long before it all fell apart. That was the point where even Ben, with his preternaturally sharp eyesight, could no longer see her and she could drop her guard.

Well, now she'd done it. She had lied to Ben, the one thing she had sworn she would never do. The truth was important to both of them, vitally important, but how on earth do you tell the man you're about to marry that you would rather walk barefoot on burning coals than see his daughter again?

Any woman worth her salt would do exactly what Laquita had done: run for her life. She had shamelessly offered her services at the hospital on her day off, which just happened to be the day Gracie was due back in town. If that had failed, she might have thrown herself under a truck.

Gracie had been the one girl in school who intimidated Laquita. She was tall, smart, pretty, ambitious, disciplined, and determined to achieve her goals despite the formidable odds against her. Next to her, Laquita had felt like a short, round slug. How she had envied Gracie's only-child status, her room of her own, the fact that she could think her own thoughts without having to fight for space to breathe. The only time she had ever felt remotely Gracie's equal was the day they had bumped into each other one early morning in a motel parking lot outside of town. *So you're human,* she had thought, noting the blush of embarrassment on Gracie's throat and face and the way she clutched Noah's hand. But then there was Noah, arguably the best—if least reliable—catch in town. Rich, smart, wild, great-looking. They were an unlikely match and yet, to Laquita's way of thinking, inevitable. Temporary but inevitable.

All of Laquita's romances before Ben had been temporary. *Romance.* Now there was a funny term for you.

There had been very little that was romantic about her encounters in bars and motel rooms and the backseats of more cars than you'd find in the parking lot during a Patriots game. Sometimes she had been looking for sex, for the oblivion that came with the act, but most of the time she had been looking for the kind of comfort and security she could only find in the arms of an older man or a bottle of vodka. She'd seen a shrink a few years ago, not long after she and Ben started living together, in an attempt to understand why she had done the things she did, and the shrink focused on the obvious answer: She was searching for a father figure.

"I have a father," she had told him. Darnell was a kind-hearted man who loved his kids, all eleven of them.

"But you have to share him," the shrink had pointed out. "You didn't share the other men."

But of course she had shared them—with their wives and other lovers. Until Ben Taylor came into her life, nobody had ever loved her totally and completely to the exclusion of others, and it was a feeling she cherished and returned in full measure. Her feelings for Ben were unlike anything she had ever known before. It was more than sex, more than security, more than the comfort of a pair of strong arms around you in the heart of the night. It was about wanting to share the good and bad of life, someone to sit down with over dinner at night and breakfast in the morning. Ben knew her darkest secrets, same as she knew his. They had faced down the monsters in the closet and were still standing.

She wanted Gracie to know these things. Gracie and Ben had had a terribly troubled relationship, and there was no doubt in anyone's mind that the blame lay solely at Ben's feet. He had failed miserably as a parent, and Gracie deserved all the credit for turning out as well as she had. But Ben had changed, was changing, and more than anything Laquita wanted Gracie to appreciate that fact, to get to know her father before it was too late.

Because the clock was always ticking. The days passed and then the years, and next thing you knew, it was time to say good-bye. Every time she looked at Ben, she wondered how much time they would have left and knew it wouldn't be nearly enough. Her family teased her by calling her an old soul, and it was true. She had always been older than her years, able to see the end of things where her friends could only see the beginning. It was part of the reason she had never really enjoyed the company of men her own age. They didn't understand how precious it all was or how quickly it passed.

Ben did. It was one of the many reasons why she loved him.

Another wave of apprehension swept over her. Ben was so happy that Graciela was coming home for the wedding. Happy and anxious and hopeful—so hopeful that it almost broke Laquita's heart. He wanted to make things right between himself and Gracie. Laquita had told him that they had come a long way over the last few years and that he should be proud of the progress he and his daughter had made toward becoming a family. She had also told him that he shouldn't expect miracles. Maybe Gracie had gone about as far as she was able to go with him, and he should accept it and be grateful to have this much.

He had no idea that Laquita was praying for a miracle.

Everyone had said she and Ben would never last, that the age difference would put an end to them before they had a chance to get started, but they were wrong. The only reason she ever wished Ben could be younger was so she could have him with her longer. Other than that, she wouldn't change a thing.

Except to give him back his daughter.

•   •   ∘

"Can I get you anything else, Mrs. C.?" Rachel Adams wiped away an imaginary streak from the crystal-clear library window of the house on the hill. "Another pot of tea, or some of that pumpkin bread maybe."

Ruth Chase smiled and shook her head. "Nothing, thank you, Rachel. I'll be more than fine until dinner."

"Are Noah and Sophie eating dinner with you?"

Ruth's smile widened, and Rachel smiled back at her. Grandmotherhood was proving to be as delightful as everyone had said it would be. "Sophie loves your Greek salad. If we have some feta, perhaps you could—"

"Done," said Rachel. "It's good to see the little one smile after all she's been through."

"That it is." She pointed toward a stack of books near the doorway. "I found some wonderful books on the Renaissance for Storm. She's welcome to keep them as long as she likes."

Rachel thanked her. "I'll send her in to get them as soon as she comes home from school."

"No hurry," said Ruth. "They're here waiting."

Storm was Rachel and Darnell's eleventh and last child. Storm was fourteen years old, beautiful, and more charming than the law allowed. Ruth thoroughly enjoyed having the child living under her roof. In truth, she enjoyed all of the Adamses, including their extended family of brothers and sisters, nieces and nephews, and the scattering of in-laws. Ruth had first opened her home to them three years ago, right after the flash flood that had washed away the homes by the river and everything in them. Two of the Adams children had been badly hurt, as had Darnell himself when he tried to save them, but God was kind that day and let them live. The Urbanska family hadn't been that lucky. All six of them, lost to nature's fury.

The town had leaped into action. The fire department organized a food drive. The police department collected

donations of money, clothes, household goods. Families
took shelter where they could, but the huge Adams clan
faced being split until Ruth heard about their plight and
offered her home. "I'm rattling around this place like a
marble," she said when Darnell expressed reluctance to
accept her generosity. "I'd love the company. Why should
all those bedrooms go to waste?"

Darnell and Rachel finally agreed but with the proviso
that they be allowed to work around the house to earn
their keep. The plan worked out so well that a temporary
arrangement quickly turned into a permanent situation that
was highly agreeable to all.

If someone had told her twenty years ago that the family of hippies who lived down by the river would move
into her house and turn it into a home, she would have
laughed out loud. If someone had told her that her son
would return at last from Europe with a beautiful little
daughter in tow, she would have been astonished. Life,
she had learned, was nothing if not surprising.

Like the fact that Rachel's eldest, Laquita, was marrying Ben Taylor. Ruth was too old to be shocked by much
of anything, but that news did give her a moment's pause.
The age difference alone was reason enough to think
twice, but given both Ben's and Laquita's personal his-
tories—well, there had certainly been more than a fair
share of gossip about both of them. Still, there was no
denying that something about them seemed right, as if
each supplied what the other lacked, and together they
were stronger than anything life could throw their way.

Rachel had mentioned that Ben invited Gracie home
for the wedding. Once, a very long time ago, Ruth had
seen Gracie and Noah together, embracing in the shadows
of the lighthouse, and she had felt a pain in her heart that
still had the power to take her breath away. They'd never
stood a chance, of course—Simon would have seen to

that—but the sight of them together had reminded her again of how powerful young love could be.

Ruth had been a widow now for a little over eight years, and in that time she had discovered many things about herself. She had learned that the human heart was very adaptable. The pain of losing Simon so suddenly had never really left her, but the unbearable grief had faded with time until it became as much a part of her being as her pulse or respiration. You could live with pain, Ruth discovered. To her surprise, it was possible to go on.

Living with regret was something else entirely. She had many regrets. Some of them were as wide and deep as eternity.

The first year without Simon had been difficult. In one tragic afternoon she lost her husband to death and her son to circumstance, leaving her to deal with the aftermath alone. Simon had always been the one to deal with the unpleasantnesses of life. He paid the bills. He took care of keeping the cars in good running order, made sure insurance policies were up to date, kept tabs on household repairs, and still managed to write for and publish the *Gazette*, even though readership wasn't half of what it used to be.

"Sell, Ruth." That had been Ed Hinkemeyer's advice when they met to discuss her financial future a few weeks after Simon's funeral. He showed her the latest offer from the Boston newspaper syndicate that had been their most persistent suitor. "You want my advice? Take the money and run."

She had come very close to doing just that. The *Gazette* had fallen into disfavor. The reputation it had enjoyed during those heady days after Simon's Pulitzer was a thing of the past. Now it was just another daily tabloid dose of town news, police blotter updates, and supermarket circulars, like every other small-town New England paper. Letting it go had seemed the better part of valor, and Ruth had been prepared to do exactly that until the day she went into the office to speak to the employees. Unadorned numbers in a ledger were replaced with names and faces who came with families and stories, and she knew she had no choice but to hold onto the *Gazette* a little bit longer.

For one thing, it made her feel closer to Simon, as if she were somehow making up for a lifetime of mistakes. They had both been very good at making mistakes. She was grateful he went to his grave not knowing anything about hers.

Her broken hip this spring had slowed her down, but so far it hadn't stopped her. She had let Noah think she was more frail than she was, which could be called manipulative, but she was certain the circumstances warranted such measures. She had caused so much damage already. She wouldn't cause anymore. This was a time for healing. Her last chance to get things right, to know that just once she had thought of Noah's happiness before her own.

She had asked him if he would take over some of her responsibilities while he was home, and he agreed. He needed a place to be right now, both for his own sake and for Sophie's, and that place might as well be Idle Point. It would do him good to drop in at the *Gazette*, to take Sophie to school in the morning and pick her up in the afternoon, to show her where he used to go sledding on the rare Christmas break when they stayed home. It would do them all good to be a family again.

"Take a seat, Gracie," Ben said after she took off her coat and let a suspicious Pyewacket out of his carrier. "I'll fix you a cup of coffee."

"You don't have to do that," she said. "I can—"

"Sit." He pointed toward the beautiful pale cream and yellow sofa near the front window. "You're the one who just spent eight hours on the road."

She was reasonably certain she had stumbled into some kind of alternate universe. Few other explanations seemed to fit. If the house didn't still boast the same slanted hallway floor and staggered ceilings, she would think her father had razed the old house and built a new one from the ground up. This house was quiet and serene. Soft white walls, white curtains, white sofa with the faintest touches of yellow and green. Tables of bleached oak. The hardwood floor had been sanded then stained the palest maple and polished to a comfortable glow. The house breathed happiness and exhaled contentment, much as her father himself. Her father's reading glasses rested on the coffee table next to an empty cup. A copy of the latest Tom Clancy novel lay open on the end table nearest Ben's chair. She couldn't remember ever seeing her father read for pleasure. Gracie had always been the one with her nose in a book, letting the magical words inside transport her to Singapore and Tibet, the African coast and the North Pole. Her father had found his escape in a bottle of booze.

If she had ever wondered whether the change in Ben was real or an illusion he managed to maintain for a weekend visit every now and again, she had her answer. This oasis of calm and control told her everything she needed to know. She looked about for signs of Laquita and found a nursing textbook on the bookshelf near the television, a copy of the newest Danielle Steel, a small lipstick in a silver-toned case, and three back issues of *U. S. News and World Report*. She had no doubt Laquita was responsible for most of the changes in Ben's life, and she wondered what changes Ben had brought about in Laquita's life as well.

He seemed so happy, so filled with plans for the future. If Laquita only loved him half as much, they would be guaranteed a wonderful life. But then, when did life ever come with guarantees?

"Laquita had a pot of chowdah on the stove," Ben said as he came back into the room with a tray piled high with goodies. "I put some in a bowl for you, a few crackers. You look like you could use a good meal."

"I've always looked like I could use a good meal," she said, laughing.

"You take after your grandmother," he said, and there was a fondness in his tone she couldn't remember ever hearing before. "She ate and ate and stayed skinny as a broomstick."

Do I really take after Gramma Del, Dad? Can you tell me if her blood and yours really flow through my veins? She pushed the thought from her mind. What did it matter, anyway? All that mattered was the fact that they were there together in that strange yet familiar living room on this cold November evening, with a bowl of good chowder and the sounds of the ocean winds beating against the house.

Asking for more might be tempting the gods.

"I hate to eat alone," she said. "You look like you could use a good meal yourself."

He glanced at the clock on the mantel. "It's after six," he said. "Wouldn't hurt to have some supper with you."

She followed him into the kitchen where he fixed himself a bowl of chowder, too. She found a can of cat food in her bag and emptied it onto a paper plate for a grateful Pyewacket. There was so much history between Gracie and her father, so much that was dark and hurtful, that this simple act of breaking bread together in the house where she had grown up was nothing less than a small miracle. They sat down opposite each other at the old wooden table where Gramma Del had made a thousand meals, and she saw her life moving past her eyes. The last time she had seen this room, this table, was the day she lost Noah forever. She had left the letter for him right here, not six inches away from her right hand, tucked between the salt shaker and the sugar bowl. *How many letters were here when you finally came home, Dad? Did Noah read his? Did you ever wonder why I never came home again?*

She had spent many nights wondering if she should have stayed and confronted Simon and Ben and forced all of the secrets out into the light, but she had been a product of her upbringing, raised on a diet of keeping family secrets hidden away in the shadows.

She told herself not to ask for the moon, to be satisfied with this tiny piece of it, but she couldn't help wishing for answers to the questions she could never ask.

". . . parents work for Mrs. Chase at the house. The youngest, Storm, is fourteen . . . doing Thanksgiving dinner there . . ."

Gracie tried hard to pay attention, but the combination of warm soup, a cozy sofa, and exhaustion were taking their toll. She had already nodded off three times while her father was talking, and she was determined not to nod off a fourth time.

"You should get a little shut-eye," he said, reaching down to scratch Pye behind his left ear. "You're out on your feet, Graciela."

She started to protest, but he was having none of it. "Get some sleep. We'll have plenty of time to jaw tomorrow when Laquita's home."

Gracie barely stifled a yawn. "I wanted to stay up and see her tonight."

"She won't be in until after two," Ben said. "I don't

think there's a way in hell you could stay awake that long."

She looked at the clock. It read ten-fifteen. "You're right," she said. "I'll never make it." She stood up and battled that yawn one more time. "I really enjoyed this, Dad."

He stood up and gave her an awkward pat on the right shoulder. "So did I."

"Am I sleeping in the sewing room?"

"No," he said. "Laquita fixed up Gramma's place for you. We figured you might like a little privacy."

"That's wonderful," she said, appreciating the gesture. "What a nice thing to do." Mending fences was hard work. They would all benefit from a little breathing room.

"It is yours, after all."

She stopped midstretch. "I keep forgetting that."

"Things have changed, Graciela."

"I know." She hesitated, then leaned forward and kissed him on the cheek. "I'm glad."

Ben helped her unload the Jeep. She carried a squirming Pyewacket across the rain-soaked yard and deposited him in the front room.

"You sleep well," her father said, giving her an awkward pat on the shoulder.

"You, too." She looked away for a moment. "Please apologize to Laquita."

"We'll see you at breakfast?"

She nodded. "Absolutely."

She went to lock the door after him then remembered where she was and she laughed softly. She was back home in Idle Point.

Mornings were the worst. Sophie didn't like mornings at all, and no matter how many times Noah told her it was time to get up, she burrowed more deeply under the covers and clung to sleep as if her life depended upon it.

"Come on, Soph." He shook her tiny shoulder. "You're coming to work with me today, and we can't be late." Okay, so that wasn't strictly true. His family owned the *Gazette*. He could be as late as he wanted.

She opened one sleepy eye. "No school today?"

"No school for two days," he said as she sat up and yawned, tiny fists pressed against her mouth. "You're on suspension."

"What's that?"

"A punishment," Noah said, "for biting your classmates." He reminded her of the fact that Mrs. Cavanaugh was still quite displeased with her behavior, but he couldn't tell how much of an impact that news had on his little daughter.

"Can I play with a computer?"

"Sure," he said, "but you can't go to the office and play with the computers if you don't get dressed."

I'll be damned. He watched as she ran barefoot to the bathroom and started brushing her teeth. A little good old-fashioned bribery, and he was in business. Why hadn't anybody told him that logic and reason were for the birds? Bribery was the only real way to a child's heart. There was a lesson to be learned there, and it wasn't one that Dr. Spock would have embraced.

The truth was, he barely knew Sophie. Each day he learned something new about her, something that reminded him either of himself or, now and again, of Catherine. Or what little he knew of Catherine. Their affair had lasted only six months. They had parted amicably when Catherine's acting career took her from London to Sydney. Neither one of them had suggested Noah join her. He had that effect on women.

He took a little pair of jeans out of the closet, a white shirt with a lacy collar, and a pink sweater, then laid them down on the bed. He tapped on the bathroom door. "Sophie, do you need help in there?"

"Go away!"

Five years old and guarding her privacy. He had kept the bathroom door open until he was twenty-two. "Okay, Soph," he said, stepping away from the door. "I'm here if you need me."

He waited. And waited. And waited a little bit more. Finally he knocked on the door again and was treated to an explosion of words uttered in such a thick English accent that he couldn't understand any of them. *Temperament? A problem? Something only a woman would understand?* He was stumped. He and Sophie not only had a bit of a language problem, but also they had a gender problem.

It was going to be a long day.

He was determined not to run to his mother with every problem he encountered with Sophie. He had been away from home for eight years. He had built an independent life. His mother had had more than her share of problems while he was gone, and she hadn't run to him for help. The least he could do for her now was work out his own difficulties with his daughter.

Unless Storm was around.

Sophie liked Storm Adams. Storm was much the way he had remembered Laquita at that age: remarkably self-possessed, quiet, almost Zen-like in her acceptance of the vicissitudes of life. The antithesis of his live-wire daughter. Seeing your home and belongings swept away in a flash flood had to have been a devastating experience, but you would never know it by Storm. His mother seemed very fond of Storm. She encouraged the girl to use their personal library anytime she liked, and he had noticed Storm reading quietly in a corner of the room the last few nights.

He stepped out into the hallway. No sign of anyone. He walked over to the landing and looked down at the foyer where Rachel Adams was polishing the mirror that hung over the small table where they stacked outgoing mail. She caught sight of him and looked up.

"Morning, Noah. Breakfast's ready when you are."

"Thanks, Rachel," he said. "Is Storm around anywhere?"

Rachel shook her head. The movement made her hip-length ponytail sway. "Band practice this morning." She grinned up at him. "Girl trouble?"

"You could hear her down there in the foyer?"

"Couldn't understand a word, but the intent was pretty clear."

"I think she's having a problem with her hair."

"It starts early," Rachel said, barely containing a laugh. She reached into her pocket and withdrew a crinkled circle of soft hot-pink fabric. "Your secret weapon."

He bounded down the stairs and took it from her. "Does this secret weapon have a name?"

"Ask Sophie," she said, turning back to the mirror. "She'll know."

Rachel was right. Sophie hollered. "Scruncheeee!" then made a lunge for it. Even though Noah was new at the parenthood game, he recognized a power position when he saw it. Maybe there was hope for him yet.

Gracie woke up a little after six to the sound of the morning paper hitting the front door. Pyewacket slept curled up next to her; his purr almost drowned out the sound of the wind off the ocean. She felt groggy, not quite all there, even though she'd managed almost eight hours of sleep. She had been dreaming about Gramma Del, one of those talky dreams where much was said and little remembered. *You wouldn't recognize this place, Gramma. Laquita*

made new curtains, re-covered your sofa and your favor-
ite chair. She painted the walls white. Can you imagine
that? White walls and pale yellow scatter rugs. She even
filled the fridge for me with milk and orange juice and
eggs and arranged for the paper. And she writes notes.
Remember how you were always trying to get me to write
my thank-you notes? Bet you wouldn't have had any trou-
ble with Laquita—

Good grief. She sat up straight, suddenly wide awake.
Laquita was about to become Gramma Del's daughter-in-
law, or she would be if Gramma were still alive. She
would be Gracie's stepmother, which meant Rachel and
Darnell, the hippies by the river, would be her father's
parents-in-law, and they'd be related to all of the Adams
kids and whoever they ended up marrying—it was all too
confusing.

The note from Laquita was on the nightstand. Gracie
rolled over on her side and reached for it. She had been
so tired last night that the words had run together like
melted candle wax. Okay, it was a simple welcome note.
Warm but not too warm. Brief but not terse. Very much
in keeping with the low-key manner Gracie remembered
when she thought about Laquita. Of course, there was also
the matter of Laquita's sex life. She had slept with half
the men in town by the time she turned twenty years old.
Gracie felt like a bit of a bitch for thinking it, but she
couldn't help wondering if her father's intended found
monogamy a good fit.

"None of your business," she said out loud. "None of
your damn business."

She swung her legs out of bed, then did a few stretches.
Faint streaks of light pushed their way through the oyster-
white fabric shades at the windows. She pushed the shade
aside and peered across the yard at her father's cottage.
The blinds were drawn. She could see there were no lights

on inside. A red Toyota, probably Laquita's, was parked in the driveway next to Gracie's Jeep.

Domestic tranquillity, she thought, then turned away from the window. Who would have thought Ben would find it long before his daughter?

"We're up shit creek," Andy Futrello announced to Noah the moment he and Sophie walked into the newsroom, "and Levine's got the paddle."

Noah looked pointedly at his little girl then back at Andy. "Let's watch it, okay?"

"Sorry. I'm not used to seeing a kid around here."

"Yeah, well that makes two of us." He helped Sophie out of her jacket and settled her down at an empty desk with her crayons and coloring book. "So what's wrong?" he said to Andy.

"Mary Levine's in the hospital," Andy said. "Heart attack, and it looks like she won't be getting her column in on time."

"How is she?" Noah had grown up with newspaper types. He knew all about their mastery of understatement.

"I don't know how she is. All I know is that we've got a hole in the editorial page, and it needs to be filled in the next forty-five minutes, or we're in trouble."

"We've been in trouble for quite a while," Noah observed. "Levine isn't going to tip the scales much either way."

"Check out the list of advertisers yet, Noah? Levine brought in half of 'em. She goes, they go."

"What is it exactly that Levine writes?"

"That family shit—" Andy glanced toward Sophie. "I mean stuff. Warm fuzzies, like if you crossed Donna Reed with that Martha Stewart dame and they gave birth to somebody who could write."

"And that pulled in the house and garden money."

"That pulled in house and garden and bookstores, and it grew from there. Without the revenue Levine pulled in, we'd be dead and buried."

"They'd bolt after missing one column?"

"Who the hell knows? But I sure don't want to risk it. I don't have good feelings about this, Noah. We don't have that kind of cushion to play with."

"If my mother ends up selling to Granite News Syndicate, that won't be a problem."

"A lot's been happening the last few months, and your mother—and don't get me wrong, she's a great woman, really knows what's going on—but since your mother went in for the broken hip and all that, she's stepped away from the fray, and let me tell you, it's a lot rougher now than it was." He told Noah that Granite News was getting cold feet, and any slip in circulation would be enough to kill the deal.

There was a part of Noah that wouldn't be disappointed at all if that happened. Granite News was your typical conglomerate, one more concerned with syndicates and cutting costs than with providing good jobs for good people who loved the newspaper business. He had tried on more than one occasion to question his mother about her choice, but each time Ruth had neatly changed the subject. He wondered how committed she really was to the venture.

He turned his attention back to Futrello.

"So we need some stories while Mary's on the disabled list. You're a writer, Andy. Give us some."

"I'm a sportswriter. I can't do that home and hearth crap."

"There's got to be somebody who can handle it."

"Most of us are straight news guys. We report what we see. Your old man knew how to write the essays that got noticed. Mary knows how to write the ones that bring in money."

"So you're saying we're up the creek."

"Yeah," said Andy. "That's what I'm saying." He paused, then continued, "You did some writing over there in Europe, didn't you?"

"Some," Noah conceded, "but it was mostly ad copy. I sold a few op-ed pieces to the American papers and—" He stopped cold. "I'm not on staff."

Andy started to laugh. "You *own* the staff."

"Yeah," said Noah, starting to laugh himself, "I do, don't I?"

"So why don't you give it a try? It's not like we have anything to lose."

Noah glanced over at Sophie, who was twirling her scrunchie around a bright blue crayon and humming softly to herself. The moment of absolute powerlessness he'd felt this morning when she refused to come out of the bathroom came back to him in vivid detail. Andy was right. They had nothing to lose.

He sat down at the computer and started to write.

All they did at the newspaper office was yell. Sophie had been playing Go Fish at one of the computers, trying to pretend it wasn't so noisy and scary in there. She hated yelling. Every time grown-ups yelled, bad things happened.

Sophie had lived with a lot of different people since she was a baby, and she knew all about how these things worked. First the grown-ups yelled at each other, then they yelled at her, and then the next thing she knew, her bags were packed and she was on her way to another new house where the people didn't really want her.

Even her new father was yelling. He and the fat man were yelling right into each other's faces, and it scared

Sophie. They spoke really fast in those strange American accents. She could only understand some of what they were saying, but she was sure they were yelling about her.

"I don't know much about bringing up kids," her new father had told her the day they went to court in London to sign the papers, "so I hope you'll help me." He had given her a big hug, but she had held herself all stiff in his arms. "We're in this together, Sophie, you and me. We're a family now."

He said that her new name was Sophie Chase and that she would be his daughter forever.

Sophie didn't believe him. If he loved her so much and was so happy that she was his daughter, then why was he so busy yelling at people and hammering the computer keys with his big fingers? If she ran away, it would probably take him a fortnight to realize she was missing.

Try as she might, Gracie couldn't find any traces of Gramma Del left in the old cottage. Except for the boxes tucked away in the attic, the place was stripped clean of old memories. It left her feeling disoriented, as if she'd made a wrong turn somewhere and this wasn't Gramma Del's at all. She flipped through the *Gazette* but didn't find much of anything to hold her interest there. She didn't recognize most of the names and faces, something she thought would never happen in Idle Point. Finally she dressed, then let herself out the front door to take a walk. She used to walk all the way into town in the days before she was old enough to drive. This seemed as good a time as any to see if she could still do it.

She wondered if Gerson's Bakery was still at the corner opposite the barbershop. She craved bagels and cream cheese and maybe some of those delicious sticky buns with the nuts studded all over the top. Maybe she would buy some freshly ground coffee beans, too—she was sure coffee mania had reached Idle Point by now—and bring them back to share with Ben and Laquita. The more she thought about the idea, the more she liked it. She wasn't a guest; she was family, and family contributed to the pantry.

Truth was, she was a little apprehensive about actually meeting Laquita again after all these years and seeing how her dad and old schoolmate fit together. Going for a long walk was one way to burn off nervous energy and center herself. Gracie always had a lot of physical energy to burn; she had quickly discovered that the best thing about living in Manhattan was the walking. Nobody thought you were strange if you walked forty or fifty blocks at a time, Battery Park to the Upper West Side, East River to the Hudson. Still, Manhattan wasn't Idle Point. Manhattan didn't smell like ocean kissed by pine trees. When you could find the sky, it was never storybook blue.

Not that the sky was blue that morning. It was a deep, brooding pewter gray with rain that was more than a mist but less than a storm. She wore jeans, a heavy black sweater, and her favorite jacket. Tina had told her she looked like a runaway Trappist monk in the jacket, but Gracie loved it. It was too big and too old to be fashionable, but Gracie had never been one to worry about that. She loved disappearing inside the jacket when she walked the city, letting the hood fall over her face, obscuring her identity. It made her feel mysterious.

Gerson's was gone. A sandwich shop had opened in its place. The bank boasted a face-lift and a brand-new name, while the grocery store, candy shop, and dry cleaners all looked exactly the way they had when she left. Herb's Camera Shop was still next to Leonard Insurance, which was next to Samantha's Bridal Shop, which was next to

Video Haven, which was next to Patsy's. And everybody knew Patsy's was next to the *Gazette*.

She was cold and hungry and wet and she needed caffeine. The lights from Patsy's down the block splashed out onto the rain-swept street. She remembered Patsy's blueberry muffins with great fondness. A blueberry muffin with a huge mug of hot coffee with lots of sugar and maybe some scrambled eggs. What was she hesitating for? Simon Chase was dead. Noah was on the other side of the Atlantic Ocean. Sure, she would probably run into plenty of people she knew, but they could never break her heart. Besides, why had she come home to Idle Point if she wasn't going to reconnect with old friends and familiar faces?

The rain was slicing down faster. She ducked her head and let the hood fall over her face, limiting her vision to just a few inches of sidewalk in front of her. She could almost taste the coffee, hot and sweet, as—

The little girl came out of nowhere. One second Gracie was the only person on the street, the next second she was almost knocked over by a child with a curly blond ponytail who burst out of the *Gazette* office as if she had the hounds of hell at her heels.

"Whoa, honey!" She backed up a step and put her hands on the child's slender shoulders. The child was shivering already, and no wonder. No coat, no sweater, nobody paying attention. "Where are you running to?"

The child looked up at her with huge blue eyes framed by dark lashes thick and long enough to make a grown woman weep. She had only known one other lucky person with such beautiful eyes. The child's hair was golden blond. Her skin was fair and pink. She looked positively angelic as she hauled off and kicked Gracie hard in the shin, then ran off down the street.

"Why, you little—"

Gracie took off in hot pursuit. If that little brat thought she was going to get away with a stunt like that, she had another think coming. The kid was fast but short. Gracie was fast and tall. She captured her assailant before they reached Samantha's Bridal Shop and swept her up into her arms.

"Where are your parents?" Gracie demanded as she marched the wet, wriggling child back up the block toward the *Gazette*. "How could they let you run around in this rain without a coat?"

The kid tried to kick her again, but Gracie held her out and away from her body the way she once held an angry fox terrier.

"Oh, no, you don't. One free kick is all you get."

"Bloody hell!" the little girl yelled. "Why don't you sod off?"

Gracie was so shocked she almost dropped her. "Somebody should wash out that mouth of yours with a bar of soap."

It was the kid's turn to be shocked. Her eyes widened as she stared up at Gracie, then she giggled. "Soap!"

"Yes, soap. Exactly what a little brat with a dirty mouth needs."

"You can't tell me what to do."

"I can tell you you're not going to kick me in the shin and get away with it." She tucked the child under her right arm. "Now, who do you belong to?"

The girl thrust her little pointed chin out and pressed her lips tightly together.

"Silent treatment, is it?" Gracie muttered. "Don't worry. I'll find out." She pushed open the door to the newspaper office. The place buzzed like an angry hive.

"Does anybody here own this child?" she called out.

Nobody paid any attention. They went on running to and fro, typing away at their workstations, ignoring her.

The kid, however, landed another sharp right that made Gracie cry out.

"If somebody doesn't claim this child in the next thirty seconds, I'm taking her to the police station before she breaks my leg."

The kid tried to make a run for it, but Gracie held on tight.

"Papa!" The kid had a pair of lungs on her a hog caller would envy. "Help!"

"Sophie?" A male voice rang out from one of the cubicles.

That voice . . . Sweat broke out on Gracie's brow. It couldn't be. God wouldn't possibly play a trick like this on her. She heard footsteps. She knew that rhythm: hard right, soft left; hard right, soft left. The rhythm of his walk, the sound of his voice, the smell of his skin—they were all part of her soul's language. She put the little girl down. Every instinct told her to run, but she couldn't move. She had been running for eight years, and she couldn't do it any longer.

TWELVE

The woman stood in the middle of the front office. Her tall, slender body was hidden inside a jacket that was easily three sizes too large for her. Her face was obscured by a hood that made her look like the Ghost of Christmas Future. Sophie, soaking wet, extremely angry, and inexplicably barefoot, stood next to her.

"Sit down over there," he ordered Sophie, pointing toward the chair against the wall. "I'll deal with you in a minute." She muttered something dark and terribly British but did as she was told. He wasn't fool enough to think compliance meant anything at all.

"Thanks," he said to the mystery woman. "I'm going to have to put a bell on—"

"Hello, Noah."

He knew before he knew, if such a thing was possible. There was an instant before the realization coalesced into thought when he registered her presence with his very skin.

"Gracie?"

She shook off her hood in a gentle arc of raindrops, and the years fell away when he saw her again. *Damn you.* He couldn't control the anger that ripped through him. *Damn you for leaving.*

"I didn't know you were back in Idle Point," she said, all cool and calm as if they'd seen each other the day before yesterday. "How long have you been here?"

So this is how you're going to play it, like you didn't walk out on me on our wedding day. "A few weeks. What about you?"

"Last night."

"You know about Ben and Laquita."

"That's why I came home."

"To try and stop it?"

"To attend the wedding."

She had lived a life he knew nothing about, would never know anything about. "Things are okay with you and your father?"

She nodded, and her hair, the same soft, shiny brown he saw in his dreams, drifted across her cheeks. "We've come a long way."

That was good. He was a father now; he knew how much it mattered. He wanted to tell her that, but he was choking on his anger. *It was always you, Gracie. There's never been anyone else.*

She glanced toward Sophie. "She kicked me."

He nodded. "She does that."

"Who is she?"

"Her name is Sophie," he said. "She's my daughter."

Gracie felt as if she'd been stabbed. He knew it in his own gut. The pain pierced through her muscles, her ribs, straight into her heart. It hurt to breathe, to think. Of all the things he could have said or done, nothing could have hurt her more deeply than this living proof that he had loved somebody else. He couldn't wish Sophie away, though. He wouldn't. She was the one shining triumph in eight dark years.

Noah watched her carefully. His words had found their mark. He could see the pain in her eyes, and he was glad.

That's how it feels, Gracie. Now you know.

"She's beautiful."

He nodded his thanks. "She's having trouble adjusting. Mrs. Cavanaugh put her on a two-day suspension."

"Kicking?"

"Biting."

"She sounds English."

"Her mother is from London."

"Oh." Her gaze swept the room. "Is your wife here?"

He shook his head, pushing away the question, the conversation. "I can't do this, Gracie."

Her brown eyes filled with tears—her emotions had always been so close to the surface—and for a moment he almost loved her again the way he used to love her, back in the days when he thought they could have it all.

Oh, God, Gracie thought. *Please don't let me cry in front of him.* The whole thing was bad enough without losing her dignity in the process.

"Neither can I," she said. "Take care, Noah."

"You, too."

She was gone before he had the chance to change his mind and ask her to stay.

Gracie made it halfway down the block before she realized she couldn't breathe. No matter how hard she tried, she couldn't pull enough air into her lungs to make a difference. The ground rolled beneath her feet. The horizon tilted at a crazy angle. She leaned against the window of Samantha's Bridal Shop and prayed she wouldn't vomit.

He had a wife. That little girl was his daughter. Noah and his wife had created that beautiful, bad-tempered little blonde she'd found running barefoot in the rain. Noah and his wife had held each other and loved each other, and out of that love had come a miracle: their daughter.

She didn't think she could hurt this much and still live. The pain was white hot. It sliced through all the protective layers she'd built up over the years and split her in two. He had gone on with his life. He had picked up the pieces and moved forward the way she had said he should, the way she had told herself she had wanted him to do, the way she had lied to herself about every single day for the last eight years.

Sophie should have been theirs. She would have been theirs if—

Don't think about it. There's nothing you can do about any of it. You had to leave. . . . You had no choice. . . . You never had any choice. . . .

Noah was an impossible dream, and it wasn't because he had a wife and child. It was thanks to Simon Chase and her mother.

For eight years Noah had wondered what he would do if he ever saw Gracie again. Letting her walk away again had never been one of the options.

He collared Andy. "Watch Sophie for me. I won't be long."

"She bites," Andy said, looking nervously in Sophie's direction.

"You're fifty-three," Noah said. "She's five. I think you can handle it. Get Sarah from Accounting to help you."

Morning traffic rolled slowly down the rainy street. John Templeton and Myrna DeGrassi waved at Noah then disappeared into Patsy's for morning coffee and town gossip. A big yellow school bus idled at the corner, its exhaust sending puffs of gray smoke into the chill air. Stan Foxworthy bent down to retrieve a copy of the *Gazette* from a stand at the opposite corner. Tess Moore waved at him, then unlocked the front door to the jewelry shop.

And there at the far end of the block was Gracie, bent

over double in front of Samantha's Bridal Shop, swamped inside that big coat. Every line of her body was familiar to him. The graceful curve of her back, her long slender arms, the spill of golden brown hair. His anger began to shift and sharpen as he ran toward her. He bridged the last eight years in forty-six strides.

"Don't do this, Noah." She said it without looking up, without looking at him. The weariness in her voice sharpened his anger yet again.

"You owe me." He didn't recognize his own voice. It held a mix of sorrow and pain held close for too long.

She lifted her head and met his eyes. "No," she said. "Not anymore."

"The hell you don't."

"It's over, Noah. It's been over for a very long time. Let it rest."

"Tell me why. That's all I want to know. Give me a reason, and I'll turn and walk away." He needed answers. He had spent too many years wondering what he had done wrong, wondering if he had imagined love, wondering if there had been one moment when he could have turned left instead of right and none of this would have happened.

"I left you a letter."

He slammed his hand against the window of Samantha's Bridal Shop. "That letter was bullshit."

He reached for her arm as she pushed past him, but she was too fast. All he got was a fistful of sleeve. She broke into a swift, spare run, dodging puddles, darting around knots of children, ignoring the fact that he was in close pursuit. There was no hesitancy, no uncertainty about her flight. She wanted to put as much distance between them as she possibly could.

He took ten steps, then the absurdity of the situation stopped him cold. He'd been looking for answers and he'd found them. They weren't the answers he had wanted, but that was life. Icy rain stung his face and arms, but still he stood there, watching her run out of his life for the second time. She'd answered all of his questions without saying a word. The sight of her slender body in retreat told him everything he needed to know and more.

This time, though, he had Sophie. Sophie would keep him from disappearing down that black hole of loneliness and anger. Sophie needed him almost as much as he needed her. A child didn't care if your whole world was falling apart. A child's needs were immediate and all-encompassing. Unconditional love, every day for the rest of your life. Once you had that worked out, then you could start worrying about everything else.

He would never know what made him turn back at that exact moment, just in time to see her trip over the curb, almost recover her balance, then crumple to the sidewalk.

At least he didn't see me fall.

That was the first thing Gracie thought when her ankle went one way and the rest of her body went the other. Bad enough that she had completely lost her composure at the first sight of his beloved face and ended up running away from him through the rain like the heroine of a very bad French movie. Knowing that he had seen her collapse in a tangle of limbs and embarrassment would have been enough to send her back to New York right now. His footsteps had dropped off somewhere before the middle of the last block, and she was grateful for that fact. It was the only good thing about what was shaping up to be an extremely bad morning.

She scrambled to her knees in the icy mud puddle, tried to stand, then fell back down again. Her right ankle throbbed, and she knew it was already beginning to swell.

"Oh, damn," she muttered, sitting back on the curb, lost

inside the mud-splattered folds of her Trappist monk jacket and more memories than she could handle even on a good day. "Damn damn damn."

She rested her forehead on her knees and let the tears fall, too. Of all the stupid, ridiculous, idiotic things to do, this one took the cake. She wasn't even in town one day, and already her entire world had been tilted on its ear and she'd made a fool of herself besides. Now what was she supposed to do, stuck there with a bad ankle, no car, and almost two miles away from home in a town that didn't believe in public transportation of any kind for anyone over the age of puberty? She'd noticed a few school buses making their wet way down the street toward Idle Point Elementary. Maybe Celeste was still driving, and she could beg a ride. At least her future stepmother was a nurse—

The thought was so absurd that she started laughing. Her father was about to marry the girl who'd sat behind his daughter in high school. The only man she'd ever loved had a snotty little brat who kicked when she wasn't busy spewing insults at strangers. And Gracie was sitting on her butt in the middle of the street in the middle of a budding nor'easter with a sprained ankle and a bruised ego and the realization that maybe you really couldn't go home again, no matter how much you wished you could.

She jumped at the touch of a hand on her shoulder. "I'm fine, I'm fine," she said to whoever was looming over her. "Just let me catch my breath and—"

"You're not fine," Noah said, and she wished fervently for a swift death, free from pain and any more humiliation. "You wouldn't be sitting there in the middle of the street if you were fine."

"Go take care of your daughter," she snapped, unable to pretend anything but a strong desire to stay as far away from him as possible. "I'm fine."

He crouched down next to her, so close she caught the smell of shampoo in his hair. He went to touch her ankle and she yelped. "Is it broken?"

"Keep your hands to yourself," she said. "It's not broken. This happens all the time."

"You yelped like it's broken."

"I didn't yelp."

"Yeah, you did. All I did was—"

She yelped again. "Do you get some kind of sadistic kick out of hurting me? I have a weak ankle, okay? It's none of your business."

The change in him was immediate. She could feel the difference along her nerve endings and she wished she could pull back her words.

"Listen," she said, "you really don't—"

"I never hurt you, Gracie. Not now. Not then."

She wanted to look away but couldn't. After all these years, she owed him at least that much. The expression in his eyes was etched with a sorrow so deep it threatened to engulf them both. She had only seen an expression like that one other place in her life: in her own mirror. "I know that," she whispered.

"Your ankle's swelling," he said, the mask back in place. He was a stranger to her. The boy she had loved had been replaced by the man who stood before her. "You'd better get it looked at."

"There are no breaks," she said. "All I need is some elevation and compression. It'll be okay."

"You sound like a doctor."

"I *am* a doctor," she said. "A vet."

"You did it."

"I did it." She couldn't keep the note of intense pride from her voice. *I did it, Noah, I actually did it.*

"Where do you practice?"

"Manhattan," she said, carefully avoiding any mention of her suspension.

"So you got what you wanted after all."

"Don't you have a wife and daughter to take care of?" She didn't want him to know that his words had found their mark.

"Daughter," he said, maintaining that intense eye contact. "No wife."

No wife . . . no wife . . . She had to remind herself that it didn't matter and never could. "Your daughter—"

"Sophie."

"Sophie was drenched. You don't want her to catch cold." *Are you divorced, Noah? A widower? Does Sophie look like her mother? Does her mother still have a part of your heart?*

"You're a doctor. You should know you catch cold from germs, not the weather."

"I remain unconvinced."

"I left Futrello in charge. He has six kids. He'll know what to do."

"Andy Futrello? The dockworker who used to play for the Red Sox farm team?"

"That's the one. He's our sportswriter."

"He came back to Idle Point."

"Looks like we all do, sooner or later."

"I'm only here for the wedding."

"And I'm only here to sell off the *Gazette.*"

"I'm going back to New York right after the reception."

"Sophie and I return to London as soon as I find the right buyer."

"Not Paris?"

He shook his head. "Not Paris."

We were going to see Paris together, Noah. Do you remember? We had all of those wonderful dreams, all of those plans . . .

He stood up and held out his hand. "Where's your car? I'll drive you back to your father's place."

"I walked," she said. "I wasn't expecting to twist my ankle." She waved away his offer of help. "I'll be fine. Go back to the office. I'll wangle a lift from somebody."

"In case you haven't noticed, there's a storm blowing in. Why don't you quit acting like you give a damn about my time and let me drive you home before we both waste anymore of the morning than we already have."

"Fine," she said, stung. "Terrific. Drive me home. That'll be great." They had nothing to hide anymore, did they? They were adults now. They both had lives of their own. One of them even had a child.

He held out his hand in a gesture that was familiar enough to break what was left of her heart. She saw them on the beach, in the shadow of the lighthouse, saw the faded blue blanket and the way his skin gleamed like burnished copper in the moonlight. She saw it all and more in that one gesture, and she knew that he saw it, too. It was there in his eyes, in the set of his mouth, in the warmth of his hand as she reached for him.

She tried to stand, but her ankle couldn't support her weight. "Lean on me," he said, but she resisted, determined not to fall any deeper under the spell of memory than necessary. Pain, however, made the choice for her, and she let him help her. He was bigger than she remembered, but then that really shouldn't surprise her. He was a man now, not the boy she had known. The boy she had known no longer existed except inside her heart.

They took two steps, and Noah swore under his breath. "Hold on," he said. "I'll try not to hurt you."

Too late, Gracie thought as he swept her up into his arms. From the looks of Sophie, at least five or six years too late.

•　•　•

She was stiff as a two-by-four in his arms. She looped her slender arms around his neck, but she didn't rest her head against his shoulder the way she would have years ago. If it was possible to maintain your dignity despite the fact that you were cold, wet, muddy, and nursing an ankle the size of an airbus, Gracie was accomplishing it. The hood of that ridiculous tent she was wearing caught the wind like a sail and kept slapping him in the face. He didn't care. The smell of her, the warmth of her body, the way her wet hair plastered itself against his cheek, even the slap of that hood—he wanted to burn each of these sensations into his memory before the anger came rushing back in on him again. His body remembered things his brain had worked hard to forget. Holding her this way was like being eighteen again but without the uncertainty. This time he knew they weren't going to have a happy ending.

He walked past Patsy's, and a crowd rushed out to greet them.

"Looks like an old Doris Day–Rock Hudson movie," Patsy remarked, standing under her red-and-white striped awning. "Welcome home, Gracie. It's been a long time."

Gracie, her face as red as the stripes, gave Patsy a weak smile.

"Kidnapping's illegal in Maine," Chester Brubaker called out. "Better take her over the state line if you know what's good for you."

He could feel Gracie's indignation bubbling through her veins.

"Ignore them," Noah advised her. "If you say anything, it'll just get worse."

"I sprained my ankle," she called out, trying to lift her right leg up to show them. "I don't have my car, so Noah's driving me home."

The crowd in front of the coffee shop exchanged looks, then burst into laughter.

Annie Lafferty, who had graduated with Gracie, cupped her hands around her mouth. "Good to see you two together again! Just like the old days."

"I told you to ignore them," Noah said as they hurried past the *Gazette*.

"Why do they have to say things like that?" Gracie asked. "Don't they have anything better to do?"

His mother's late-model Lincoln Town Car was parked in the first row in the spot marked Owner. He fumbled around with the keyless entry system, almost dropping Gracie in the process, then managed to get the passenger door open and deposit her on the front seat. He ran around to the driver's side and slid behind the wheel.

They maintained an uneasy silence during the three-minute drive to her father's house. Everything seemed both strange and familiar, an odd blend of the past and present. He wondered if she sensed it, too. How many times had they been alone together in a car, the two of them enclosed in a private hideaway of glass and steel? How small their world had been then: a stretch of beach, the front seat of a sports car. It was where he had learned that a man could hold the universe in his arms and want for nothing more.

For the first time in her life, Gracie was afraid of him. The car seemed too small for the emotions it contained. Loud, ugly emotions that threatened to tear off the roof and kick out the windows. The kind of emotions that she'd been running from since the day she left Idle Point.

She had hurt him badly. She could see it in the way he held the wheel, the rhythm of his breathing, the thrust of his jaw. Simon Chase's revelation had shattered what sense of family she'd had and had come close to destroying her sense of self. She couldn't face Noah or Ben, knowing the truth but unable—or unwilling—to burden them with it, too. And so she ran. She had thought she was setting him free of the memories, but neither one of them was free, not in any way that mattered. They were still bound together by promises whispered in the dark a long time ago, and nothing, neither time nor circumstance, had changed that fact.

He rounded a curve halfway between her house and town, took it too fast, and she turned to look at him. Their eyes met, and she saw herself reflected back, saw the future as it could have been, and she started to cry.

"I shouldn't have come back," she said. "I never thought you would be here."

"I wouldn't be if I'd known," he said. "I wanted to live the rest of my life without you in it."

"I'm sorry," she said. "I'm so sorry—"

He skidded to a stop along the side of the road.

"Noah—"

"Shut up."

He gathered her into his arms, his touch rough and sweet and filled with hunger. She could fight him, push him away, she knew that, knew she had the power, but the second his mouth found hers she was lost. Years of missing him, years of emptiness and longing overwhelmed whatever reason she had left, and she melted against him. Nothing mattered but his mouth on hers, the heat of his body beneath her hands, the smell of his skin, the taste of it beneath her tongue, the delicious ache building deep inside her. She was tired of being alone, tired of being lonely, of being far away from her home, from Noah, from everything she had ever loved and lost and longed for. He was her home—more than Idle Point, more than that stretch of beach near the lighthouse, more than the little cottage where she grew up—and nothing would ever change that.

Noah was drunk on her scent, on the silky wet feel of her hair between his fingers, of the sounds she made when he touched her. She had always been so joyous, so responsive, so eager to give and receive pleasure as if it were a sacrament of the flesh. All of those sweetly carnal memories flooded his heart as he touched and kissed and tasted her. She was the other half of his soul. Time had changed nothing at all. He wasn't free of her, not even close. She was there inside his head, his heart, his blood, where she had been from the very beginning, where she would always be, and he hated her for the power she still held over him.

He deepened the kiss, drawing her very breath into his soul. He cupped her face between his hands and memorized every plane and angle, the short straight nose, the generous mouth, the warm, intelligent brown eyes glittering now with desire, and then he remembered a note left propped on the kitchen table with the words "Good-bye" scrawled at the bottom; the anger and pain was as fresh and cutting now as it had been eight long years ago.

Cold water couldn't have worked any better.

He sat back against his seat and clutched the steering wheel. He was breathing hard.

She adjusted her jacket and smoothed her hair. Her hands were trembling.

They didn't say another word until he dropped her off at the front door of her father's house, and then the only word they said was good-bye.

THIRTEEN

Noah let her off at the top of the driveway, as close to Gramma Del's front door as possible. He offered to see her inside, but she refused. He lingered in the driveway and didn't begin rolling back down toward the street until she turned and motioned that it was okay for him to leave. A gentleman to the end.

At least she hadn't bumped into Ben or Laquita. She felt too exposed right now, too vulnerable, to make small talk. All she wanted to do was slip into Gramma Del's cottage unnoticed and try to make sense of the fact that the boy she loved was now a man with a child.

Unfortunately, she wasn't fast enough, because the side door of her father's house opened, and Laquita stepped outside.

"Knee or ankle?" Laquita asked, falling into step with her.

"Ankle." Gracie made a face. "A sprain. I'm a chronic klutz."

"Lean on me," Laquita said. "A little ice, a little elevation, and you'll be good as new."

"That's what I was thinking."

"That's right." Laquita looked up at her. "You're a vet.

So, tell me, what do you do when an Irish setter sprains her ankle?"

"I'll let you know when it happens," Gracie said.

Laquita pushed open the door to Gramma Del's cabin, and they stepped inside. Pyewacket strolled toward them with the world-weary air of one to the manor born. "That can't be Sam!"

"This is Pyewacket. Sam died five years ago." Now there was a conversation stopper for you. Nothing like talking about dead pets with your new stepmother.

Laquita motioned toward the chair. "Take off that wet jacket, then sit down and put your foot up on the coffee table while I get some ice."

"Funny," said Gracie as she shrugged out of her jacket, "but I don't remember you being this bossy when we were in school."

"Really?" Laquita walked back into the room carrying a large bag of mixed vegetables. "I don't remember you being so klutzy."

Gracie laughed, even though she sensed maybe the slightest edge to Laquita's innocent words. Then again, she might have been guilty of that herself.

"No ice," Laquita said, kneeling down in front of Gracie. "This'll have to do."

Gracie jumped as the bag of vegetables touched her skin. "It would be easier to go out and play in the snow."

"Assuming we had snow. The weather's been unnaturally warm. I can't remember ever reaching Thanksgiving week without snow." Laquita claimed the corner of the sofa next to Gracie, then Pye claimed Laquita.

Traitor, thought Gracie. *Fair-weather friend.*

"So, was that Noah's car I saw backing out of the driveway?" Laquita absently stroked behind Pye's ear with the finesse of a woman who was accustomed to cats. Pye looked like he was in heaven.

Gracie nodded. "He found me sitting on the curb and gave me a lift home."

"You should've asked him in. I have some cookies for Sophie."

"You know Sophie?"

Laquita lifted her left pant leg and pointed toward a fading bruise on her shin. "I know Sophie."

"What's with that kid?" Gracie leaned forward to readjust the makeshift ice pack. "I hear she bites, too. Why don't Noah and her mother do something about it?"

"Noah's trying," Laquita said, "but it's tough being a single parent."

"Wait a second," Gracie said. "Back up. I thought Sophie's mother was in the picture."

Laquita looked at her strangely. "Noah didn't tell you the whole story."

Gracie hesitated. "He told me that he isn't with Sophie's mother. That's about all."

"I thought you two were old friends."

"That was a long time ago." She shifted position, although her discomfort wasn't just physical. "So what's the story?"

"Apparently Noah just found out about Sophie a few months ago." She went on to tell Gracie about a holiday romance that ended amicably when Noah returned to London and the woman in question, an actress, went away to Sydney. No angst. No strings. Except for the fact that the woman was pregnant. Catherine was Catholic, and she chose to have the baby, even though she had no desire to raise a child on her own. Fiercely independent, Catherine never contacted Noah. When the little girl was born, she gave the baby to childless relatives to raise and went on with her life.

"They adopted her?"

"Nothing that formal," Laquita said. "Remember, this

is all third-hand information, but I hear the baby was passed from relatives to friends then back again. Not much of a life for a little girl."

Damn it. The last thing Gracie had wanted was to feel something for Noah's child. "The mother didn't care?"

"Who knows?" Laquita said. "I assume she believed the girl was being well cared for."

"So how did Noah end up with Sophie?"

"The authorities contacted Sophie's mother after Sophie ran away from home and they found her asleep on the steps of a church. To make a long story short, they were going to put Sophie into the system, and the mother decided maybe it was time to let Noah in on the fact that he had a five-year-old daughter." Noah flew over to England, met the child, and immediately took on responsibility for her future."

"And that's why he came home to Idle Point, for Sophie?" There was a lump in Gracie's throat the size of a dinner plate. The thought of Noah meeting his little girl for the first time brought back all the years she'd prayed that her own father would open his eyes and really see her for who she was.

Laquita nodded. "That and the *Gazette*. He has a lot on his plate right now."

"Seems so." Noah had wanted to write the great American novel, not be pinned down behind a desk at a newspaper office. She had a million questions, but she didn't trust herself to say anything more, not with her emotions so close to the surface. The thought of Noah with a daughter of his own awoke so many memories inside her heart, so many of the dreams she had put aside. The thought that his daughter shared her blood made her want to weep. A cruel twist of fate had joined them together forever in that angry little child. Nothing about her return home was the way she thought it would be, not even close.

"Ben would love to make you his special scrambled eggs," Laquita said after an uncomfortable silence, "but if you're not up to—"

"I'm fine," Gracie jumped in. "I'd love to try Dad's scrambled eggs." She was almost thirty years old, and this was the first time she could remember her father doing anything special for her.

Laquita's serene expression turned downright joyful. "He'll be so pleased." She leaned forward and touched Gracie's forearm. "You don't know how much this means to him. He's so excited that you came up for our wedding."

Gracie's smile was noncommittal. She certainly couldn't tell Laquita that the only reason she had agreed was because Ben caught her at a weak—and unemployed—moment. "It'll be fun, I'm sure."

"I probably shouldn't tell you this—Ben will kill me if he finds out—but he's going to ask you something, Gracie, and if the answer's going to be no, I'd really like the chance to prepare him." She took a deep, bracing breath that inflated her already considerable chest to alarming proportions. "He wants you to stand up for him."

"Be his best man?" Gracie couldn't keep the surprise from her voice.

"Be his witness," Laquita corrected gently. "You have no idea how much it would mean to him. I know your life hasn't been perfect and that most of that is Ben's fault, but he's made such progress, and he loves you so much. If you would consider it, I'd be in your debt forever."

"You don't have to be in my debt," she said. "Of course I'll be his witness."

Laquita leaped up and hugged Gracie around the neck. "This is wonderful! I'm so pleased."

"One question though," Gracie said. "Do you love him?"

Laquita stepped back and met her gaze head-on. "Yes," she said. "I love him enough to be faithful."

"I didn't ask that."

"But you wanted to."

"Yes," Gracie admitted. "I wanted to."

"I know we look like the odd couple, but it's real, what we have. We're going to last forever."

Gracie didn't bother to tell her that sometimes forever wasn't very long at all.

"This is great!" The managing editor, a seen-it-all type named Doheny, turned away from the computer screen and looked up at Noah. "How'd you come up with this stuff, anyway? I wouldn't have figured you for the type."

"Beats me," said Noah, and it was the truth. The words seemed to pour from his fingertips like magic. All of the frustrations he had felt with Sophie, his anger toward Gracie, the bittersweet memories hiding around every street corner—they were all there, willing to be transformed into words and phrases meant to move the reader. It wasn't anything like his usual style, which tended toward the brittle and manipulative—pure gold in advertising—but more real, more emotional than anything he had ever written.

"Can you do us up another one for tomorrow?"

He raised his hands and took a step back. "Hey, I'm not looking to take over Mary's job, Doheny. I'm on the other team, remember."

"I talked to Mary's husband, and it doesn't sound like she'll be back anytime soon."

"Fine," Noah said. "We'll pull over Eileen or Gregory from the Lifestyle section. I've seen their work. Maybe we could rotate their columns."

"They're both maxed out. Besides, Eileen's going out on maternity leave next week."

"Let me level with you," Noah said as the two men stepped into Doheny's cubicle. "I'm not looking to be a columnist at the *Gazette*. I have my own job back in London, and as soon as we can get this thing sold, I'll be going back to it."

"Great," said Doheny, looking underenthused, "but that doesn't change things. You want top dollar, you need a strong circulation. It's that simple."

Just hold the fort, Doheny said. Give them a few column inches until they could plug in a replacement for Mary Levine. Noah reluctantly agreed. He'd poured a lot of drivel out onto his keyboard and called it a column. When it came out tomorrow and the cries of outrage from subscribers reached Doheny's ears, he'd see who was right.

Noah spent the rest of the day in conference with the money men. For a moment, when they talked about the *Gazette*'s illustrious past, he had experienced grave misgivings about the entire process. The *Gazette* might not look like much at the moment, but there had been a time when it had commanded worldwide respect and, strangely enough, that respect had been largely the result of his father's folksy but powerful editorials. Simon's anti–Vietnam War views had been shocking in those days, the years before even Walter Cronkite was voicing an opinion against the slaughter. Simon had stood alone for peace, and he had been noticed. The *Gazette* office had been fire-bombed twice. Simon had received numerous threats against his life. At one point he had apparently sent Ruth away for her own safety. But still he clung to his beliefs, and in time the rest of the country came to see it his way.

The thought of allowing the *Gazette* to pass out of family hands didn't sit well with Noah, and he wasn't quite sure why. He had loved and respected his father, but he hadn't liked him very much at the end. There had been a terrible bitterness at the core of Simon's soul, and by the time of his death, that bitterness had spread to his family. Simon had lived a life of privilege and accomplishment, and it was difficult to see what he had to be bitter about. There was only one battle he had lost in his sixty-two years of life, and that was the battle for the heart of Mona Taylor. You wouldn't think Simon Chase had been the kind of man to carry a forty-two-year-old torch.

Then again, maybe father and son were more alike than Noah cared to admit. Any illusions he might have had about being over Gracie had gone up in flames this morning when he kissed her. Hell, his illusions had vanished even before that, when he'd seen her standing there in the lobby of the *Gazette* in that enormous coat of hers. She had never had any clothes sense at all. Her clothes had always been an afterthought, an idiosyncratic assemblage of whatever she happened to grab from her closet. He had always loved that about her. She was utterly without vanity when it came to the way she looked. She had no idea how beautiful she was. Not pretty, but beautiful. Noah was very clear about the difference. The sleek line of her hair in the rain, the curve of her hip, her endless legs. Her wit, her intelligence, her drive. She had grown from an attractive girl into the kind of woman who caught your eye and kept it. There were so many layers to her appeal that a man could spend the rest of his life discovering them.

He loved her. He hated her. He wanted her. He hated himself for wanting her. There was no future for them. Even this morning, when he was crazed for the touch and smell of her, he knew that, but somehow it didn't matter. He could have lived the rest of his life without seeing her again, but now that he had seen her he didn't know how he could bear to lose her a second time.

The thing to do was lay low until after Ben and Laquita's wedding. If he confined himself to the *Gazette* and caring for Sophie, he would be okay. When they swept up the last of the orange blossoms and rice, Gracie would go back to New York where she belonged, and once the *Gazette* was sold, he and Sophie would return to London, and it would be as if none of this had ever happened. His future wasn't here. It never had been. Not without Gracie.

If he never saw Gracie's face again, he just might be able to find a way to live without her.

The *Gazette* hit the front door at six forty-five the next morning.

Laquita hit the front door at six fifty-five.

Gracie, who was fortunately an early bird, invited her in. "I made coffee," she said, "but the toast isn't ready yet."

Laquita waved away Gracie's words. "Did you see it?" she demanded, holding the *Gazette* under Gracie's nose. "Did you read it?"

"I've only been up twenty minutes," Gracie said. "I thought I'd skim it over breakfast."

"Read it," Laquita ordered, very obviously an oldest child. "I marked the column right there on page eighteen."

She noticed Noah's byline and pushed the paper away. "I'll read it after breakfast."

"I think you should read it now."

"I can't read on an empty stomach. I need caffeine and calories."

"Make an exception."

"I don't have my contacts in."

"You don't wear contacts."

"You don't know that."

"Lucky guess. I have to get ready for work. Please read it, Gracie. You won't be sorry."

Gracie delayed as long as she could after Laquita left,

but her curiosity finally got the better of her, and she glanced down at the first sentence.

She walked in out of the rain with my daughter in her arms.

She put down the paper and pushed it away. She poured herself a second cup of coffee, even though her heart was beating as if she'd mainlined caffeine. She drummed her fingers on the tabletop while she tried to convince herself she didn't want to read the rest of the column. She almost believed it, too, until the phone rang and Don Hasty said, "So when's the wedding?" which was followed by a call from Annie Lafferty who said, "I knew it when I saw you yesterday morning. . . . I just knew it!"

She quit answering the phone after Joann, Tim, and Patsy from the coffee shop all called to weigh in on the subject. She picked up the newspaper and forced herself through the rest of the column. She felt like a voyeur; his view of the workings of a man's heart was undeniably moving. There was no doubt that Noah was a gifted writer. He had managed to say so much about the two of them and their past and still never say anything at all. He never called her by name. He never identified her by either family or career or the color of her hair, and yet short of publishing her fingerprints, he had turned the spotlight on her just the same.

It was a love letter of sorts, angry and bittersweet enough to catch the eye of half the town, but when Gracie examined the text, she saw that he wrote more about his little girl and her bad hair day. So why did she see herself in every line? How was it she knew he was telling her that he loved her and hoped he never saw her again?

"He did it again," Laquita said at six fifty-one the next morning. She had highlighted the most moving passages in Noah's second column in Day-Glo yellow. "Read this one, but make sure you have your tissues handy."

"I don't want to read it," Gracie said. "It's bad enough everyone else in town is reading it." She frowned. "Has Ben seen it?"

Laquita shook her head. "But he knows all about it. Ben won't go near the *Gazette*."

"Then he's the only one in town who won't. I think I've heard from everyone else."

"He can't believe there was ever anything between you and Noah. I have to admit the idea doesn't make him too happy."

"Right now the idea doesn't make me very happy, either."

She tasted like moonlight, of summer nights spent in the shadow of the lighthouse.

His words angered her. He had no right resurrecting their past this way. It was over. They were over. Did he have to make her feel as if her heart had been sliced in two? Payback, that was what it was. Payback for leaving him with his heart in his hand and a wedding ring in his pocket. She wanted to stuff those words down his throat, noun by noun. He had no idea what he was doing with these columns, what forces he was unleashing. It was too late for the truth. The truth would only hurt Ben and Ruth and Noah and even Sophie. If he kept up this ridiculous string of columns, something terrible was bound to happen. You couldn't play on emotion this way and not pay a price somewhere down the line. She pulled the telephone number off the masthead and dialed up the *Gazette*, enduring layer after layer of voice-mail nonsense until she finally reached Noah. Except that it wasn't Noah at all but his voice mail. She slammed down the phone without leaving a message.

He had no right to do this. All they had left between them was the secret of the love they had shared. They had been apart for over eight years now. He had taken lovers. He had a daughter to love, while she had a cat named Pyewacket and a few memories. What more could he possibly want?

The storm had yet to turn into a full-fledged nor'easter, but it was bad enough to keep her inside most of the day. Laquita had taped her ankle, and thanks to the ice and elevation, Gracie could get around with only the slightest limp. She ran out once to buy some more apples and brown sugar at the market and was forced to endure some very embarrassing comments from Raymond at the register and half the produce department. Despite the possibility of even greater embarrassment, she swung by the animal hospital to see Dr. Jim, who greeted her warmly.

"So you're back," he said as they grabbed coffee in his office. "How's the big city treating you?"

"Not too well," she said, suddenly tired of putting a good face on everything. "I screwed up royally and I'm on suspension."

She gave him the details, sparing nobody, and he nodded.

"What would you have done?" she asked him. "Would you have suspended me for saving a healthy animal from being put down?"

"Yes," he said, "and then I would have taken you out to dinner to thank you for doing it."

He didn't ask why she had left Idle Point, but she did notice an open copy of the *Gazette* on his desk.

"Will I see you at the Adamses' Thanksgiving table tomorrow?" he asked.

"Absolutely," she said, hiding her surprise. She had had no idea that the Adamses and Dr. Jim were friends. "Please tell me that Ellen is making her famous candied yams." She remembered them fondly from church suppers when she was a little girl.

His face clouded, and she instantly knew she had said something terribly wrong.

"Ellen died last year," he told her, his dark eyes welling with tears. "She put up a brave fight, but in the end she lost."

She didn't know what else to do, so she hugged him.

"Come back home to stay, Gracie," he said as she said good-bye. "You know this is where you're meant to be. Don't wait until it's too late."

Dr. Jim's words lingered with her as she pared apples and rolled piecrust. *Don't wait until it's too late.* She was barely thirty years old. Not even at the halfway point in her life.

"Dr. Jim said the strangest thing to me today," she said to Ben, who was putting together a window seat for Pyewacket. Pye watched the endeavor from atop the television set across the room. "He said I should come back to Idle Point before it's too late. Do you have any idea what he meant by that?"

Ben put down his hammer and considered her question. "He's still pretty raw from losing Ellen. That can make a man sit up and take notice of how quickly it all spins by."

"I'm not exactly AARP material yet," she said dryly as she reached for the cinnamon. "There's plenty of time."

"I thought that, too, Graciela. I was only forty-one when your mother was killed in that car crash."

She stopped what she was doing. She all but stopped breathing. This was the first time in her entire life that he had directly referenced her mother's death.

He leaned back on his heels, hammer dangling from his right hand, and met her eyes. "You've probably heard some talk along the way about your mother and me."

She leaned against the counter for support. "Yes," she said. "I have."

"Most of it was true," he said. "We had what you'd call a difficult marriage, but I loved that woman with all my heart, and in the end I know she loved me, too."

"I-I'm sure she did, Dad." *You don't know what Simon told me, Dad. She was leaving you, taking me with her. She was going to run off with another man.*

"We had our troubles, don't get me wrong. At one point we were going to throw in the towel and call it quits once and for all, but then out of the blue you came along, and it was like God opened up the gates of Heaven and let us in."

She looked down at her hands, willing herself not to cry. For almost thirty years she had dreamed of the day her father would open up to her, and now that he had, she wanted to turn and run. *You're pretty good at that, aren't you, Gracie? You proved that Monday with Noah.*

"I wasn't her first choice," he said. "She loved somebody else all through high school, but I was always there. I knew what I wanted, and I was willing to wait. The best-looking, most popular couple at Idle Point High. King and queen of the senior prom. The ones most likely to elope on graduation night and live happily ever after. Except it didn't happen that way," Ben said with a small laugh. "You see, the king of the prom wanted more out of life than your mother could give him. He loved her, but he didn't love her enough to look past her family and the fact that she lived in one of those shacks near Milltown. He tried, I'll give him that, but in the end he couldn't separate the girl he loved from the family she came from, and he married somebody else."

"Ruth Marlow," she said in a whisper.

"You knew?"

"I saw the yearbook a long time ago," she said.

"Your mother was a beautiful woman," he said, memory softening his weathered features. "Prettiest girl ever to come out of Idle Point."

"I've heard . . . things," she said, forcing each word out with increasing effort. "That my mother was—" How do you ask your father if your mother, his wife, had been unfaithful to him?

"She was a good mother," he said fiercely. "The best. She loved you with her heart and soul, and she would never have done anything to hurt you."

"I know, but—"

"When we found out she was expecting you, everything changed. After all those years of praying for a miracle, we had one right there growing in her belly—" He stopped for a moment as the memories threatened to overcome him. "I didn't ask," he said fiercely. "She came to me with a miracle. I wasn't about to ask why."

Or how. He didn't say the words, but Gracie heard them just the same. Simon had been telling the truth. She had often wondered how he could hate his own child, the child of the woman he loved, and maybe this was the answer. Her birth had brought Ben back into the picture for good.

"The day of the accident," she began, her voice quavering. "Where was she going?"

Ben looked at her curiously. "You had an appointment with the pediatrician. One of those six-month checkups. The doctor said he had never seen your mother look happier or more beautiful."

"You're sure we were on our way home?" she persisted. "You're positive?" Simon had said that she was on her way to be with him, that the three of them were going to run away together and leave Idle Point and everyone in it far behind.

"Yes," he said. "She stopped at the convenience store

for a quart of milk and the chocolate donuts I like. Eb found them in the backseat."

Gracie's knees gave way, and she grabbed for a kitchen chair. Truth mixed with lies. Lies mixed with truth. She saw clearly now how much Simon must have hated her. Her birth had put an end to his dreams of a future with Mona. Whatever else her mother had done wrong in her life, in the end she had chosen to stay with the man who had loved her unconditionally right from the start.

Ben helped steady her. "I shouldn't have told you all of this," he said, looking so much older and sadder than he had a few minutes ago. "We weren't saints, your mother and I, not by a long shot, but in the end we found our way back to happiness because of you. You were the one who turned us into a family."

He placed his hand on her shoulder. She reached up and placed her hand on top of his.

"I love you, Graciela," he said, his voice breaking on her name.

"I know," she said, leaning her head against his arm and closing her eyes. "I know you do." She wanted to tell him how she felt, but the words weren't there. Not yet. But for the first time in her life, she knew it was only a matter of time.

FOURTEEN

⁓⊙⊱⁓

Ben had headed out around two o'clock to a bachelor party given by his AA friends from Bangor. He asked her to tell Laquita that he would pick up the wedding favors from the printer while he was there. Gracie finished the pies around four-thirty. There was something comforting about rolling dough and arranging the strips in a lattice-work pattern the way Gramma Del had taught her to do. It made her feel connected to family and tradition, and after so many years away from home, that felt good.

She set the pies to cool on the counter, then cast a sharp look at Pyewacket. "You wouldn't, would you?" she asked the sleeping feline, then set up a barrier just to be sure. Laquita had called a while ago to say she'd swing by around five o'clock to pick up Gracie so they could shop for a wedding outfit for her, which meant Gracie had less than thirty minutes to shower and change.

Apparently there was more to being her father's witness than she had realized. There was wardrobe, for one thing. Laquita had suggested that she wear a variation on the bridesmaid dresses, and when Gracie asked where she could purchase one on such short notice, Laquita had laughed and said she'd show Gracie after work.

"Very funny," she said when Laquita pulled up in front of the big house on the hill that evening. A wicked wind drove the rain into the windshield at an alarming rate, making the brightly lit house look like a haven. "The Chases are selling bridal wear these days?"

"Not quite," Laquita said, "but you do need a dress, and this is the best place to find one."

"I'm not following you. Don't tell me Mrs. Chase is a seamstress."

"Not that I know of," Laquita said as they both exited the car, "but my mother is."

Gracie felt like the slightly slow third cousin twice removed. "And your mother is—"

"Living here," Laquita supplied. "Along with my father, three brothers, and my baby sister Storm." Plus three cats, two dogs, and a half-dozen parakeets. "I can't believe nobody told you. It was big news around here for quite a while."

Gracie tried to imagine the stately mansion bursting at the seams with pets and children, but that was more than her brain could handle. She wondered what Gramma Del would think of this remarkable turn of events. Somehow it made sense in a strange kind of way. She would never forget the sight of Mrs. Chase laughing at the kitchen table with Laquita's flamboyant aunts as if they all shared a particularly juicy secret. *How long ago was that?* she wondered. *Another lifetime at least.* Mrs. Chase had looked as comfortable at that old Formica table as she did in her own drawing room, and Gracie remembered being struck by that fact. It had seemed most remarkable at the time.

"I can't go in there," she said, thinking about Noah and all that had transpired between them. "Especially not after those newspaper stories."

"Oh, don't worry. You won't bump into anyone. We

respect each other's privacy. Mrs. C. gave my family the entire downstairs, except for the main rooms. We have the garden extension, the rooms built off the kitchen, the old servants' quarters. I haven't seen Mrs. C in at least two months."

All Gracie could do was stare at Laquita in amazement. For a town that hadn't changed an iota in its two-hundred-plus-year history, it had sure been busy the last ninety-six months. Next thing she knew, she would find out Ruth Chase had taken a lover and was planning to move to Monte Carlo.

"There's no way I'm coming here for Thanksgiving dinner tomorrow."

"Will you stop worrying? I told you, we have completely separate living quarters. Besides, I hear Noah is taking his mother and Sophie out to some fancy restaurant in Portland."

They hurried through the downpour to the back door, the one she remembered so well from the days when Gramma Del cooked for the Chases. She even remembered the gouge the size of a quarter dug into the frame when six-year-old-Noah accidentally hit it with a baseball bat. The kitchen itself was much the same as Gracie remembered it, a warm and inviting haven on a cold and rainy night. Rachel Adams had added touches of her own that had made it even more appealing. One wall was now lacquered a deep red and hung with shiny copper pots of varying shapes and sizes. The cabinets had been restored to their original pine and the floors tiled in a shade that reminded Gracie of toasted almonds. Pots of flowers hand-picked from the greenhouse graced the countertops, the table, the refrigerator. The smells of cookies and pies and breads were downright intoxicating. Huge piles of fresh vegetables awaited tomorrow's Thanksgiving feast, while a big pot of chili simmered on the back burner.

The second that door closed behind her, she was five years old again with Gramma chopping carrots at the sink, Noah coloring at the kitchen table, and Ruth Chase hovering nearby. Some of her happiest moments had been spent in this kitchen. Some of her very best days. She had to shake her head to physically drive away the memories.

"Rachel!" Laquita's voice rang out as they approached the back hall. "We're here for a fitting."

Two shaggy mutts bounded into the room, both with tails at full mast.

"They're the image of Wiley!"

"They should be. They're his offspring." Wiley was almost fifteen years old now. He spent his days sleeping at Ruth Chase's feet, dreaming of his youthful exploits.

Gracie knelt down on the tiles and let the animals sniff her hands and forearms before she started to pet them. It was one of the first things they'd taught her at veterinary school, and it had saved her numerous trips to the ER. "Are they yours or the Chases'?"

"Both," Laquita said. "The lines get blurrier every year."

An alternate universe, that was what it was. *Gramma Del, are you watching this? The Adams-Chase household! Can you imagine?*

"Let's check out the sewing room," Laquita said. "They're probably all in there."

"Great." Gracie was a shameless snoop. She peeked in every room they passed as they walked down the back hallway toward the sewing room. She saw a beautiful den with two sofas and a fireplace. She saw three bedrooms, each one more handsomely appointed than the one before. Two baths. One jacuzzi. A laundry room that would make the Maytag repairman proud. There wasn't a fingerprint or speck of dust anywhere. Gracie had seen operating theaters that weren't as perfectly maintained.

The sewing room was at the end of the hall, to the right of the door that led out to the garden. Shouts of female laughter spilled into the hallway. Gracie felt a sharp pang of envy that Laquita had been lucky enough to be part of such a happy family. When she was a little girl, she used to wish she could be part of Laquita's family, just sneak into the little house by the river and blend right in with the crowd. Ben was a lucky man. No more lonely Christmases, no more New Year's Eves spent with a bottle of Scotch and a handful of memories. The Adams clan would see to that.

"Well, there you are!" Rachel Adams leaped to her feet to greet them. "We were wondering if the two of you had forgotten about us."

"You knew I had to work," Laquita said with the weary sound of affectionate exasperation Gracie had heard in the voices of countless other daughters over the years. "We didn't even stop for supper."

"Of course you didn't," Rachel said, enveloping her oldest child in a big hug. "You knew I was making chili for everybody."

Gracie stood in the doorway, feeling awkward and jealous and all points in between. The room was a jumble of midnight blue satin, ivory lace, a large black sewing machine near the window, teacups, platters of cookies, and more adorable young women than you would find on the pages of *Seventeen* magazine. They all looked like variations of Laquita with long, shiny dark hair and deep brown eyes and lush figures.

Rachel stepped away from her daughter and opened her arms wide. "Gracie Taylor!" she exclaimed. "Welcome to the family."

So many familiar names attached now to almost grownup bodies. Even Storm, the baby, looked like a young woman and not a little girl.

"I feel so old," Gracie said with a laugh as they all trooped into the kitchen for bowls of chili and homemade bread. "What happened to all the little kids I remember?"

"They grew up," Rachel said with a shake of her head. "Sometimes I think that's why I had so many of them. I was hoping one of them would stay little for me."

For a moment Gracie understood. How hard it must be to watch your child grow up and move away from your circle of protection. Still, if appearances were any indication, Rachel and Darnell had done a great job with their kids. She asked about the boys—Morocco, Sage, and Joe—and wasn't surprised at all to hear they were in college and doing well. They were expected home any minute for Thanksgiving Day weekend.

"Laquita was our wild child," Rachel said, casting a fondly bemused glance at her eldest daughter. "Sometimes I think we asked too much of her, and that's why she needed to rebel."

Laquita, who was about to bring a spoonful of chili up to her mouth, groaned. "Like Gracie really wants to talk about that," she said. "Helloooo, Rachel. I'm about to marry her father, remember?"

"This is a small town," Rachel reminded her daughter. "We don't have any secrets. Besides, I'm just commenting on how well you turned your life around."

Giggles erupted from the knot of teenage sisters at the far end of the table. Gracie's heart sank.

"I love the *Gazette*," the one named Cleo piped up, her lovely dark eyes dancing with mischief.

"Me, too," said Vienna, her twin. "Especially that new column . . ."

They convulsed with laughter that garnered a sharp look from their mother.

"Quiet," said Rachel in a tone Gracie could only describe as maternal-warning mode. "I'm sure Gracie has been teased quite enough about Noah's column."

Gracie couldn't help it. She groaned, then rested her forehead on the tabletop. "Why does everyone think he's writing about me?"

The explosion of laughter from all quarters was answer enough, but Cheyenne couldn't help adding a postscript. "You two are legendary around here," she said over Laquita's protests. "I mean, you both disappear on the same day a million years ago and you give old Eb a million dollars and Noah goes off to Paris and you're a famous doctor in Manhattan and then *boom!* You're both home again for the wedding and Noah's carrying you through the rain. . . ." She sighed melodramatically. "I mean, it's only the most romantic thing anybody's ever seen around here."

"Don Hasty and Joann told Sage that you two used to meet on the beach by the lighthouse every night during the summer. They could see you from Hidden Island." Storm seemed proud of her contribution to the legend. Gracie must have looked shocked, because Storm quickly added, "But only when they used their binoculars."

"Out!" Rachel commanded, pointing toward the door. "Take your chili and eat in the den."

Cheyenne looked legitimately puzzled. "Why? I like it in here."

"So do we," Rachel said, "and we want Gracie to like it here, too. I expect you back here in fifteen minutes to finish the beading."

Mother and daughter launched into a stream of friendly sparring that made the other girls roll their eyes and retreat with their bowls of chili.

"Don't you dare take that chili into the front room," Laquita warned, "or I'll kill you."

"Just cook for us," Cheyenne shot back. "That'll do it." She raced from the room before Laquita could retaliate.

"Like I said, Gracie, welcome to our family." Rachel reached back and adjusted her ponytail. Her hair was still very dark and lustrous with only the faintest icing of silver around the temples. "Not too many secrets allowed around here."

Gracie smiled weakly and concentrated on her chili. The truth was, she was beyond speech. The fact that so many people had known so much about her and Noah amazed her. Wouldn't you think one of them would have known Mona and Simon's secret, too?

"There's plenty of chili in the pot," Rachel reminded them, "so help yourselves to seconds."

Gracie didn't need another invitation. She pushed back her chair and helped herself, amid a flurry of teasing comments about her rail-thin figure.

"We're all built like my mother," Laquita said with a loud sigh. "Hips the size of a VW."

"We're womanly," Rachel said. "Our hips are made for childbearing." She gave her daughter a stern look. "Your problem isn't genetics, Quita. It's the gallon of Ben and Jerry's you devour every week."

That led to another spirited discussion of calories, aerobic exercise, and quality of life. Gracie hadn't heard this much conversation since she lived in a dorm. The affection between Laquita and Rachel was obvious. Their teasing was gentle, funny, and inclusive. Not for one second did Gracie feel like an outsider. They meant it when they said she was family, and she could feel her guard dropping with every second that passed in their company. She tried to imagine what it had been like for Laquita, growing up the oldest in such a big and boisterous family. She had always seemed older than her years to Gracie, self-contained and serene. A lot had been expected of her. In some ways she was almost a surrogate mother to her brothers and sisters, which meant she had been responsible for other human beings since she was old enough to read. Gracie thought about the haven Laquita had created for herself and Ben, a soothing adult oasis of calm and quiet, and another piece of the puzzle fell into place.

Ruth listened to the sounds of laughter floating down the hallway toward the library where she had been sitting for hours. She loved the sounds of family, the sense that the house was barely large enough to contain the lives being lived within its four walls. In the early days of her marriage, she had believed that was how it would be for her and Simon. "We'll fill this house with babies," she had promised him on their wedding night. "Sons and daughters to carry on your name." That was one of many promises she had been unable to fulfill.

Rachel's family was on their way home for the holiday weekend. The boys were hitching a ride up from Storrs, while the girls made their way in from various points on the eastern seaboard. They came home, though, each and every one of them, which was no small testament to Rachel and Darnell.

Wiley stirred slightly in his sleep. He spent most of his time now dreaming of days gone by. They had that in common. Lately Ruth had spent a good deal of time thinking about the past. She had made so many mistakes along the way, kept too many secrets, and now it seemed as if they were all coming home to roost.

Don't blame yourself, Ruth. How could you have known it would turn out this way?

Noah and Gracie had been little more than teenagers at the time, barely old enough to drive, much less fall in love. Ruth couldn't have been expected to understand the depth of what they had felt for each other. She couldn't possibly have known the repercussions. Who could blame her for believing it was a teenage romance that time and distance would turn into a dim memory.

The paper lay open on her lap, folded neatly to the page with Noah's essay.

I waited at the edge of town for her. . . . the marriage license was tucked in the glove compartment. . . .

How well she remembered that day. Blazingly hot, too hot even for August. The air had hung heavy as a wet sponge. Simon had been agitated for days since Del's death. She remembered that the doctor had been worrying about him. "Watch him carefully, Ruth. Stress is the worst thing for that heart of his." Oh, how carefully she had watched him. She had watched him fall more deeply into a depression that not even the doctor's strongest mood-elevating drugs could touch. "Give it time," she had begged Simon. "You're recovering from a heart attack and major surgery. Your body needs time to heal." But he was beyond hearing her. Del's funeral had cast a bright light on Noah and Gracie. When Noah defended her against her father, their relationship became fodder for town gossip.

Simon talked endlessly about Noah, about how he could do better than Gracie Taylor, how he owed it to himself to see the world and not settle for some plain little townie with a drunk for a father. Ruth told herself it would blow over in a matter of days. Gracie was getting ready to return to school in Philadelphia. Noah would go back to Boston and see if his father's influence could reopen the doors to B. U. one more time. Life would shift back into a more recognizable pattern.

When Simon took off in his Town Car that last afternoon, every fiber of Ruth's being had registered alarm, and she did something she had never done before; she searched his desk. She wasn't certain what she was looking for, but when she discovered a fax of a marriage license in the names Noah Chase and Graciela Taylor on top of the copy machine and the carbon of a withdrawal slip in the amount of ten thousand dollars, she knew exactly what Simon was up to.

She could have done something to stop him. She could see that now with the wisdom of hindsight. She could have headed him off at the bank or followed him to the Taylors' house by the docks. But the truth was, she did neither of those things. She sat by the window in the library and she waited while her husband played God with the lives of two good kids who deserved better than the families life had parceled out to them.

Three hours later, her husband was dead, her son had vanished, and Gracie Taylor had left town for good.

The fire in the hearth was barely an ember. She considered calling Darnell and asking him to build a new fire, but it was the night before Thanksgiving. She was sure he had many other things to do. There had been a time when she could tend to such chores herself without thinking twice about it, but those days were gone. She was old now, in body and in spirit, and she was alone.

There were some people in this world who were meant to be together. She understood that now. You could call it fate or destiny or whatever New Age term you might care to conjure up, but it was a force that should never be trifled with. Simon had turned away from Mona when he was young and acquisitive, more concerned with social status than with love. He found her again in middle age, that dangerous time when a man begins to feel the cold breath of eternity at the back of his neck. Ruth had fought back the only way she knew how, with the oldest weapon in a woman's arsenal. She went away for a while and when she came home, they had a son named Noah. A man like Simon might walk away from his wife, but he would never walk away from his son. She had counted on that, and she had been right.

She closed her eyes as tears slid quietly down her cheeks. What should have been the happiest time in their lives had been filled instead with anger and bitterness. Simon felt trapped. He wanted to love Noah, but he couldn't find it in himself to separate fatherhood from paternity.

Ruth had always believed that as long as Mona Taylor lived, her marriage didn't stand a chance, but she quickly learned that happiness could never spring from tragedy. Mona Taylor's death had breathed life into Ruth's marriage, but at a terrible cost. A husband whose heart would never belong to her alone. A son who grew up in boarding schools because his mother didn't want to rock the boat. A widower who found solace in a bottle of booze. A little girl who lived on the fringes of other people's lives.

She couldn't undo any of it. She wasn't a good enough woman to wish that she could. Her life had been an imperfect one, but it had been her choice each step of the way. She had stayed with Simon because she loved him. She would make no apologies for that. But Simon was gone and she was here and her mistakes were settling in around her in a way she could no longer ignore.

FIFTEEN

~~~~≈◎≈~~~~

He wrote about a Thanksgiving ten years ago, about turkey sandwiches and clam chowder at a little hole-in-the-
wall in Plymouth, about watching the snow fall while they
cuddled in a booth and talked about their future.

*She wanted four children, two boys and two girls. I
said I would settle for six. We would live in a house by
the ocean and we would be happy together for the rest
of our lives.*

Gracie sat on the edge of her bed Thanksgiving morning and saw it all through Noah's eyes. She hadn't thought
about that day in many years. Like so many other days,
it had been lost in the daily rush of living and her powerful need to forget. With six hundred perfectly chosen
words, Noah had given that snowy Thanksgiving Day
back to her, with all of the sights and sounds and smells
as real and vibrant as they had been at the time.

She saw him with Sophie last night. She had been
standing in the doorway, looking out at the night while
Rachel pressed some seams, when he pulled his rental car
into the driveway. The rain had finally stopped, and a few
stars twinkled tentatively overhead. She closed her eyes
for a moment and made a wish, the same wish she had

made every night since she was five years old and starting kindergarten. *Keep him safe from harm.*

The rhythmic sweep of the lighthouse's beam washed the sky, punctuated by the occasional bleat of a foghorn in the distance. She was half drunk on the sheer smell of the night, a potent combination of wet leaves and pine and the ever-present smell of the sea.

He flung open his door, then climbed out of the car. She watched, scarcely breathing, as he looked up at the sky. She knew what he was doing. He was wishing on a star, too. She had taught him that their first summer together in the shadow of the lighthouse, in their summer of love. *It's the same for you, isn't it, Noah? No matter how far we run, this will always be home.* He had wanted to see the world, to shrug off the traces of Idle Point and create himself anew. *Are you happy, Noah? Is it all you thought it would be?*

She had watched, as he opened the back door and, after a minute or two, lifted a sleeping Sophie out of the car. The little girl murmured something—the soft sweet sound lifted and rose on the wind like a prayer—then curled up against Noah's chest. All of her fire, all of her fears, forgotten in the secure circle of her father's embrace. One day when Sophie was all grown up, she would remember that feeling of being deeply loved and she would gain strength from it.

I see her as she was then, reflected unexpectedly in my daughter, and I want to make things right for both of them. . . .

He didn't know what he was doing, dredging up all of these memories. There could be no happy ending, not the kind of romantic resolution they had dreamed about years ago. He needed to know that, and he needed to know why, or none of them would ever find happiness. Sophie deserved a family, a real family, with a mother and father who loved her and each other, and that was something that could never happen unless she told Noah the truth.

Ben knew the truth. He had told her as much yesterday afternoon. She was reasonably certain Ruth Chase suspected the truth as well. She would ask Noah to help her shield them as much as possible, but hurting them was a chance they had to take for Sophie's sake.

One thing Noah had learned since he became an instant daddy three months ago was that Murphy's Law was not only true, but also it had probably been discovered by a single father. No matter how much time he allotted to getting Sophie ready, he always fell short by at least twenty minutes. He wasn't taking any chances today. He decided to start right after breakfast so they'd have a shot at making it to the restaurant for Thanksgiving dinner at three o'clock. And it was a good thing he had, because it seemed just combing her hair might take most of the day.

She had pulled another one of those disappearing acts last night that aged him another five years. Not at the First Thanksgiving reenactment where Sophie had been enthralled by the Pilgrims with their shiny shoe buckles and exaggerated manners, but at the *Gazette* again. They had stopped at the office so he could knock out his column, and when he looked up, she was gone. She had left her shoes behind, her coloring book, her sweater, and disappeared. One of the local cops found her peering in the window of Samantha's Bridal Shop where Noah caught up with them.

After the cop left, Sophie took Noah's hand without any prompting, and he understood again why parents would lay down their lives to keep their children safe.

He had a clear vision of Gracie at that age, reaching up for his mother's hand on the way home from kindergarten. She had looked uncertain at first, then hopeful, and then when his mother took her hand, almost giddy with delight. It hadn't made sense to him at the time. What was so special about holding his mother's hand, anyway? His mother's hand was always within reach. It wasn't until he was sent away to St. Luke's that he began to understand what Gracie and Sophie had known almost from birth. The parent-child connection was as deep and wide as the ocean, as mysterious as heaven, as impossible to explain as love. The best he could do was follow his heart and pray.

"Papa!" Sophie squirmed out of Noah's reach. "Ow!"

"Sorry, Soph." He kissed the top of her head. "I'll be more careful."

Her perfect little face contorted into a scowl. "I'm a girl," she reminded him.

"I know that," he said, barely containing a chuckle. He knew his fierce little girl wouldn't appreciate that one bit. "Hair is very important to girls, isn't it?"

"Very," she agreed. She twisted around in her chair, trying to see his progress in the mirror.

"Not bad, huh?" He wasn't above soliciting compliments wherever he could get them.

She shrugged, and he had the feeling she was almost disappointed to see he could cope with a French braid.

"You know, Soph, your curly hair is so pretty it seems almost a shame to scrape it back into a braid."

"I like braids," she said. "Marla at school wears her hair braided, and everybody likes her."

Dangerous parenting territory dead ahead. "I'll bet Marla doesn't bite or kick."

"Maybe she does," Sophie said. "I only met her last month."

"I remember when I was your age. The popular kids never bit anybody."

"That was a long time ago."

"That's true," he said, "but I'll bet it's the same at your school, too. I'll bet your friends don't like it when you kick them."

"No," she said. How a five-year-old managed to sound like the Queen Mother was a mystery to him. "I think they like it quite a bit."

Okay, so he wasn't Dr. Spock, but it was a start.

The first person Gracie saw when she stepped into Rachel's kitchen was Noah. He was sitting at the counter with Sophie on his lap, and the two of them were topping and tailing string beans. She pulled Laquita into the alcove. "I thought you said he wasn't supposed to be here."

"He wasn't," Laquita said, looking as surprised as Gracie felt. "Ruth must've changed her mind about going out."

She forced herself to walk over to father and daughter and say hello. "Is this your first Thanksgiving, Sophie?" she asked, making sure she was out of kicking range.

Sophie nodded. "Uh-huh. The Pilgrims bought the turkey from the Indians."

"Or something like that," Noah said.

"I like your dress," she said to Sophie. "You look very pretty." She looked more than pretty. The child was beautiful with her huge blue eyes and blond curls, both set off perfectly by a sapphire-blue velvet jumper and lacy white blouse. Noah's child. Her blood. The range of emotion she felt made her dizzy.

"Gracie paid you a compliment, Sophie. What do you say?"

Sophie thought about it for a moment. "Thank you."

Rachel motioned to her from across the room. God bless the woman's timing. She offered a fake smile to Noah and his daughter. "Looks like I'm being called to

KP duty," she said, then hurried away before either one could say another word.

"Mrs. C. and Noah and Sophie will be joining us for dinner," Rachel said to Gracie. "I don't know why she changed her mind at the last minute, but I'm so pleased she did. She suggested we use the big dining room, so we need to move everything from here to there. We could use an extra pair of hands, if you don't mind."

Mind? Gracie could have kissed Rachel for giving her something to take her mind off her decision to tell Noah everything. She had never been very good at sitting still, especially not when she was feeling uncomfortable or apprehensive. She gratefully disappeared into the smaller dining room and began to gather up the silverware in a large soft towel. She was admiring a particularly beautiful serving spoon that looked like it belonged at Windsor Castle when she realized Sophie was standing next to her.

"What are you doing?" Sophie asked. She looked like the poster child for perfect behavior.

"See this spoon?" she asked, handing it to the little girl. "I was thinking that it's so beautiful that it belongs on a queen's table."

"You don't have a queen in America, do you?"

"No, we don't," Gracie said, swallowing a few terrible jokes about imperial presidencies. "We have a president."

"Does she eat turkey, too?"

"To be honest, Sophie, we've never had a woman president." She told her a little bit about the man in the White House and how every year he pardons the biggest turkey—of the poultry persuasion—in town.

"Papa took me to see the Pilgrims yesterday." She wrinkled her nose. "I don't like cranberries."

What an odd little girl. She could tell you to sod off one moment, then charm you with her almost Victorian manners the next.

"What are you doing?" Sophie asked. "Are you stealing the silverware?"

Gracie laughed out loud. "I'm moving it from Rachel's dining table to your grandmother's table. Here," she said, handing the girl a handful of teaspoons. "You can help me."

Sophie didn't look entirely pleased with the prospect, but to her credit she trooped after Gracie with five teaspoons and a stack of perfectly starched and ironed linen napkins clutched in her hands.

I know you, Gracie thought as they arranged the silver at each place. *I know all about you.* She didn't know all of the details of Sophie's life, but she did know how it was to feel all alone in a very big and scary world, how it felt to wish you fit in. That was why the child struck out the way she did. You didn't need a master's in psychology to figure that one out. Raise a child in chaos and you'll end up with either a people-pleaser like Gracie or little Stands-With-Fists. The best thing Noah could do was offer her stability and love, both in equal measure. Gramma Del had done that for Gracie, and it had made all the difference.

"My grandmother changed her mind and said families should spend Thanksgiving at home, not in restaurants," Sophie said out of nowhere. "She and Papa yelled at each other this morning." The little girl shuddered. "I don't like yelling."

"I'm sure they were just having a disagreement."

"No." Sophie sounded quite positive. "They were very loud. They sounded like my aunt Giselle before she said I had to go away."

Gracie took a deep breath, crossed her fingers, then jumped in. "My father used to yell all the time when I was a little girl. I used to hide in my closet with my fingers in my ears."

Sophie considered her for a moment. "I run away."

"I thought maybe you did."

"I wish grown-ups wouldn't yell."

"I know, Sophie, so do I. But sometimes that's the only way they can make themselves heard."

Sophie nodded. "Can I carry in the teacups now?"

It took Gracie a second to shift gears. "Carefully," she said. "They're china teacups and very delicate."

"I'll be careful," Sophie said.

"Promise?"

The child nodded. "I promise."

His mother found Noah in the side yard. He was gathering wood for the fireplaces in the main dining room.

"She's very good with Sophie."

He looked up from a pile of kindling he was separating. "Who is?"

"Gracie. I heard them talking in the dining room. They were very endearing together."

He wanted to brush off his mother's comments with a smart-ass remark, but Sophie's welfare was too important for that. "What were they doing?"

"Setting the table. Gracie was trying to explain why adults raise their voices."

"Damn it," Noah said, tossing a piece of firewood across the yard. "Sophie heard us this morning."

"It would appear so."

"Did she sound very upset?"

His mother nodded. "She seems to believe loud arguments are the only way adults communicate."

"I know," he said. "Apparently she heard a lot of them the last few years." He didn't blame Catherine's relatives for not wanting to take on the responsibility of an active, angry little girl. Most of them were in their fifties and sixties, looking forward to retirement and a life of reduced stress and strain.

"I didn't realize Gracie would be here today."

He met her eyes. "Yeah," he said, "you did. That's why you canceled our plans to eat out."

"The two of you need to talk."

"A little late for romantic advice."

"I'm trying to help."

"And I'm trying to salvage the *Gazette* and figure out how to be the best father I can be for Sophie. I don't have time for the rest of this."

She leaned more heavily on her cane. Noah noticed once again that Ruth's life required more effort from her these days than it ever had before. "I've been reading your column, Noah."

Funny how he hadn't really made the intellectual leap from the act of writing to the discomfort of being read. "Mary Levine is out on medical leave, and I was pulled in to sub for her."

"If what I've read so far is any indication, you are immensely qualified."

He muttered his thanks. They were private dreams made public before he had realized what he was doing. "Just filling in until we can put together a deal to sell the *Gazette*." He launched into an explanation about ad space availability and rates, but his mother raised her hand to stop him.

"It's more than that, Noah. You're writing from the heart."

"I'm writing for a paycheck," he said, trying to deflect her words.

"You're writing for Gracie Taylor."

"I'm writing for Sophie."

"In part, perhaps, but Gracie is at the heart of it all."

"It happened a long time ago," he said after an uncom-

fortable silence. "She ended it. I wouldn't have." He had
asked a lot of her. He knew that now. Not even love gave
a man the right to expect a woman to put aside her dreams
and follow him to Paris.

"A moment ago you said you wanted to salvage the
Gazette," Ruth persisted.

He said nothing.

"You could do it, if you set your mind to it, Noah.
You're talented. You have great vision. You care about—"

He stopped her with a look. "You asked me to put
together a deal with Granite. That's what I'm doing."

"I've only been the *Gazette*'s caretaker while you were
gone, Noah. Now that you're back in Idle Point, you
should be the one to decide its fate."

*And the fate of the men and women who were its life's
blood.* She didn't say those words, but Noah heard them
just the same. They were a tightly knit group at the *Gazette*, second- and third-generation employees who cared
about the craft of journalism as deeply as they cared about
their town and each other. The *Gazette* was a family op-
eration, built on trust and loyalty. Noah's grandfather had
understood that. So had Simon. After his death, when the
Gazette had been in danger of going under, his mother
stepped into the breach, and her warmth and good common sense had kept them afloat.

Now it was his turn. He knew that if he sold to Granite
News, the conglomerate would fold the *Gazette* into their
larger family of newspapers, and within a year all of the
people he had come to know and care about would be out
of work.

If he didn't sell, he would be committing himself and
Sophie to making a life in Idle Point.

". . . she needs a home . . ." his mother was saying, as

if she'd read his mind. "Idle Point is a good place to raise a child."

Then why did you send me away?

But there was no point in asking her that, same as there was no point in believing a life in Idle Point was possible for him without Gracie at the heart of it.

Gracie had grown up to be a lovely young woman. She was still reed thin, still soft-spoken, but there was a strength about her that Ruth found compelling. Ruth had always admired strong women, mainly because she had never considered herself to be one. She had always deferred her desires to Simon's will, keeping his secrets, dreaming his dreams. Her rebellions had been sly rather than decisive, and the repercussions devastating. There was the sense about Gracie that she could handle what life threw her way.

Except when she looked at Noah.

Oh, she was discreet about it. Her glances were quick and well concealed, but the longing in her eyes when she looked at him cut Ruth to the quick. They were all seated at the long cherrywood table in Ruth's little-used dining room with two satellite tables set up for the children at either end. Rachel didn't believe in place cards. Seating was a matter of friendly negotiation and a touch of pushing and shoving that made for much good-natured teasing and laughter. The fact that, when all was said and done, Gracie and Noah were seated opposite each other escaped no one.

The connection between them was almost palpable. Soul mates, Ruth thought not for the first time. She felt the weight of the eight years they had lost in every corner of her soul. She told herself that it hadn't been her fault. She had been hurt by Simon's actions, too. Noah and Gracie couldn't possibly blame her for all they had lost.

Gracie's eyes had filled with tears when she turned and saw Ruth walk through the back door. "Mrs. Chase!" she had exclaimed, then dashed over to say hello. Her gaze lingered on the elegant cane Ruth had been using since she broke her hip that spring.

"Don't worry," Ruth said, "I won't break. Now, come give me a hug, Gracie Taylor."

"Chanel No. 5," Gracie said, laughing as they hugged. "Do you know that I always think of you when I smell Chanel No. 5?" There had been nothing but love and respect in the young woman's demeanor, and Ruth felt singularly unworthy of either gift.

Gracie swore she could feel her heart grow two sizes larger as she glanced around Rachel's table. How could she have stayed away from Idle Point and these beloved people for so long? She felt more connected to the world here in this tiny seacoast town than she ever had in the middle of Manhattan.

Rachel Adams raised her glass and smiled at the guests assembled around her dining room table. "I'm thankful for each and every one of you, those related to me by blood and those by my own good fortune." She turned to her husband.

Darnell stood up and held his glass high. "I'm thankful for another year spent in the company of the people I love." He turned to Laquita.

Laquita squeezed Ben's hand, then raised her glass. "I'm grateful for every second I've been granted with this wonderful man"—she looked toward Gracie—"and for my renewed friendship with his daughter."

The chain of thanks moved its way around the table. Gracie found herself giving thanks that she was at the end of the line. Who would have suspected that the hippie family down by the river was actually the Waltons in disguise? She looked across the table at Ben. How well he fit in with the family. He was an odd cross between patriarch and peer, and it suited him down to the ground.

Noah stood up and raised his glass. "I'm thankful I found my daughter Sophie and that I had sense enough to bring her home to Idle Point."

He looked at Gracie, then sat down again. It wasn't as if she had expected him to say he was thankful she had walked out on him eight years ago. Still, she felt disappointed.

Sophie pressed her face against Noah's shoulder and refused to talk, as did Sage's son Will.

Dr. Jim stood and turned toward Gracie. "Come home where you belong, Dr. Taylor. My door is always open to you." He was thankful for the gift of love his late wife Ellen had given to him, for friends, for good food, for life renewing itself in unexpected ways.

Finally it was Gracie's turn. Twenty-four people lifted their glasses in anticipation of something witty or profound as befit her new big-city-girl persona. She raised her glass, ready to offer her thanks for the wonderful welcome, and to her horror she found herself so overcome by emotion she could barely speak.

"I'm thankful to all of you for making room for me at your table. I hope to be able to make room for you at mine one day."

The room burst into applause and laughter, but all she saw was the look in Noah's eyes.

Sophie wasn't sure what she thought of the turkey or the stuffing, but she loved the yams and the mashed potatoes. She sat perfectly straight in her chair, looking like an angel in her blue velvet jumper and frilly white blouse. The snowy napkin lay neatly on her lap. She handled her knife and fork with a distinctly European flair that had everyone showering her with compliments. Whoever had taught his daughter table manners had done a great job. Noah was prouder of her facility with a knife and fork than he was of any of his own accomplishments.

"I think we have a vegetarian in the making," Ruth observed as she placed her utensils across her plate and leaned back in her chair.

"The aunt who took care of her last year is a vegetarian." Giselle was a perfectly lovely sixty-year-old woman who didn't want the responsibility of raising her niece's child. He couldn't fault Giselle for that; her niece had felt the same way.

Sophie tugged at his sleeve. "When is the dessert?"

"First dinner, then dessert," he said.

"Even on Thanksgiving?"

"Even then."

Sophie looked across the table at Gracie. "Do you like cranberries?"

Gracie nodded. "As long as they're soaked in sugar. It's the American way."

Sophie giggled. "You put marshmallows on your potatoes."

"Candied yams." She leaned across the table and lowered her voice to a stage whisper. "Don't tell anyone, but I eat ice cream cake for breakfast on my birthday."

"Really?"

"Yes, but that's after my tuna salad sandwich. First the healthy stuff, then dessert."

"You eat tuna for breakfast?" Sophie looked shocked.

"Sometimes," Gracie said. "And some nights I eat cereal for supper."

Sophie seemed downright enchanted. "When I'm grown up, I'll have trifle for breakfast every day of the week."

"You might want to mix a little protein in there," Gracie said, tapping her forehead with her index finger. "You need to keep the brain cells well fed."

"I have a lot to think about," Sophie said, and Noah's heart did one of those little half-twists that seemed to happen every time she opened her mouth and spoke.

"Yes, you do," Gracie said. "Life is very complicated, isn't it?"

Sophie nodded. "It is!"

Sophie seemed happier and more relaxed than he had ever seen her. Gracie had a way of talking with his daughter that worked magic. She didn't condescend. She didn't patronize. She talked with Sophie the way she talked with Dr. Jim or his mother, and apparently Sophie sensed the difference and responded in kind.

His mother reached over and patted his hand. "Don't worry," she said softly. "It will work itself out."

"I know," he said, but he was lying.

SIXTEEN

Sleeping Adamses and their friends were scattered from one end of the den to the other. Rachel and Darnell had shooed everyone out of the kitchen while they finished cleaning up, and Gracie laughed as the clan beat a hasty retreat. Ben and Laquita were napping on the sofa with one of Wiley's offspring curled up between them. The football game droned on in the background, but nobody seemed to be paying any attention to it. Sage, Morocco, and Joe—and their offspring—were outside playing a game of touch football with two of their sisters, while Cheyenne and Storm retreated to the sewing room to work on their dresses. They begged Gracie to let them do one more fitting on the pants suit Rachel was assembling for her, but Gracie said if she tried it on tonight, they would have to let out all of the seams.

Ruth had excused herself to go upstairs and rest. Noah and Sophie had just plain disappeared. Gracie felt restless and unsettled. The house, big as it was, felt too small to contain her emotions, and she found herself craving a lonely sweep of rocky beach. How wonderful to be able to walk out a door and step onto the beach. Everyone had said she was crazy to keep a car in the city, but she had needed the means to escape whenever the noise and the crowds became too much for her. Taking the subway to Coney Island or the bus to Rockaway wasn't the same as driving east through Queens to Long Island, where she followed the signs to Jones Beach. That wide, smooth expanse of civilized sand was nothing like the unforgiving beaches of her childhood, but knowing that the same ocean crashed against the shores of Idle Point soothed her soul.

She grabbed her coat from the hall closet, then let herself out the back door, the one that led out into the garden. Two late roses, blood red and just beginning to unfurl, bloomed near the stairs. Beach roses used to line the path to the rocky beach by the lighthouse. Once upon a time, in another life, Noah had trailed a beach rose over the curve of her hip, the line of her thigh. The gesture was both sensually charged and painfully sweet, the kind of gesture a woman never forgot. She remembered the look in his eyes, the faint smell of salt on his skin, the callused tip of his index finger, the velvety softness of the petals of the rose against her bare skin. If the world had ended at that very moment, she would have died knowing her life had been blessed beyond measure.

She didn't have him—she couldn't—but she had those memories and sometimes she even managed to convince herself that those memories were enough.

Sophie was fearless. She flew across the rocky beach in her fancy velvet dress and heavy parka as if she had been born there in Idle Point instead of on the other side of the ocean.

"Sophie, be careful!" he shouted into the wind. "The rocks are slippery!"

She didn't hear him. He probably wouldn't have been able to hear a warning at her age either. She was so small, a tiny scrap of humanity against the enormity of the wind and tides. If he had his way, he would lock her in the house until she was forty.

She leaped from rock to rock, arms outstretched, mimicking the gulls that swooped and soared overhead. She reminded him of Gracie as a little girl, so filled with physical energy and enthusiasm that the span of her arms reached the edges of the world.

"She looks like she was born here."

He was surprised he hadn't felt her presence before he heard her voice. "I was thinking the same thing."

Gracie cupped her hands around her mouth. "Soooo-phie!"

His daughter stopped, perched on a huge rock near the water's edge, and waved.

Gracie waved back, her oversized coat billowing in the wind like a woolen parachute. "Has she seen a gull open a clam yet?"

"I don't think so."

She scanned the area. "I remember the first time you saw that gull drop the clam onto the rocks and break it open."

"You opened my eyes," he said. The natural world had been invisible to him until Gracie came into his life.

"You should go catch up with her," she said, wrapping her arms around her slender body as the wind kicked up. "Low tide's a perfect time to start teaching her about the shore."

"Like Gramma Del did for you."

She peered out from beneath her hood. "You remember that."

"I remember a lot of things, Gracie."

She was halfway across the rocks before he realized she was in motion. She ran the way she did everything, with speed and grace. She never slipped, never faltered.

This beach, this place, was her heart's home and always had been.

The rocks fought him as he made his way toward his daughter and Gracie. They shifted and moved beneath his feet. Moss, slippery as ice, threatened his balance. He had been denied whatever gene it was that enabled Gracie and Sophie to navigate these rocks as if they were on flat dry land. At least it was still daylight. He wouldn't want to be out there in the dark with the tide rolling in.

Gracie used to laugh at him during those hot summer nights when he refused to venture too far from the shadow of the lighthouse. She didn't understand because she was born to be part of this place, while he had somehow always felt as though he was just passing through.

He looked up and saw that Gracie and his daughter were way up the beach already, walking along the shoreline with their heads down. He could see Gracie pointing at various bits of aquatic flora and fauna, and if Sophie's body language was any indication, the child was spellbound.

He knew just how she felt.

They looked right together, the three of them. Gracie could easily imagine the picture they made as they walked the beach at sunset. Handsome man, hardworking woman, happy child.

They looked like a family.

Tell him, Gracie. It's time. Do it for Sophie if you can't do it for Noah or yourself.

"Ben and Laquita look happy," he observed as they followed the bouncing Sophie up the gilded beach. "What odds do you give them?"

"I think they're going to make it," Gracie said, bending down to pick up a beautiful striated rock. "They're an odd couple, but somehow they work."

"We would have made it," he said, his gaze fastened on his quick little daughter.

"Yes," Gracie said, "we probably would have." *Tell him, Gracie. Now is as good a time as any.* There was no reason for her to keep Simon's secret any longer. It was time to move on.

"I didn't get it, Gracie. Remember when you used to call me the rich kid? You were right. I didn't get how it was for you . . . what I was asking you to sacrifice."

She took a deep breath and dived in. "You're right," she said. "We need to talk about what happened. You deserve the truth."

His expression held a thousand shades of emotion, all of which broke her heart. "I see us everywhere. The way you looked in the moonlight—"

"Don't," she said. "We can't—"

"I didn't love Sophie's mother."

"I don't want to hear this."

"I liked her. We enjoyed each other's company." He forced her to meet his eyes. "She reminded me of you. She was ambitious. Focused in a way I've never had to be. I wanted something with no strings, no chance of hurting anyone or being hurt myself."

"What did she want?"

"Sex and laughs." He grew quiet for a moment, his gaze returned again to Sophie. "Catherine wasn't one for getting sidetracked."

"Which would explain why she let Sophie go."

"I'm not sure anything explains that." A clean letting go would have given Sophie a permanent home right off the bat, not years of being passed from relative to relative until somebody thought about letting the father know he had a child.

"You're giving her a good life."

"I can do better."

"You will," she said, "but from what I can see, you're doing everything right."

"Which doesn't explain the biting and kicking."

"She's scared. She doesn't have too many ways to express it."

"She could try telling me."

"I'm sure she will once she believes you're a sure thing."

"A sure thing?"

"That you're not going to bail out on her the way every other adult in her life has."

"I've told her that from the beginning."

"So did Ben. Prove it to her, and then she'll start believing you."

Another silence.

"I'm planning to go back to London after I work out a deal to sell the *Gazette*."

"Because you love London?"

Don't go, Noah. Stay here. Make a life for you and Sophie here in Idle Point.

"Because being here is too hard."

"I know," she whispered, unable to contain her emotions. "It is for me, too." Their dreams waited for them on the corner. Their hopes were still right up the road by the lighthouse.

"What about you?" he asked. "I suppose you're going back to New York after the wedding."

"I don't know what I'm going to do after the wedding."

"I thought you had a big job down there."

" 'Had' being the operative word." She kept her eyes trained on Sophie who was a fair distance away. "I'm on suspension." She told him why in fifty words or less.

"You haven't changed."

"I'm not sure how to take that."

"I wouldn't complain if Sophie followed your lead."

"She'll find a better way," Gracie said, bypassing the compliment. She hoped Sophie would find a way that wouldn't break her heart.

Sophie stopped running. They watched as she bent down to inspect something at the shoreline.

"I've missed you, Gracie," he said.

"I've missed you, too." *You're the other half of my heart. You always will be.* She whispered a silent prayer, then pushed forward. "I want to tell you why—"

Sophie's scream shattered the mood.

They were at her side seconds later. Sophie threw herself against Noah, sobbing wildly. A small gull, horribly tangled in fishing line, lay dying on the beach. A barbed hook was embedded in the side of his neck. He had lost a great deal of blood; it puddled beneath him on the hard sand. Gracie knew instantly that it was a lost cause, and she shook her head at Noah when Sophie wasn't looking.

"It's okay, Soph." He held her close while she cried. "Gracie is an animal doctor. She knows what to do."

Gracie did indeed know what to do, but it wasn't something she would tell the child. Sophie had dealt with enough of life's ugliness. She wasn't about to visit anymore of it on her.

"He's hurt!" Sophie cried, turning toward Gracie. "Make it stop hurting him, Gracie! Make it stop!"

It would only be a matter of a few minutes. Gracie could tell by the gull's shallow breathing, the utter lack of fear at human contact. She was about to shrug off her coat and wrap the bird in its folds when Noah offered up his jacket instead. She thanked him, then motioned for him to divert Sophie's attention while she quickly wrapped the dying bird in his jacket.

"What are you going to do?" Sophie asked, keeping her face pressed tightly against her father's shoulder.

"I'm going to keep him comfortable," Gracie said,

walking the fine line of truth and falsehood.

"You'll make it stop hurting him?"

"Yes," Gracie said. "I promise you I will."

Sophie wanted to follow Gracie around back to find Dr. Jim, but Noah wouldn't let her.

"You're cold and wet," he said to his daughter. "Let's go upstairs and get warm first."

He should have known the quiet afternoon was too good to be true. Her crying about the injured seagull suddenly turned into a mini–temper tantrum. The tantrum fell short of kicking and biting, but it wasn't a whole lot of fun for either one of them. Sophie was crying so hard she could hardly breathe by the time he got her upstairs to her room. So much for progress. Every time Noah felt as if he'd gotten a handle on fatherhood, he hit another speed bump.

"Take off your clothes," he told Sophie, "and put on your robe while I start a bath for you."

"I don't want to take a bath."

"A nice warm bubble bath will make you feel better."

"I don't want to feel better."

"I don't want you to catch cold, Soph."

She made a run for it. He managed to catch her at the top of the staircase. He tucked her under his arm and carried her back to her room.

"I want to help the bird, Papa," she said, struggling against his efforts to remove her wet clothes. "I have to find Gracie and help her."

"Gracie is an animal doctor," he reminded Sophie, "and so is Dr. Jim. They'll make sure the bird doesn't hurt anymore."

"But I am the one who found him. He'll be looking for me."

"He's being cared for, Sophie. I'll bet Gracie will be

up here by the time you finish your bath and put on your nightgown." How did you draw the line between the painful truth and a comforting lie?

Sophie didn't seem convinced, but most of the fight drained out of her. He wasn't above taking advantage of that fact.

"There was nothing we could have done, Gracie." Dr. Jim put an arm around her shoulders and gave her a swift hug. "He didn't have a chance."

"I know that," Gracie said. "I know all about the food chain and the ways of nature. Believe me, I've dealt with that and more down in New York." She knew the difference between a lost cause and convenience. In fact, knowing that had cost her her position at the hospital where she'd worked. "It was the look in Sophie's eyes . . ."

"The little one's been through a lot," he said. "It's natural you'd want to protect her."

"She's not mine," Gracie said. "I don't know how Noah wants to handle this." Every parent treated the topic of death in a different way. She only knew she didn't want to lie to Sophie.

"Seeing you and Noah together took me back a lot of years," Dr. Jim said. "I always hoped you would end up together."

"So did I," Gracie said with a soft laugh.

"So what's stopping you? I saw the way you looked at each other over Rachel's turkey. It's clear nothing has changed."

"A lot has changed, Dr. Jim."

"Nothing essential."

She had to stop this now before it went too far. "I'm hoping we can find a way to be friends again."

"And that's your polite way of telling me to mind my own business."

"I'd never tell you that."

"No," he said with a smile, "you wouldn't, but I'll do it just the same."

They stood together in silence for a few minutes, watching the sun slide behind the hills.

"There's a place for you here, Gracie," he said as they hugged good-bye. "I meant what I said at the dinner table."

"I know you did," she said, "and I love you for it."

She lingered a few moments more, then stepped back into the house where Laquita found her a second later.

"Your father's getting tired," Laquita said, "and I'm working the midnight shift. If you don't mind, I think it's time to head home."

Gracie hesitated. She had finally worked up the nerve to tell Noah what had happened the day she left him, and the right moment kept slipping between her fingers. "Why don't you two go ahead without me." She told Laquita about Sophie and the injured bird. "I think I'll stay and see if Sophie wants to talk."

"How will you get home?"

"I hadn't thought of that."

Laquita pulled her car keys from the pocket of her bright red down jacket. "Here," she said. "Use my car."

"What about you and Dad?"

"I have ten siblings," she said with a grin. "If I can't bum a ride off one of them, it's a sorry world."

Gracie thanked her, then Laquita rushed off to find someone to drive her and Ben home. That was part of being a family, this kind of give and take. *Here, take my car. . . . Hey, how about a ride down to the corner. . . . It's cold . . . you'd better borrow my sweater . . . Do you remember when we used to . . .*

She could have that and more if she moved back to Idle Point. It was there for the taking, almost everything she had ever wanted from life. A big, loud, loving family, even if most of them were imported by marriage. A relationship with her father. The chance to work with Dr. Jim. She could even have Noah in her life—Sophie, too—although not in the way she had always dreamed. All she had to do was say the word, and it was hers.

"Do you know where Noah is?" she asked Rachel, who was putting away the last of the dishes.

"He was looking for you," Rachel said, closing the glass doors to the china cabinet. "Sophie wants you to give her a bath."

Second floor, third door on the left.

Gracie flew up the stairs. The signs were all there. She had motive and she had opportunity. She was tired of living only half a life, and she wished for more for Sophie and Noah. This wasn't the happy ending she had dreamed about, but it was more than she had believed possible these last eight years. *Tell him tonight. Tell him before you leave this house.* They couldn't be lovers, but they could be part of each other's lives. She could be his friend, grow old with him, watch Sophie grow up. And even though it hurt more than she sometimes believed possible, it was so much better than being without him.

She tapped on the door to Sophie's room. "I hear somebody needs a bath," she called out.

"C'mon in!" Noah shouted from inside the room. "You're not a minute too soon."

She opened the door and stepped into the bedroom she wished she'd had as a little girl. Open and airy. Pink and white. A window seat. A nightstand piled high with *Madeleine* and *Harry Potter* and the *Complete Dr. Seuss.* Paradise!

Sophie, naked and highly annoyed, stood in the middle of the room.

Noah, fully clothed and completely at a loss, sat on the edge of her bed.

They both looked toward Gracie as if she were the answer to their prayers.

"Barbie's Dream House!" Gracie couldn't believe her eyes. There it was in all of its plastic prefab glory to the left of the window seat. "Sophie, you have Barbie's Dream House!" She knelt down in front of the pricey piece of real estate and admired each detail.

"Did you have Barbies when you were a little girl?" Sophie asked, clearly skeptical.

"I sure did," Gracie said. "Mine was one of the beach Barbies. She carried a surfboard and had a year-round tan."

"They had Barbies when you were little?"

"Prehistoric Barbie," Gracie said with a straight face. "Ken came with a loincloth and a club."

"I have two Barbies and one Ken." Sophie lowered her voice and leaned closer to Gracie. "They pulled his legs off."

Gracie met Noah's eyes over the top of Sophie's head. He was trying hard not to laugh out loud.

"Sounds like they're Biker Barbies," Gracie said, inspecting the two innocent-looking blondes for signs of aggression. "A pair of tough chicks."

"They didn't mean to do it. Sometimes these things happen."

"Ken better watch his step," Gracie said, matching Sophie's serious tone.

"Oh, yes," said Sophie, "or something bad might happen to him."

That did it. Both Noah and Gracie burst into laughter. Sophie looked at them with annoyance at first, and then she started laughing, too, obviously pleased to be the source of such good-natured amusement.

"Okay, Soph." Noah stood up. "Time for that bath you've been putting off for the last half hour."

Sophie looked toward Gracie. "Will you wash my hair for me?"

"I've never washed a little girl's hair before," Gracie said. "Are you sure you want me to do it?"

"You really never washed a little girl's hair?" Sophie asked.

"I shampooed a cocker spaniel," she said, and Sophie giggled. "I shampooed poodles and Dalmatians. I even shampooed my cat once, and he sneezed soap bubbles all over me."

Sophie tugged at her sleeve. "You can't shampoo a cat."

"Sure you can," said Gracie, taking her hand. "I didn't say he liked it, but you can do it."

"I had a cat named Fred when I lived with Aunt Sarah and Uncle Hamish. He wouldn't go out in the rain."

"Uncle Hamish?" Gracie asked, wide-eyed with pretend innocence.

"No, silly!" Sophie was overcome with giggles. "Fred!"

They kept up the silly banter while Noah ran the tub and filled it with fragrant bubbles. They tried to imagine Gracie's Pyewacket swatting the bubbles with a lazy paw, and that only made Sophie laugh even more.

If this was all Gracie could have of Noah, it would be enough.

Ruth was engrossed in the newest Dick Francis novel when Dr. Jim stepped into the library to say good night.

"Thank you for opening your home to me, Ruthie." He sat down on the edge of the sofa next to her chair. "You made my first Thanksgiving without Ellen much easier."

"There's no need to thank me, Jim, even though I loved

your company. Rachel put everything together. I was
nothing more than a party crasher."

Jim's smile always made Ruth feel the world was a
better place. "And some party it was," he said. "I feel like
everyone in town dropped by at some time or another."

"Rachel and Darnell are lucky people."

"That they are. They raised themselves a fine group of
young men and women, didn't they?"

They chatted for a bit about Laquita and Ben's upcom-
ing wedding, then talk turned quite naturally to Noah and
Gracie.

"If ever a man and woman were meant for each other,
it's those two," Jim said with a shake of his graying head.
"I never could figure out what's been keeping them apart."

"Whatever it is, it's between them," Ruth said primly
in an attempt to hide her own complicity. "I wouldn't dare
ask either one of them about it."

"Not suggesting you should," Jim said easily. "Just
making conversation."

Ruth slipped off her reading glasses and gently mas-
saged the bridge of her nose. "I'm sorry if I sounded
sharp, Jim. The holidays stir up a lot of old memories,
some of which are better left undisturbed."

"Don't I know it," he said, rising to his feet. "It's just
when it comes to Gracie, I can't seem to help hoping for
the best."

"I feel the same way," she said. "About both of them."

"I just wish there was something I could do to make
things right." He bent down and kissed her on the left
cheek. "Guess it's best left in the hands of God."

Ruth sat staring into the fire for a long time after Jim
said good night, wishing she had the courage to try to
make things right, but the thought of disturbing the graves
of so many long-buried secrets was more than she could
contemplate.

If Noah and Gracie were meant to be, they would find their way to each other without any help.

For the first time in the three months he'd known Sophie, Noah felt some of the tension leave his body. It was the sound of her laughter that did it. He wasn't sure he'd ever heard it before, certainly not so much of it or so freely given.

Noah went to place Sophie in the warm tub, but she wanted Gracie to do it.

"Are you a poodle?" Gracie teased his daughter.

"No!"

"Are you a cocker spaniel?"

"No!"

"Then I'm not sure I know how to give you a bath."

A second later, Sophie was immersed in bubbles with nothing but her heart-shaped face and halo of blond curls visible.

"You'd better take your coat off," Noah suggested to Gracie. "She splashes."

Gracie looked surprised. "My coat! I completely forgot I was wearing it." She shrugged it off and hung it from the hook behind the door. "Now where were we?" She pushed her sleeves up over her elbows. "That's right. I was going to bathe a cat."

Sophie loved every second of it. Gracie claimed no prior knowledge of bathing young children, but she handled it like a pro. Certainly a hell of a lot better than he had his first time around. She made sure no soap got in Sophie's eyes. She protected her ears with tiny wads of cotton. And when the bath was over, she rinsed Sophie squeaky clean then wrapped her in the biggest, warmest towel she could find.

"Do you have a blow dryer?" she asked Noah.

He removed one from the vanity beneath the sink.

"Oh, good," said Gracie. "It has a diffuser."

"A diffuser?"

"See this?" She pointed toward the wide attachment over the mouth of the dryer. "That's for curly hair."

"Yes, Papa," said Sophie. "Everyone knows that."

"First I've heard of it," he muttered then stepped back into the shadows where he belonged.

Gracie put the dryer on the lowest setting, and in no time at all Sophie's hair was a mass of shiny, sweet-smelling curls. There had always been a sadness about Gracie even during her happiest moments, but the air of sadness about her that night was almost palpable. The look in her eyes when Sophie took her hand for the walk from the bathroom to the bedroom would stay with Noah for a long time.

"You look beautiful, mademoiselle," Gracie said as Sophie did a pirouette in her pink terry cloth bathrobe.

"Okay, Soph," he said, as he slipped her prettiest nightgown over her head, "time for bed."

"No!" She stomped one tiny bare foot on the thick pale pink carpet. "Not yet!"

"It's late," he said, "and you've had a long day."

"No, I haven't."

"Sophie, I'm telling you—"

"No!"

Gracie quietly went into the bathroom, and when she came out she was wearing her big floppy coat.

"Don't go!" Sophie cried out. "I don't want you to leave."

"And I don't want to leave," Gracie said calmly, "but if you and your daddy are going to fight, I think I'll go home."

"I don't want to fight with Papa."

"Remember when we talked about how sometimes

grown-ups talk real loud because they think that's the only way they can be heard?"

Sophie nodded.

"That's what you were doing."

Sophie look up at him with big teary blue eyes, and he was tempted to run out to Toys R Us and buy her a dozen Barbie Dream Houses to make her smile again.

"Gracie's right, Soph," he said instead. "But we're both learning, aren't we?"

Sophie was quick to anger but equally quick to forget what she had been so angry about. A moment later he had her laughing again, and she was still laughing when he tucked her into bed. He read her another scene from a Harry Potter book while Gracie gently stroked her hair. Then it was Gracie's turn, and she told Sophie a story about her brand-new cat Pyewacket and his adventures on the road from New York City to Idle Point that actually had Noah sitting on the edge of his seat.

Sophie's eyelids fluttered closed. They waited a moment and then, when they were sure she was asleep, tiptoed from the room.

"Does Pyewacket ever go home to New York?" Sophie called out as they reached the door.

"I don't know yet," Gracie said, glancing at Noah. "Pye will have to let me know."

Sophie yawned. "What about my seagull? Did you and Dr. Jim make him all better?"

Gracie's heart sank to her feet. She had been waiting for this question and when it hadn't come by lights out, she'd thought they were home free.

"Did he—?" Noah whispered.

"Yes," she said. "I don't want to lie to her."

"I don't want you to, either."

It was a small thing, but she deserved the truth.

"The gull was hurt very badly, honey," Gracie said,

crouching down at the side of Sophie's bed. "Dr. Jim and I did everything we could to make him comfortable."

"Is he all better?"

"We lost him, Sophie. I'm so sorry. We tried our best, but he was hurt too badly for us to be able to save him."

"You mean he's gone?"

"Yes, honey."

"Then I should go find him."

"No, Soph, you don't have to do that." Noah bent down to talk to her. "What Gracie's saying is that the gull died."

Sophie thought about that for a moment. Neither Gracie nor Noah knew just how well she understood the concept of death.

"Where is my seagull now?"

"Dr. Jim has him," Gracie said. "He'll take him back to the beach where he belongs." Nature was unforgiving at best, but there was comfort to be found in the notion of life renewing itself. At five and a half, Sophie was too young to understand that concept, but in time she would.

They waited until Sophie's eyes grew heavy a second time, then slipped from the room. Sophie's pink night-light was on. Its faint glow spilled out into the darkened hallway. The house seemed very quiet after the Thanksgiving Day commotion.

"Listen," Gracie said, tilting her head to the right. "Not a sound. She's out like a light."

His face was inches away from hers. The look in his eyes was filled with both pain and wonder. "You were great with her."

"I think we speak the same language."

"She's had it rough," he said. "She's been passed around since the day she was born, then some guy from another country comes along and says, 'I'm your father, kid,' and takes her across the ocean."

"She's lucky you found her. You'll give her the family she deserves."

"No," he said. "I'm the one who's lucky. She's the one good thing to happen to me since I lost you."

"It hurts so much, Noah," she whispered, her voice breaking. He was so close she could smell the dried sea spray on his skin. "When you told me she was your daughter, I hurt so much I thought I was going to die."

"Now you know," he said, his tone fierce with rage and longing. "That's what you did to me, Gracie, when you left me."

"Oh, God, I never wanted to hurt you. That's the last thing I wanted to do. I was scared. I didn't know which way to turn. I did the only thing I could do. I had no choice. It was the only option left to me."

"I pushed too hard," he said, his mouth only inches from hers. "I asked you to give up everything you'd worked for. I wanted you all for myself."

"No, no, that's not what I mean . . . Oh, God, this is so hard . . . seeing you again . . . seeing you with Sophie—"

They fell into each other's arms as if that was the only safe place on earth to be. And maybe it was. Their kisses were open-mouthed and hungry, hot and wet and impossible to deny. She wanted to taste every inch of his body. She wanted to bite the flesh of his inner thigh and mark him as her own. Years of longing erupted, and she was on fire for him. She knew it was wrong. She knew there could be no future for them. She knew it all, but she didn't care. She wanted this one night, this one gift to hold onto for the rest of her life.

He pressed her against the wall, trapped her there with his body, his hands, his heart. She clung to him, desperate for more, more of his kisses, his touch, everything he had and was or would ever be.

He was a half step away from madness. Her slender

curves hidden inside that foolish coat awoke a thousand memories. She had been so excited, so eager, so unbearably lovely that first time. He carried those images with him every day of his life. He'd dreamed of holding her again, tasting her skin, hearing her soft cries. And now here she was in his arms, and he wasn't dreaming. She moved against him, on fire and unashamed, matching him in passion and love and need, all that she had been before and more, so much more, because now he knew how it felt to be without her. At once he saw her as she was and as she had been, past and present coming together in a blaze of anger and love and desire that almost brought him to his knees.

"I love you," she murmured, her lips hot against the base of his throat. "I've never stopped loving you."

He pushed the coat off her shoulders, unbuttoned her sweater. "I've never loved anyone but you, Gracie. Never . . ."

"Those stories . . . the things you wrote . . . so beautiful . . ."

"I remember everything about you . . . everything—" Every breath she took, every word she had uttered. He remembered it all.

Rachel's voice drifted up the staircase. They needed to be alone, away from the world. He swept Gracie up into his arms and carried her down the hallway to his room, three doors down. The bedroom was dark. He reached for the lamp, but Gracie stopped him.

"They'll see the light," she whispered as he stripped off her clothes then shed his own.

They were greedy for each other, avid, intoxicated by the feel of bare skin against bare skin, the wonder of touch. Words of love spiraled between them, striking sparks in the darkness. Their bodies were strange and yet familiar; the rhythm of love was part sense memory, part miracle. He needed all that she had to give, to find the other half of his heart. She needed to make him part of her body the same way he had been part of her heart and soul for as long as she could remember.

Remember . . . remember this moment . . .

Remember the way he looked in the moonlit bedroom. Remember the words he murmured against her skin. Remember how it felt to be happy again.

Remember the moment when he pulsed deep inside her body, holding her as if he would never let her go, the way her body answered his with a fierce shattering of her defenses that was triumphant and heartbreaking all at the same time, because she knew it could never happen again.

He unfurled the future for her like a flag of silk. The fact that they would have a future seemed like a miracle to him, like the first snowfall or a baby's smile. They had been handed a second chance, and he wasn't about to waste a moment of it.

Words poured from his mouth the way they had poured from his fingers onto the computer keyboard. She was the key to everything. Without Gracie by his side, life was nothing more than a counting down of the days. He created castles in the air for her, castles with a foundation of unshakable love, and after a bit he realized that she lay curled on the bed next to him but hadn't said anything at all.

"Gracie?" He rolled on his side and looked at her through the darkness. "Is something wrong?" He reached out and touched her cheek. It was damp with tears. "Did I hurt you?"

She took his face between her hands and ran her thumbs across his cheekbones, down to the corners of his mouth. "I love you so much," she said. "Nothing will ever change that."

He felt the icy breath of fear against the back of his neck. "What is it?" Eight years was a long time to be apart from the one you love. He knew nothing about that time. Had she been sick? Was there something he needed to know? "You can tell me anything."

"I tried to find the nerve to tell you all day, but there was one interruption after the other." She sat up straight with her back against the headboard. "I don't know. Maybe I was looking for a reason not to tell you at all."

"This is about that day, isn't it?"

"Yes." The look in her eyes scared him. Sadness was in her eyes and regret. She drew in a deep breath, and the sound struck him like a physical blow. "Your father knew about us. A friend at the courthouse in Portland sent him a copy of our marriage license."

The icy breath grew colder still. "How did you find out?"

She clasped her hands together, but her fingers still shook. "He came to my house that afternoon. He told me we were all wrong for each other, that I would only hold you back—"

"But you were the one with the ambitions. I—"

She wouldn't let him continue. If she stopped she would never manage to say the words and she needed to say them more than anything in the world. "He knew me, Noah. He knew what made me tick. But I wouldn't give in. I told him I loved you, that I would make you happy, that you were the best thing that ever happened to me. He even tried to buy me off, as if money was the one thing I couldn't refuse, but I wouldn't give an inch."

Noah leaned back against the pillow as the story took shape in front of him. He'd found his father parked along the side of the road not far from the docks where Gracie lived. Simon's dying words had been about Gracie. Why hadn't he realized that before?

"Did he threaten you? What did he say that made you run?"

"He told me about my mother, that they had loved each other." Her voice broke, and the sound tore at Noah's heart. "He said they were going to leave their spouses, take me, and run away. They were only forty, he said, still young enough to build a new life. I didn't want to believe him, but all the bits and pieces suddenly started to fit together, all those things about my life that had never made sense before—"

"Spit it out," he demanded, as fear downshifted into anger. "What does any of that have to do with us? I don't give a damn what happened between them. All I want to know is what made you throw away our dreams."

"Oh, God, Noah, don't you see?" She knelt in front of him, forcing him to meet his eyes. "Simon was my father, too."

SEVENTEEN

Words.

English words.

They tumbled around inside his head like Scrabble tiles.

"Say that again." Maybe if he heard the words a second time, he'd be able to make sense out of them.

She was crying. He saw that. He understood that. She knelt in front of him, knees sinking into the mattress, her slender body illuminated by a thin ribbon of moonlight spilling through the window.

Then she said it again. "Simon Chase was my father, too."

His father. Her mother. Years of secrets and lies and plans that ended on a sunny afternoon in May when Mona Taylor died.

"It doesn't make sense," he said, struggling to find one shred of sanity in the sordid mess. "If you were his child, why did he hate you so much?" He remembered his father's withering sarcasm whenever Gracie's name was mentioned. His seething resentment of his cook's grand-child had always seemed out of whack to Noah. "You were all he had left of the woman he loved. You should have been—"

"He blamed me. I was the reason she stayed in her marriage. My birth brought her and Ben back together. Don't you see? In Simon's eyes, it was all my fault, and he hated me for it."

"Why didn't you come and tell me?"

"Your father was a very powerful man, Noah. He told me he would ruin what was left of Ben's life, break your mother's heart, and"—she hesitated a moment—"he said he would cut you off without a penny."

"Do you really think I gave a damn about his money?"

"No, but we were so young, Noah! He was going to take school away from you, everything that was part of your life. I knew what it was like to be poor, but you hadn't a clue. How could I do that to you?"

"Are you sure you weren't looking out for yourself?"

His words stung like a slap. "I think you know the answer to that."

"There was money involved. I heard the stories."

"Ten thousand dollars cash," she said without hesitation. "He left it in an envelope on the kitchen table. I found it when I was leaving the notes for you and for Ben." She told him about old Eb and his surprise. "I like to think he had himself a good time on it."

In a twisted way, everything she had said made sense. Each piece fit perfectly with the piece next to it and the pieces above and below.

He swung his legs from the bed. "Get dressed."

She stared up at him as if she'd never seen him before. "What did you say?"

"Get dressed. We're going to talk to my mother about this."

"No!" She leaped from the bed and faced him. "Leave Ruth out of it. I don't want her to be hurt by this."

"I need some answers, and she's the only one who might be able to give them."

"You can't do this, Noah. She's old. She hasn't been well. You can't throw the past at her this way. What if she doesn't know about this?"

He pulled on his pants and a sweater, jammed his feet into his shoes. "Then I'm afraid she's about to find out. This is the rest of our life we're talking about, Gracie. Don't you need to finally hear the whole story?"

The last thing Gracie wanted was to hear the whole story in all of its sordid detail, but Noah was out of his mind with anger and pain. She'd never seen him this way before. This Noah hadn't existed when they were young and their future stretched out before them, bathed in the golden light of innocence. She quickly slipped back into her clothes and ran down the hall after him.

The loud voices were what woke Sophie up. She tried to cover her ears with the pillow to keep them out, but it didn't work. Papa's angry voice found her anyway. She thought she heard Gracie, too, but Gracie didn't sound angry. She sounded scared and very sad, like she was about to cry.

Sophie hated loud voices unless they were hers. She didn't like the way grown-ups shouted at each other and then made the children pay the price. She lay there for an awfully long time, listening to the sounds. Her mind danced all over the place. She thought about all the people she had met today. She thought about how much fun she had playing outside with Sage's and Morocco's children. She thought about the food and the music and Gracie and the poor bird she had found on the beach. She didn't want to think about the bird, but every time she closed her eyes she saw him lying there, scared and cold and alone on the rocky beach.

What if there were other birds on the beach who needed help, too? There could be lots of them all tangled up in

fishing line, hoping somebody would come along and save
them. The more she thought about the birds, the sadder
she felt, until there was nothing left to do but go down to
the beach and see for herself.

At least at the beach she wouldn't be able to hear Papa
and Gracie fighting.

Ruth had been about to retire for the night when Noah
and Gracie burst into the room. Their clothes were wrinkled. Gracie's hair was decidedly untidy. She would have
thought they were fresh from a romantic encounter if the
air between them hadn't sizzled with anger.

"What is it?" she asked, trying to seem her usual calm
and placid self. "Is something wrong?"

"We need to talk," Noah said. He didn't sound like her
son. The fierceness of his tone made her uneasy.

"Noah has some questions," Gracie began, and Ruth
could see the fear in her eyes. "If this isn't a good
time . . ."

"It's about my father and Mona Taylor," Noah inter-
rupted.

Ruth's eyes closed for a moment. Just hearing Mona's
name brought back so many memories, both painful and
sweet, that she felt overcome with emotion. She drew in
a deep breath, then looked at her son. "They dated in high
school," she said, "but you probably already knew that."

"I don't give a damn about high school," he said. "I
want to know about after."

"There is no 'after,' " she said quietly. "Mona married
Ben the year after graduation. I married your father three
months later. There isn't much to tell."

*You're a coward, Ruth. He deserves better than this.
. . . They both do.*

"Is that what you wanted to know?" she asked.

Gracie pulled at his sleeve. "This isn't a good time," she said. "Your mother's tired."

"Not at all," Ruth lied. "It's just a very old story. I'm surprised you're interested."

"He loved Mona, didn't he?" Noah persisted. "He loved her enough to leave you for her."

Ruth laughed nervously. "Where on earth did you hear such a thing?"

"That's how Gracie's mother died. She was on her way to meet my father . . . they were running off together—"

"No!" Gracie broke in. "That's not true. Simon was lying. My mother was on her way back home from taking me to the pediatrician for a checkup. She had a quart of milk in the car, Noah, and donuts for Ben. She wasn't running off with Simon. She was going home."

"Gracie's right," Ruth said, taking another step toward releasing her burden. "I saw Mona at the convenience store just before the accident, and she had laughed about those donuts with Willie Sloane, who was at the register that day. She said Ben's belly was bigger than hers had been at nine months along. She saw me standing near the newspapers, and we just looked at each other across the store for what seemed like the longest time, then she gathered up her change, grabbed her groceries, and left." It was the last time Ruth saw Mona alive. "I always wondered if I could have stopped it somehow . . . if I had said something to her . . . delayed her for five or ten seconds . . . maybe—" What was the point? Mona was gone, and Ruth was here, and there were days when Ruth wasn't sure which woman was the luckier one.

Gracie cried softly. Ruth's words had found their mark deep inside the young woman's heart. It was her mother, after all, who had been at the center of the drama. It was her mother who had died. Noah, however, hurt too much to hear what she was saying. Ruth had lived with the truth

for so long now that she had almost forgotten the way
unbearable pain obscured everything but the source. It
was a lesson she had prayed her son would never have
occasion to learn.

*See what you've done, Ruth? It's all catching up with
you* . . .

Noah grabbed Gracie by the shoulders and spun her
around to face Ruth.

"Look at her!" he demanded. "Take a good look and
tell me she's not Simon's daughter."

Gracie was a grown woman now, but Ruth could still
see the child she had been, that needy little girl who had
reached up to hold her hand as if Ruth could somehow
make it all better. She looked at the child and saw the
mother, gone now almost thirty years, and it almost broke
her heart in two.

Hope was a painful emotion. For the space of three or
four seconds, Gracie believed they might have a happy
ending, but then Ruth's eyes filled with tears, and she
said, "I'm so sorry, Gracie, I wish I could—" The ocean
roared in Gracie's ears, and she ran blindly from the library.

She'd been a fool to believe they had a chance to be
together. Tonight had been a terrible mistake, one she
would pay for for the rest of her life. It was easier to live
with the absence of happiness than it was to lose it again.
They had come so close, so painfully close, to making
their dreams come true at last. If only she hadn't let herself believe they could bend reality to fit their needs, then
maybe this wouldn't hurt the way it did.

She was halfway to the door when she realized her coat
and the car keys were upstairs in Noah's room. She didn't
want to see him again or his mother. She wanted to run
out the back door and disappear. *I understand why you*

do it, Sophie. Sometimes there's just no other way.

Noah was in so much pain. She remembered how it had felt when she first discovered that there could be no future for them. The enormity of it, the finality, had been devastating. How do you come to terms with the fact that nothing you could do, nothing you could say, could ever make things right again? Not even love was powerful enough to change this central fact of their lives.

"Oh, it's you, Gracie." Darnell poked his head into the hallway. "I heard the back door slam, and I was wondering."

She struggled to regain a degree of composure. "I wasn't anywhere near the back door, Darnell."

He frowned. "That's strange. I could've sworn I caught sight of someone running by, then heard the door slam shut. Must've had too much white zin with dinner."

"Didn't we all. That's part of the Thanksgiving—" She stopped. "Oh, my God," she said. "Sophie!"

She tore back through the hallway, past Noah and Ruth, and ran upstairs to Sophie's room. The door was ajar. Her heart was racing with apprehension. "Sophie," she whispered, pushing the door open wider. "Sophie, are you asleep?"

The bed was empty.

She flew back downstairs to Noah and Ruth. "Sophie's gone. Her bed is empty. She's not in the bathroom." She told them about Darnell and the sound of the back door slamming.

"Call the cops," Noah told his mother, "then call Sage and Morocco and ask if they'll help."

"Get some flashlights," Gracie said. "I'll tell Darnell and Rachel and the others to start combing the house and the yard."

"She's a little girl," he said, aging before Gracie's eyes. "She couldn't get very far."

Gracie didn't have the heart to tell him how wrong he was.

Storm and two of her siblings began searching the house from basement to attic for Sophie. In a big house like that, there were a thousand places where a little girl could hide. Ruth was in the kitchen talking to one of the local policemen while Rachel brewed pots of coffee. Darnell had gone out in his truck to search the local roads while his sons headed off into the woods. That left Noah and Gracie to check the yard, the garage, the tool shed, and the carriage house.

"She can't have gone very far," Gracie said. "We'll find her very soon."

"I should have seen this coming." Noah paced back and forth in front of Gracie. "You did."

"Where does she usually go when she runs?" Gracie asked.

"No place special. For the most part she just runs." He struggled to corral his thoughts into something useful. "Whatever caught her eye earlier: the bridal shop, Patsy's—"

They looked at each other.

"Jesus," he said. "The beach."

Sophie followed the path that twisted and curved behind the garage and led down the slope to the beach. The closer she got to the beach, the rockier the ground became, until she found herself stepping from one slippery perch to another. She wished she had put on her shoes and socks and maybe even a heavy coat. There wasn't a single bird out tonight. In fact, the water seemed to be coming closer, lapping over her ankles and sliding up her legs.

She felt very small out there alone in the dark. The world was bigger here than it had been back home in

England. Even the smells were different. During the day she didn't mind so much, but now all of those things seemed to be lurking in the shadows, laughing at her.

She wished she had stayed in her nice warm bed in the pretty pink room with the Barbie Dream House. It was scary being out here all alone. Even the moon looked spooky as it slid behind some dark clouds. She didn't like the slithery feeling under her feet or the way something long and feathery kept brushing up against her legs. There were lots of strange things lurking about underwater, eels long and skinny as snakes, big ugly sharks with jagged teeth and dead eyes, even dead bodies like she had seen on the telly.

Maybe she should go home and come back tomorrow when the sun was shining and the seagulls were awake. That sounded like a good idea. She turned to retrace her steps when suddenly her right foot slipped a little and she tried to stop herself, but it was too late. Her foot slid down and wedged itself between two rocks. She tried to wiggle her way out, but each time she moved the jagged edge of the rock pressed deeper into her ankle.

She cried out for her father and then she called for Gracie, too, but there was no answer except for the shrieking sound the ocean made as it rose higher all around her.

You couldn't miss the fact that high tide was rolling in, but only Gracie realized they had no more than ten minutes to find Sophie before the thin strip of remaining rocks vanished altogether. She knew this stretch of beach well. In many ways, it mirrored the beach by the lighthouse where she and Noah had fallen in love. It was great for sunbathing at low tide when the receding water revealed hidden stretches of smooth sand, but once the water started rolling back in, you could get in trouble in the blink of an eye. If the rocks didn't get you, the currents would.

She didn't say any of that to Noah. He knew the realities of Maine beaches. She saw the way his eyes darkened when he realized the tide was rising.

"I don't see anything," he said into the wind. "The place is deserted."

She cupped her hands around her mouth and for the second time that day she screamed, "Soophiiiie!"

Noah did the same, louder still.

"Wait!" Gracie motioned for him to be quiet. "I hear something."

"I don't hear—"

"Papa!" The sound was soft, so soft it was almost lost in the rush of wind and sea. "Papa, help!"

"I see her!" Gracie pointed farther down the beach. "She's lying across the rocks. Stand up, Sophie! The tide's coming in."

Sophie tried but failed, and a chill ran up Gracie's spine.

"Stay here," Gracie said to Noah. "I'll get her. I'm better than you are at walking on these rocks."

"The hell I'll stay here. I'm going with you."

She would have been disappointed if he'd said anything else.

They struck out over the rocks, scrambling, slipping, swearing under their breaths. Even Gracie found it tough going. The sky melted into the sea; the rising tide obscured the rocks and made each step a leap of faith.

Gracie cried out suddenly as the bottom dropped out beneath her, and she found herself in at least ten feet of murky, icy water. "Stay there," she warned Noah as she dogpaddled fiercely to stay afloat. "One of us has to be able to go back for help if something goes wrong."

She did a quick crawl toward Sophie, who was shivering uncontrollably. The child looked in Gracie's direction, but there was no recognition. Hypothermia, Gracie realized. She was well on her way to unconsciousness.

"C'mon, Sophie!" Gracie cried out. "Stay awake! Don't give up on me!" Her arms were lead weights slicing through the water. Her mind was oatmeal. She peered into the darkness, but Sophie's tiny form blended in with the rocks and the water, appearing and disappearing at will. "Wave to me, Soph!" Move, scream, anything to give her something to aim for, a focal point in all of the sameness. Thank God. Sophie somehow registered her words and lifted her hand. Gracie fixed her sights on that slight movement, narrowing her concentration until there was nothing left in the universe but that faint back-and-forth movement.

A little more . . . just a little more. . . . Don't be distracted. . . . Don't look toward the horizon or you'll never get back on track. . . . You're almost there . . . almost . . .

Moments later Sophie threw her arms around Gracie's neck and clung to her as if she'd never let her go.

"Don't leave me here!" Sophie cried. "Don't let go!"

"Don't worry," Gracie promised as the current swirled around them. "You're safe with me now, Sophie. Everything's going to be all right."

Gracie tried to strike out toward shore, but the second she moved, Sophie let out a cry. Gracie realized with horror that the child's foot was stuck between the two rapidly disappearing rocks.

Ruth paced the driveway, calling Sophie's name, praying, trying not to cry. Her granddaughter. Her one chance for redemption. They had had so little time together, a handful of weeks to make up for the five years she had missed. God wouldn't be so cruel as to take Sophie now when she was so tiny, so vulnerable. Sophie had been through so much in her short life. Was it asking too much that she be allowed to have a home and family to call her own?

The thought that she might lose all three of them— Sophie, Noah, and Gracie—hit Ruth like a blow. She sagged against the side of Laquita's car and choked back a sob. She felt old and useless, trapped by time and infirmity, unable to get out there and join in the search.

She had made up her mind to tell Noah and Gracie everything, but Gracie had jumped the gun and leaped to the wrong conclusion, and see where it had led them. Sophie had run off, Noah and Gracie were at odds, and Ruth was more alone than ever before.

Simon and Mona were long gone. Ben had finally found happiness. And there was Ruth, keeper of secrets, with the chance to set things right if she only could. *Just give me one more chance to do this,* she pleaded with God, *not for my sake, but for theirs.*

Her time was over, but theirs had yet to begin.

Noah dove deep, trying to leverage his body weight and use it to pry the rock off Sophie's foot, but the natural buoyancy of the saltwater worked against him. Three times he dove and three times he returned to the surface, gasping for air and cursing his failure to free his daughter. Gracie, kicking furiously to stay afloat, used her body as a prop for Sophie to lean against. Their margin for error was quickly disappearing. Even with Gracie helping to keep Sophie's nose and mouth above the water line, it wouldn't be long before the water enveloped the child, and they would lose her.

Everything else dropped away from him. Anger. Pain. Sorrow. All that mattered was Sophie. He filled his lungs with air, then went down again. He used his legs this time, summoning up every ounce of strength and ingenuity at his command, then kicked hard. The rock slid away, freeing Sophie's foot at last.

"You did it!" Gracie cheered when he rose, sputtering, to the surface. "Noah, you did it!"

Sophie clung to Gracie and refused to let go.

"Can you make it back with her?" he asked, and Gracie nodded.

"Try and stop me," she said.

He had never loved her more than he did at that moment. She was brave and strong and when she loved, she loved with everything she had to give. She was his in every way except the one that really mattered. She could never be his wife, never be the mother of his children. They would watch Sophie grow up from opposite ends of town, watch each other grow old, watch each other grow lonelier as the days grew shorter, and there was nothing in heaven or on earth that could give their story the ending it deserved.

Gracie's legs caved underneath her when she reached the rocky shore. She tried to stand, but the combination of icy water and terror had done a number on her, and she collapsed on her side, careful not to hurt Sophie who was clinging to her like a baby monkey.

"I'm c-cold," Sophie whimpered, burrowing closer to Gracie.

"So am I, honey," she managed, hugging her tightly. "We'll get you home as fast as we can and get you into some warm clothes."

Noah took Sophie from her, and the exhausted child fell deeply asleep almost immediately, with her head resting against his shoulder. The sight of Noah and his daughter standing there on that rocky beach was almost Gracie's undoing. They looked right together, as if all that had happened between Noah and Gracie, the years of loneliness and despair, had found their purpose in the little girl who slept soundly in his arms.

Noah held out his right hand to Gracie, and she took it. Their fingers laced together automatically, the way they had when they were young and newly in love. Nothing had changed. Not the jolt of recognition she felt each time they touched. Not the sense that they were meant to be together forever. He helped Gracie to her feet, and they stood close together, foreheads touching, bodies shielding Sophie from the wind as if they had been watching out for her all of her life.

"Thank you," he said, as the bitter taste of broken dreams filled his throat. "I couldn't have—"

"We're still a great team," she said, her voice breaking with emotion.

"It's not enough. I want us to be together. I want—"

"I know," she whispered, "but we can still be a part of each other's life, Noah. Maybe not the way we wanted but—"

He leaned forward and kissed her one last time, long and sweet and desperate. "I love you, Gracie. Nothing they throw at us will ever change that."

"We'd better get Sophie home," Gracie said, taking a step back from the dream. "She needs some warm, dry clothes and a cup of hot chocolate."

He took her hand, and they made their way back to the house.

Storm set up a cheer when she saw them dashing across the driveway with Sophie, and the next thing they knew they were surrounded by people, all thanking God and good fortune that Sophie was safe. Ruth stepped out of the shadows near Laquita's car and touched a gentle hand to her sleeping granddaughter's cheek. She had touched Gracie's cheek that way, too, a long time ago.

"Look at the lot of you!" Rachel exclaimed. "We need

to get you all into warm tubs and dry clothing."

"I'm fine," Gracie said. "I think I'll just head home."

"You can't go home yet," Rachel said. "You're drenched and shivering."

"I really should get back," Gracie said. "Ben will be wondering where I am."

"No, Gracie!" The voice was loud and clear; the tone brooked no argument. "You're not leaving yet."

Everyone turned to stare at Ruth. They had never heard her use that tone of voice before.

"What I mean," Ruth said, "is that I'd like you to say a little longer, Gracie. I want to talk to you and Noah once you've changed into dry clothes."

"I don't think that's necessary," Gracie said, edging toward Laquita's car.

"Please," Ruth said, looking from Gracie to Noah. "There is one more thing I need to say."

Ruth took a steadying sip of whiskey while she waited for Noah and Gracie to change into dry clothes. There was no turning back this time. She had made a pact with God, and God didn't look kindly on people who reneged on a deal. No matter what else she had done wrong in her life, this was one thing she intended to get right.

"There's hot chocolate for you on the desk," she told Gracie when she arrived. She repeated the same to Noah two minutes later.

They looked so bereft, so terribly sad, that she thought her heart would break. What had she done to them? What had she allowed Simon to do?

She took a deep breath, then went straight to the heart of the matter. "You asked a question before, Noah, about paternity. I had started to answer when the commotion with Sophie began. I'd like to finish my answer, if you don't mind."

"That isn't necessary," Gracie said, and Noah concurred. "We know the truth. Now we have to find a way to live with it."

Ruth arched a brow. "Will you let me tell my story?"

Gracie's cheeks reddened. "Of course."

"You asked me a question, Noah," she continued, "and the answer is no. Simon was not Gracie's father." She turned to Gracie. "He lied to you, honey, and I'm so sorry I didn't tell you this a long time ago." Simon died. Gracie and Noah left Idle Point. The years flew by, and after a while Ruth convinced herself that anything Simon might have said or done no longer mattered. Surely her son and Mona's daughter had moved onto other loves by now.

But then Noah returned with Sophie in tow, and Gracie came home for Ben's wedding, and only a bitter woman, blind to the ways of the heart, could miss seeing that their love for each other had never died.

Gracie leaned forward and rested her forehead on her knees. She was having trouble taking in the enormity of the statement as a thousand what-ifs pummeled her emotions into suspended animation. If only she had stayed long enough to ask questions. If only she had demanded that the adults in her life account for their actions. If only she had been a little older, a little tougher, a little harder to undermine. Oh, Simon had read his opponent well. She had been too young, too brokenhearted to do anything but exactly what he had wanted her to do: Walk out of Noah's life—and his—forever.

Noah's emotions weren't in suspended animation; they were there on his sleeve for the world to see. The realization that the die had been cast long ago, and his future altered in ways he could never have imagined, tempered his shock and anger with a deep sense of relief. It wasn't his fault. None of it. There was nothing he could have

said or done to make it right. It had been out of his hands
from the day he was born.

"He had an affair with Gracie's mother after you were
married, didn't he?" Noah asked.

"Simon and Mona had a love affair," Ruth corrected
him. She needed to be clear about that. "Yes, he did."

"So it's possible—"

"No," Ruth said with great certainty. "It isn't possible."

Gracie was almost afraid to breathe deeply for fear she
might pop this wonderful soap bubble of hope. She
reached for Noah's hand and held on tight. "How can you
be sure?"

Ruth's eyes darted toward Noah, and a prickle of alarm
ran up Gracie's spine. *Please, God,* please . . .

"Because, you see, Simon was sterile." A childhood
case of mumps had left him unable to father a child, something he had neglected to tell his wife until it was too late.

Noah flinched, but he didn't look away or let go of
Gracie's hand. "So I'm adopted." A statement, not a question.

Ruth shook her head, looking older and more tired than
Gracie had ever seen her.

"You're my child," she said. "Simon and I separated
for a while a long time ago. I left Idle Point and went to
live in New York. I was seeing a wonderful man, an artist
named Michael Shanahan. He was the friend of a friend
of mine and he swept me off my feet. He was everything
Simon wasn't: warm and considerate and focused solely
on me. I wasn't careful about birth control. All those years
I had believed our childlessness was my fault, but it
wasn't. I called Simon when I found out I was pregnant
and I asked for a divorce. He refused. He told me that he
loved me and that he wanted me back. He would raise
my child as his own. What I didn't know was that Mona
had just told him she was pregnant with Gracie and de-

termined to make her marriage work. She loved your father, Gracie, and in the end it was your father she chose
to be with."

She was quiet for a minute or two. "I was always
Simon's second choice, but he was the love of my life. I
knew he would never love me the way I loved him, but
it didn't matter. Our lives were bound together and always
would be." She left Michael and went back to Simon, and
they picked up their life together where they had left off.

"What about Michael Shanahan?" Noah asked. His
voice was thick with emotion. "What happened to him?"

"He is a dear friend," Ruth said softly. "Little did I
know that our lives would remain bound together as
well." She motioned toward a fabric-covered box resting
on the lamp table to her right. "Everything you need to
know is in there," she said. Years of letters and notes,
newspaper clippings, gallery reviews, wedding and birth
announcements. Michael Shanahan married two years after Ruth left him and was now the father of three daughters who shared his love of art and music. She saw the
question in Noah's eyes. "He knows all about you, your
years at St. Luke's, Sophie—" She stopped for a moment.
"He told me that you deserved the whole story. It was
something I already knew, but hearing him say it—and
seeing you and Gracie with Sophie—gave me the courage
at last."

She reached into the pocket of her heavy hand-knit
sweater and removed a small white card. "This is Michael's address and phone number. He would like nothing
more than to hear from you, Noah. If you choose not to,
he'll understand, but I know how much you mean to him."

"If I mean so much, why didn't he ever get in touch
with me?"

"Because I asked him not to," Ruth said, her voice
heavy. "For Simon's sake, as well as for my own."

For almost thirty years Michael Shanahan had followed his son's life from a distance. In time, he fell in love again and started a family, but a part of his heart would always belong to his first child, the son he had never met.

Simon was the only father Noah had ever known, but it was Michael's blood that flowed through his veins. Who could say which connection was more important? Both men had had the right to claim Noah as their son, but neither had been able to love the child the way he deserved to be loved, openly and unconditionally. That loss had left shadows on Noah's soul that Ruth could never erase.

Next to Noah, Gracie cried softly. Ruth wished she could. Anything would be better than the heavy ache of regret inside her chest. But she pushed forward. The time for ducking the truth was long past.

"You have his smile, Noah. When I look at you I see the man who gave me the most precious gift in the world."

"You waited a hell of a long time to tell me."

"Yes, I did," she said, "and I'm sorry for that." It would take an even longer time to tell the entire story, to make her son understand that sometimes mistakes were made in the name of love and family, mistakes a mother would give her life to undo if only she could.

In the end Simon had made a grand gesture toward reconciliation but hadn't the generosity of spirit necessary to see it through. Simon never managed to forgive Ruth for her transgression, same as he never managed to forgive Gracie for her very existence. He had loved Noah in his own way and taken great delight in showing off the child, but before long, the truth of Noah's paternity began to color everything. Ultimately, Noah and Gracie came to represent all that had gone wrong in Simon's own life, and when they found each other, something inside him had snapped.

"Simon was a very proud man," Ruth said. "I learned early on in our marriage to keep his secrets to myself, and over the years I became quite good at keeping some of my own." She looked from Noah to Gracie. "Too good, I'm afraid. I wish I could give back to you the eight years you lost, but I'm afraid that's beyond my ability. The best I can do is tell you both that I love you and I pray that now that you know the truth, you'll be able to find your way back to each other. There is nothing that would make me happier." She rose from her chair and, leaning heavily on the cane, she left the room.

Noah and Gracie sat alone in the library for a long time, holding hands like survivors of a shipwreck. She was his anchor. He was her home. Nothing else mattered. Not the secrets or the sorrows, not even the eight years they had lost along the way.

"The first time I saw Sophie, she was sitting in a lawyer's office," he said. "I walked through the doorway and she looked up at me and I knew there was nothing I wouldn't do to keep her safe from harm." There had been no blood tests, no proof of paternity, only the deepest knowledge that this was where the fates meant him to be. "The lawyers said that we needed blood tests, that proof was required before they handed her over to me, but it didn't matter to me what the tests said. I knew she was mine." He told Gracie of the little girl's courage, the way she'd sat there and watched him with eyes that were far too old, and waited for him to determine her future. "I never want her to doubt that she's loved."

They both knew how it felt to be small and powerless, wondering why it was so hard to make their fathers love them. Sophie would grow up secure in the knowledge that she had a mother and father who loved her and who would slay dragons to keep her safe and happy. Parents whose love for each other would be the foundation upon which their family would be built.

There would be time for anger, for discovery, for healing. There would be time for forgiveness.

This moment, however, belonged to Noah and Gracie and to the future that suddenly loomed before them, golden and theirs for the taking. A future even brighter than the one they had dreamed about when they were young and newly in love.

They listened to the sounds of the old house as it settled down for the night. Soft voices from other floors. Footsteps padding down long halls. Sophie's laughter. Ruth's low murmur. Bathtubs running, doors closing, the sighing sounds of a family at rest.

"This is how I want our house to sound one day," Noah said.

Gracie leaned over and kissed him on the shoulder. "I think you need a big family to get that particular sound."

"I'm game if you are."

She pretended to consider the idea. "Nine kids might be a bit much for me."

"We could compromise at eight," he said, not cracking a smile.

"I was thinking six."

"Seven," he said, "but that's my final offer."

"Much better," she said. "Seven's a walk in the park."

"Sophie loves it here."

"She's not alone."

He met her eyes. "How would you feel about coming home to Idle Point to stay?"

"I'd say we already have."

She thought about the familiar streets and faces of her childhood, of the way the air still smelled of salt spray and pine and dreams. She closed here eyes and imagined Sophie with a cluster of brothers and sisters, playing together on the beach in the shadow of the lighthouse where Noah and Gracie first fell in love.

"Papa! Gracie!" Sophie called down to them from the second-floor landing. "You must come tuck me in!"

"Be right there, Soph!" Noah called back to her.

Gracie's heart was again three sizes larger than it had been just moments ago. "I've been thinking about what your mother said about the years we lost," she said, choosing her words with great care. "You know I would give anything to get back those years but not if it meant losing Sophie."

He met her eyes. "Not too many women would say that about walking into a ready-made family."

"We have a lot of time to make up for," she said, leaning her head against his shoulder. "Why not get a head start?"

Life was about compromise. They had lost eight years but gained a miracle, a child who needed their love as much as she needed oxygen. Little did Sophie know that they needed her even more. Sophie was their chance to get it right, to love a child the way all children deserved to be loved, with constancy and respect. They both knew how it felt to be on the outside of family life looking in, and they would see to it that Sophie never felt that way again. They would create a home that endured.

Family bonds were forged in many ways. Some were forged by blood; some by circumstance. If you were very lucky, the bonds were forged by love.

"I'm waiting!" Sophie called down to them, and they looked at each other and started to laugh.

Still holding hands, they climbed the stairs to the second floor and went to check on their daughter.

EPILOGUE

Christmas Day—the lighthouse

"Tell me again," Sophie said. "Do I throw them or drop them?"

Gracie knelt down next to Sophie and took a handful of rose petals from the basket looped over the little girl's arm. "You scatter them like this." Rose petals fell at their feet in a graceful arc. "See? All you have to do is walk very slowly and scatter the petals into the wind."

"Storm told me that flower girls are terribly important." Sophie's expression was quite serious as befit the subject. "She said that weddings aren't weddings without them."

"Storm is right," Gracie said. "I don't think your daddy and I could possibly get married today if we didn't have you here to lead the way."

Sophie's sober expression broke apart into a smile that turned Gracie's heart inside out. Lately that had been happening at least ten times a day. It seemed that her heart had an infinite capacity for love. The more she loved Noah and Sophie, the more love she had to give to everyone else who crossed her path. Why hadn't anyone ever told her about this amazing phenomenon, or was everyone meant to discover it in her own way?

Ruth appeared in the doorway. She was dressed in a bright red wool coat with a huge corsage made up of a red poinsettia and white roses pinned to her left shoulder. It fairly screamed "mother of the groom" and made Gracie smile every time she saw it.

"Father Tom wants to know if you're ready," Ruth said as she smoothed a hand over her granddaughter's mass of shiny blond curls. "The wind died down, and he wants to take advantage of it."

"We're ready," Gracie said, and the two women's eyes met over Sophie's head.

"You look so beautiful, Gracie."

Gracie blushed and did a pirouette that made Sophie giggle. "Rachel and the girls really outdid themselves on this one, didn't they?" The dress was floor-length and slim, high-necked with long tight sleeves and a fitted bodice. Laquita, a newlywed now herself, had embroidered seed pearls on the mandarin collar and along the turned-back cuffs.

"The dress is lovely," Ruth said, "but you're the beautiful one." She took a deep breath then continued in a rush. "You've always been special to me, honey. I'm so happy to be part of your family."

There had been a barrier between them since the night Ruth told her and Noah the truth. It was never easy to discover that one of your idols was only a mortal woman after all. Ruth's decisions, born of loyalty and love, had changed the course of their lives. But each time Gracie felt the pain of those lost years, she looked at Sophie's sweet face, and the love she felt for the child made her regret and anger fall away. It hadn't been so easy for Noah. It would take a lot of hard work to reestablish a relationship with his mother, but the fact that both Noah and Ruth were willing to work on it bode well for a happy future for all of them.

Noah wasn't afraid of hard work. He had thrown himself into the task of bringing the *Gazette* back to vibrant health and was quickly gaining the respect of all who worked with him. The health of the paper was still in doubt, but nobody doubted Noah's dedication and resolve.

Gracie hesitated then reached out her hand, and a second later the two women were hugging while Sophie tugged at Gracie's skirt, eager to be included. "Mommy," she said, "don't forget about me."

Gracie bent down and kissed the top of her head. "As if that could happen."

"Hate to break up this gabfest," Ben said as he, too, appeared in the doorway, "but it's time we got this show on the road."

Ruth hurried outside to claim her place near the makeshift altar.

"Ready?" Gracie asked Sophie, who was beginning to look a little nervous.

Sophie nodded. "I'm ready."

"Good luck, little lady," Ben said as Sophie straightened her tiny shoulders and straightened her basket of petals. "We'll be right behind you."

Sophie nodded. "I shall do my best, Grandfather," she said, then marched out the door.

"Grandfather," Ben said with a shake of his head. "I kind of like the sound of it."

"I'm kind of partial to Mommy myself," Gracie said. "We've come a long way, Dad. I'm glad you're here with me today."

"No place else I'd rather be." He cleared his throat, the classic male prelude to an emotional statement. "Your mother would be proud of you, Graciela," he said, his voice cracking in the middle of the sentence. "Just as proud as I am."

"I love you, Dad." A simple declarative sentence that erased a lifetime of pain. It felt good to say it. It felt even better to mean it.

His eyes welled up with tears, and he patted her hand. "Come on, Graciela," he said after a moment. "You and Noah have waited long enough."

She slipped her arm through his, and a moment later they stepped out into the bright Christmas afternoon sunshine. The lighthouse cast its familiar shadow along the beach, and for a moment she was a teenager again, racing across the rocks by the light of the moon to be with the boy she loved.

He was waiting for her now at the end of this rose-strewn path, the boy she had known, the man she would love forever, waiting with his little girl—their daughter—who stood next to him, impatient for their life together as a family to begin. Michael Shanahan, tall and graying, stood next to his son. His love and pride in Noah were unmistakable. The two men were very much alike, and it had given Gracie great pleasure to watch them get to know each other. They were all there, Laquita and Rachel and Darnell and Ruth and Don Hasty and Storm and Dr. Jim and Patsy and Michael's wife and daughters and dozens of *Gazette* employees and so many others who loved them and wished them well. Even Gramma Del and Mona were there. Gracie could feel their presence like a hug on a cold winter's day.

They took their places in front of Father Tom and all who loved them. "We are here this day to witness a miracle," the priest said as he opened his prayer book. "We are here to witness the birth of a family."

Gracie reached for Noah's hand and for Sophie's, and their life together began at last.

The Idle Point Gazette—*December 25*—
Special Christmas edition

She loves me and she loves my kid, and we both love the fact that by the time you finish reading this, we'll be a family on paper as well as in our hearts. This time we'll have our friends and family with us to wish us well. We lost eight years of our lives together, but every time I see her with my daughter, I find myself thanking God that we found our way back home to Idle Point.

So how does this story end? That's easy. It ends the way the best stories always end, with those familiar words that have resonated down through the years and made our children smile.

"And they lived happily ever after."
Right here in Idle Point.
Who could ask for more?